BEIGNETS AND BAD OMENS

BEIGNETS AND BAD OMENS

CRESCENT CITY CURSE™
BOOK ONE

KELLI ROBYNS

MICHAEL ANDERLE

DON'T MISS OUR NEW RELEASES

Join the Florid Romance email list to be notified of new releases and special promotions (which happen often) by following this link:

https://floridromance.lmbpn.com/about/sign-up-for-our-newsletter/

Published by Florid Romance
an imprint of LMBPN Publishing
2375 E. Tropicana Avenue, Suite 8-305
Las Vegas, Nevada 89119 USA

Version 1.01, January 2026
eBook ISBN: 979-8-89354-878-5
Print ISBN: 979-8-89354-879-2

Elle Beauregard stepped onto the concourse of Louis Armstrong Airport with a single goal, finalize her grandmother's estate and leave New Orleans before the city could claw under her skin. She hauled her suitcase through the press of travelers, trying to ignore the humidity curling her hair. Somewhere above the noise of announcements and distant jazz, she swore she heard Ruby's warm laugh, but it was only memory.

She reached the cab stand and gave the driver Ruby's old address. "No detours," she said, though her throat tightened as she imagined seeing the house again. The ride was a blur of faded shutters, wrought-iron balconies, and beads still hanging from last year's carnival season. Within minutes they stopped along Decatur Street. Tourists already lined up outside Café du Monde while the scent of fried dough drifted through the morning air.

Elle paid the driver and paused to smooth her nerves. Her grandmother had always claimed the city was alive with magic, an energy pulsing through every brick and cobblestone. Elle had dismissed those stories as folklore. Now Ruby was gone, and Elle clutched a purse containing the heirloom necklace that had been bequeathed to her with dire instructions: "Keep it close."

She squeezed the leather strap and headed toward the café. A plate of beignets might soften the ache in her chest. She placed her order and found a spot in the bustling open-air patio. The first bite melted on her tongue, airy and sweet. For a moment she almost relaxed.

A blur of movement snapped her back to the present. Someone brushed past, too close, and the weight on her shoulder vanished. Elle lurched to her feet in alarm. Her purse dangled from a stranger's hand as he wove through the tables.

"Stop!" She shoved through the crowd, nearly colliding with a trumpet player. The thief sprinted toward Jackson Square, darting between startled pedestrians. Elle ran harder, heart pounding, but the distance widened.

He rounded a corner near an alley shimmering with midday heat. For a heartbeat, Elle thought she saw a tall woman watching from the shadows, a figure draped in a purple shawl whose eyes glowed faintly gold. The thief stumbled as if acknowledging her presence. Then both were gone, swallowed by the maze of streets.

Elle stood frozen, panting, the image of that shadowy woman seared into her mind. She forced herself to the nearest police station. The idea of confronting the bureaucracy unsettled her, but she moved forward, reminding herself that if she wanted the stolen keepsake back, she needed an official record. She needed real faces and real words on paper.

Outside, the streets were quiet apart from sanitation trucks and a few groggy joggers passing beneath streetlamps. Light from the rising sun made the old stone walls around Jackson Square glow orange. She drew closer to the precinct, a tired building huddled at the edge of the block. It appeared older than she remembered, with its crumbly gray facade and narrow windows. A pungent bitter smell wafted through the open doorway, as if someone had neglected to toss out the used coffee grounds from the night before.

She stepped inside, where the fluorescent lighting illuminated a cramped, cluttered lobby. Rumpled posters about safety measures and community events lined one wall. Across from her, a short hallway opened to rows of crowded desks. The sharp odor of stale coffee and old dust coiled in her nostrils. She spotted two uniformed officers behind a counter, their postures betraying boredom. Neither looked up when she approached.

Good morning, I'm here to file a report. My purse was stolen yesterday, and there was an heirloom necklace inside.

One officer, a middle aged man with drooping eyelids, glanced her way. He sighed. "Fill the form," he rumbled, jerking his head toward a battered metal desk stacked with clipboards. Then he returned his attention to a half eaten pastry. He did not bother adding instructions or guiding her to the correct form. Elle stared at him in disbelief. She pressed her lips together, determined not to let that early wave of frustration spill out so soon.

She walked over to the desk and searched through the messy pile of paperwork until she found a generic theft report. The battered plastic pen on a chain scratched stiffly across the page. The form asked for details she had repeated at least twice over the phone yesterday, location, approximate time, description of stolen items. She answered each question thoroughly. Her throat tightened at the section labeled "any unique value?" She paused before writing, "family heirloom necklace, extremely sentimental." She swallowed the tightening in her throat as she thought of Ruby's gentle face, a memory that still burned behind her closed eyes.

When she finished, she brought the form to the counter. The bored officer glanced over it just enough to press an official stamp on the corner, then jerked his head again, pointing her toward a narrow hallway. "You gotta see an officer for intake. End of the hall, first door on the right," he said.

She made her way along the corridor and navigated around half open file cabinets. Bundles of papers lay stacked against the walls, and the overhead light sparked a headache behind her eyes. Voices crackled from an ancient radio at someone's desk. The hallway opened into a cramped main office area with several desks and a small break room off to one side. The smell of old coffee grew more powerful here and mingled with cigarette smoke from somewhere unseen.

She approached a tall counter where two uniformed

officers conversed in low tones, uninterested in her presence. She cleared her throat again. One looked up, raking a critical gaze over her, then nodded impatiently. "You have a file," he asked.

Elle handed over the stamped form. "I arrived this morning," she explained. "My purse was stolen in broad daylight on Decatur Street, near Café du Monde. The thief grabbed it and vanished. It had everything, wallet, ID, but most importantly an heirloom necklace." She heard the tension in her own voice and tried to rein it in. She knew that if she let her frustration boil over, they might dismiss her as another irate tourist. But she needed them to take her seriously.

The officer flipped through the pages without real interest. "People get stuff stolen all the time around here," he said. "You sure you did not just drop it?"

She fought the urge to grind her teeth. "I saw him take it. My purse was on my shoulder. He grabbed it and ran."

"Right," he answered. He waved a hand at another officer across the room. "Hey, Zeke, check the logs for me." Then, without waiting for a response, he turned back to his conversation with his colleague. Elle realized that was all she was going to get. She hovered in place, hoping for a follow-up question or at least a semblance of genuine help, but he had already dismissed her from his mind.

Her frustration rose, but the stench of stale coffee and the mind-numbing gloom of fluorescent lights made her feel small and out of place. Never had she felt so powerless. She took a breath and forced herself to remain polite.

"Is there anyone else who can look into this? The necklace is extremely important to me."

Zeke, an officer with a scowl chiseled on his face, glanced at a logbook on a desk. He thumbed through the pages. "There is a backlog of theft cases," he muttered. "We can keep an eye out for it, but it is probably lost in the shuffle by now. You might get lucky if a pawnshop flags a valuable item, but that is if it even gets sold."

Elle's nails bit into her palms. She wanted to snap that the necklace was priceless beyond monetary value, but she had the feeling it would make no difference. She needed to push a little harder. "Could you take a statement," she asked. "So there's something official in your records?"

Zeke sighed deeply, as though she had asked for a miracle. "All right. Fine."

He led her to a small cubicle near the break room. The overhead light cast harsh shadows on the mustard colored walls. She sat in a rickety chair that squeaked whenever she shifted. While Zeke typed at a computer, she heard footsteps behind her and turned her head in curiosity.

At first glance, she saw only a pair of dark slacks and polished shoes. Raising her eyes, she caught sight of a man standing by the desk clerk, speaking in a low voice. He was tall, with a lean build and short dark hair. The set of his shoulders suggested a reserved confidence. Elle sensed something in his presence that was different from the others here, something calmer or more focused.

He asked the desk clerk about a file, though Elle could not hear all of his words. The clerk handed him a thin folder. The man opened it, scanned the contents, then looked across the room. That was when he locked eyes with Elle. For half a second, she forgot Zeke's droning questions as their stares connected. His expression was unreadable, but his eyes focused on her with an intensity that made her heart flutter. She almost thought he recognized her, but she remembered she had never met him. Maybe he had seen her earlier when she was waiting to file her forms.

"Ma'am," Zeke said pointedly, reclaiming her attention. "Did you hear my question?" He tapped a pen on the desk, looking peevish.

"Sorry," she managed. "Could you repeat that?"

Zeke heaved a put upon sigh. "Height and basic description of the suspect. Best guess is fine."

Elle tried to recall details from the frantic chase. She described the thief's flash of ratty clothing and the shape of an arm grabbing her purse strap. She realized she had not seen much else. The memory was mostly a blur of panic.

Behind her, she heard the sound of footsteps receding. She glanced at her shoulder once more and saw the detective with dark hair moving down the hallway. Her heart sank a little. He was gone as quickly as he had appeared. She doubted he would be the one handling her case, but something about him felt more reassuring than any of these other officers. She wished she had a reason to talk to him, if only to see if he would take her story more seriously.

Zeke wrapped his questions in a rushed manner,

tapping impatiently whenever she paused to think. She tried to describe the purse in as much detail as possible, then explained how valuable the necklace was. He typed in short bursts, glancing at her occasionally to see if she was done, then hammered the keyboard again, as though finishing his job was a chore. When her statement was complete, he printed a summary, handed it to her without meeting her gaze, then pointed to a door at the far side of the office.

"You can leave," he said curtly. "We'll file this, but I wouldn't expect a citywide hunt for your missing purse."

Outside the office, she found herself blinking in the bright morning sunlight. A swirl of traffic and footsteps replaced the gloom of the precinct. Tourists were already assembling near the square, snapping photos of the statue at the center. Cafés bustled with early patrons crowding for beignets. The entire city seemed to carry on, unaware of her frustration. She clutched her statement, a flimsy piece of paper meant to represent official concern, but it felt like a hollow promise.

She leaned against a lamppost for a moment and let a wave of disappointment roll over her. Even when she closed her eyes, she saw the form of that tall detective, his shoulders set and his posture rigid yet strangely comforting. He had looked at her like he cared, or at least he had looked at her long enough to notice she was feeling lost. But he had disappeared, and she had nothing to show for her trouble except a printed statement and a sense of disillusionment.

Elle shoved the paper into her bag and turned toward

her hotel, unsure if she even wanted to go back to the cramped room. She had skipped breakfast, and her stomach twisted with a mix of anger and hunger. Maybe she would find a café away from the morning crowds and sip coffee by herself, attempting to banish the sting of being brushed aside.

As the day wore on, memories of the precinct's stale coffee and indifferent officers nagged at her. She tried to distract herself with phone calls to her credit card companies, hoping to freeze her stolen accounts or see if the thief had made any suspicious purchases. The process was disheartening but not unexpected.

When late afternoon arrived, heavy sunlight slanted across the hotel's lobby, and Tansy, her irrepressible yet favorite cousin, burst in. She balanced an iced coffee in one hand and a small paper bag of pastries in the other. Her bright floral dress and swirling tattoos on her forearms drew looks from a few guests, but Tansy moved through without a care. She gave Elle a hug and pressed the bag of pastries into her hands.

"You look done," Tansy said softly, concern in her eyes. "Any luck at the precinct?"

Elle shook her head and rummaged through the bag to pick out a pastry. "They barely even listened to me. I gave a statement, but they made me feel like it was hopeless. They think my necklace is just another stolen trinket."

Tansy slid her iced coffee onto a side table and guided Elle to sit on a small couch in the corner of the lobby, away from the front desk. "I am sorry," she murmured. "I know how important that necklace was for you, for all of us, really." She recounted the fleeting vision from the alley, the woman draped in purple whose eyes glimmered gold. Tansy's expression darkened as Elle spoke, and she whispered, "Some folks call her the Queen of the Quarter. If she is involved, the theft was no accident."

"I am just so frustrated," Elle admitted, biting into the sweet pastry. The sugar stung her chapped lips as she remembered how the taste of powdered sugar had once reminded her of better times with Ruby. "I need them to understand that it is not just some piece of jewelry."

Tansy nodded. "I know." A thoughtful pause followed before she brightened with a hint of mischief in her smile. "There might be a different way to find it. I know you are not big on the supernatural side of things, but I have heard about someone. They say Madame Laveau is the real deal."

"The psychic?" Elle's tone carried more skepticism than she intended. She had heard a few people mention that name. Supposedly the woman gave readings so accurate they bordered on eerie. In her grandmother's youth, fortune tellers and mediums had been an occasional presence, but Elle had never believed in them. She suspected they were mostly showmanship, telling strangers what they wanted to hear.

Still, Tansy pressed on. "Yes, her. She's known for seeing things no one else does. People claim she's helped them reclaim lost items or gain insight about situations the police dismissed. Many folks say she has roots going back to the city's biggest voodoo traditions." Tansy leaned closer, lowering her voice. "Ruby always said Beauregard blood responds to written symbols," she reminded her. "That necklace might amplify the effect if you learn to control it."

Elle stared into her coffee cup, swirling the liquid. A rush of memories threatened to surface, Ruby telling her that New Orleans had magic, real magic, sometimes hidden in corners you would never suspect. But Elle had grown up trying to brush off those stories as legends. She was no longer so certain. After the fiasco at the police station, who was she to reject any lead?

"It sounds silly," she said quietly, "but maybe I should go. I can't stand around hoping some random officer will solve this. Tansy, I hate feeling powerless."

TWO

Elle stood on the edge of Royal Street, caught between the swirl of midday humidity and her own jumbled thoughts. Across the way, a modest brick storefront bore a small sign: Madame Laveau's Psychic Readings. Gold lettering glinted in the sun, reminding her of flames. She swallowed nervously. According to Tansy, this was the place to get answers or at least a few cryptic hints about lost objects and odd happenings. Given the turmoil that had upended her life in the last few days, answers sounded better than the silence she had been living with.

Tansy lingered at Elle's shoulder, fiddling with the thin strap of her floral-print dress. "Sure you want to do this?" she asked. She kept her voice low, as if worried the psychic behind those doors might hear them from afar. "I hear Madame Laveau is the real deal, but real could also mean real weird."

Elle took a shaky breath. "We need a lead. The police barely helped, and I can't just pretend my grandmother's necklace will pop up by magic." She tried to keep her voice steady, but the memory of her stolen heirloom stung all over again. "Let me see if there's anything that makes sense in there."

Tansy nodded. She patted Elle's shoulder. "I'll wait outside. You shout if she tries to sell you snake oil or charge you extra for conjuring a ghost." Her smile came off as light teasing, though Elle recognized the worry that appeared behind her cousin's eyes.

Elle pushed open the door and stepped into a space filled with the cloying scent of incense. The room was small, cramped by clusters of pale candles, crystal clusters carefully arranged in glass cases, and more mirrors than she could count. They hung on every wall and stood propped on small pedestals, reflecting flickers of candlelight until a dim glow shimmered in every corner. It set her nerves on edge.

She heard a soft shuffling sound and looked farther inside. A curtain of beaded strings rattled, announcing her arrival. Madame Laveau appeared from the back room, a tall woman with a regal, composed bearing. She wore a long, flowing dress in muted lilac and had a faint smile on her lips. Lines of experience creased the corners of her eyes.

"Welcome," she said, voice hardly louder than a whisper. Despite the gentle tone, her words rang with authority. "I wondered when you would come."

An involuntary chill trickled along Elle's spine. She forced a polite smile. "I'm looking for a reading. I've been told you might help me find a missing item."

Madame Laveau nodded as if she already knew. She directed Elle to a small wrought-iron table at the center of the shop. There were three chairs, but only one sat behind the table. Madame Laveau occupied it in a graceful sweep of fabric, then gestured for Elle to sit opposite her. An empty seat remained at Elle's right, the only one set in the circle of mirrored reflections.

Elle sank onto the wooden seat, noticing it creaked in protest. She picked at a loose thread on her sleeve to keep herself calm, but the thick aroma of incense and all the hidden corners made her heart quicken. Every sense felt heightened as if the city's undercurrent pressed closer in this shop.

Cards rested on the table, worn at the edges, each face a swirl of muted colors and intricate designs. Madame Laveau lifted the deck gently and shuffled in a slow, controlled motion. She watched Elle's eyes, waiting for her to speak. Unsure how to begin, Elle tried not to ramble. "I lost something precious to me," she started. "My grandmother's necklace. It was, well, it was stolen."

Madame Laveau slid the cards in a neat stack, then turned them so the backs faced Elle. "Choose three," she said, her voice lilting with certainty. "We will see what shapes your path."

Nervous energy sparked in Elle's fingertips. She hovered uncertainly, then plucked three cards with no real method. She placed them face-down on the table. Her throat burned with unspoken hopes. Please let there be a path to find my heirloom. Please let there be a lead.

Laveau flipped the first card. The Lovers. Elle's gaze

fell on the entwined figures detailed in the card's center, two silhouettes poised in union, ringed by floral motifs. She had never studied tarot in depth, but she knew enough to guess it might mean choices or relationships. Her pulse quickened at the thought of involuntary, tangled alliances. Was it referencing the stolen necklace's tie to her family? Or worse, something more personal?

Without giving her time to dwell, Laveau revealed the second card. Death. A skeleton balanced on horseback, enthroned in transformation and finality. Elle stiffened, swallowing a hiss of alarm. She knew the Death card did not always mean literal demise, but seeing that bony figure so close to The Lovers made her heart slam once in protest. Her fantasies of a direct, easy message vanished. Madame Laveau's shop felt too quiet, as if the air itself waited for a reaction.

"Death can mean endings or transitions," the psychic commented softly. "Transformation, if you are ready to embrace it."

Elle nodded once, still rattled. "So I've heard."

On the third card, Madame Laveau paused. She did not flip it. She lifted her gaze instead, her dark eyes drifting over Elle's face. In the ripple of candlelight, her expression was almost impossible to read. "Perhaps we will wait," she said, lowering her hand from that final card. "The first two speak loudly enough."

Elle's stomach twisted. "Why wait? Don't you need to see the third card?"

The psychic's voice remained tranquil, yet it crackled

with an odd intensity. "You already sense the truth you seek. What more would a single card tell you?"

Uncertainty made Elle's palms sweat. "I came because the necklace is important to me. I lost it, and the police..."

"Find that necklace before the next moon cycle," Madame Laveau said, her soft tone clipping every syllable with clear meaning. "Fate wavers in your hands. If you wish to preserve your inheritance, do not let that piece of your grandmother's legacy vanish beyond your reach."

A lump formed in Elle's throat. The next moon cycle was two weeks away, more or less. She hated how quickly that deadline seemed to loom. "Are you saying I'll never get it back if I don't find it soon?"

Laveau answered by flipping the second card's edge again, letting it catch the candlelight. Death's skeletal grin glimmered. "Time devours all, child," she replied, voice echoing off the many mirrors. "Your grandmother nurtured a quiet power that runs through your blood. The item stolen from you resonates with that same power. Should it remain in the wrong hands too long, many forces acted upon by greed or fear may twist it to their purpose. The risk for you grows with each day."

Elle shivered, recalling how she had always dismissed the necklace as a family treasure, not a tool of anything beyond sentimental value. Was it possible her grandmother's talk of magic had more substance than she'd ever acknowledged? The idea overwhelmed her.

She forced out a question, voice trembling. "Madame Laveau, can you give me any real names or clues about who took it? I can't exactly roam the Quarter, searching every alley."

"You know the answer," Laveau said simply. She folded her hands on the table. "Listen to your instincts. Open your eyes to the city's hidden shapes. The Quarter's secrets speak if you dare to listen."

A flare of frustration mingled with fear. Elle wanted to demand specifics, but the the shop pressed upon her like a weight. Candles flickered in the row of mirrors along the walls. She thought she saw movement in one of the reflections behind Laveau, an inky silhouette that darted away when she blinked. Was her mind playing tricks?

Her throat felt dry. She glanced at the single remaining card, facedown on the table. "What about that one?" she murmured, unable to resist one last attempt. Even a single image or symbol might help her plan what to do next.

Madame Laveau's gaze never left Elle's. "The third card is a path you already walk, child. I sense that you do not need me to show you. When you leave here, the path will start to reveal itself, by your own choice."

A swirl of confusion blurred Elle's thoughts, but she found no real words to argue. She stood, her knees shaky. She offered the psychic some money, quietly placing it on the edge of the table. She felt compelled to talk more, to wrestle clarity from the cryptic reading, but Laveau had closed her eyes, as though in silent reflection.

Elle parted the beaded curtain and stepped outside. Bright sunlight hit her like a slap, so different from the candlelit gloom. She inhaled a quick breath, trying to reorient herself. The smell of hot pavement and the distant strains of saxophone music filtered through the street. She spotted Tansy waiting a few paces away, leaning beside the storefront window. At the sight of Elle's pale face, Tansy's expression knotted with concern.

"That was fast," Tansy said, eyebrows lifting. "Was she ambiguous as anything?" She squinted past Elle into the shop. "She always has that weirdness around her place. Spooky, right?"

Elle's shoulders slumped. "She gave me a strict warning, find the necklace before the next moon cycle. She said I already know how to track it. Which doesn't help much when I have no idea where to start."

Tansy brushed a wilted leaf off Elle's sleeve. "Madame Laveau can be dramatic. Some folks claim she's a legend, others call her overhyped. But I keep hearing these eerie stories about her predictions coming true."

Elle darted a look at the door, half expecting the psychic to materialize behind them. "It felt real, Tansy," she admitted. "Death and The Lovers. That matchup gave me chills. And the mention of my grandmother's power? I can't shake the sense there's something bigger going on, like the city is whispering in corners."

Tansy opened her mouth, unsure how to respond. She gave Elle a quick, protective hug. "Look, it could be her usual show to keep tourists spooked. That being said, you're not a tourist anymore." She pulled back and lightly patted Elle's arm. "Let's get coffee or something sweet. Mystery or not, I refuse to let you unravel alone."

Grateful for Tansy's presence, Elle managed a nod. They walked away from Madame Laveau's shop, footsteps tapping the uneven sidewalk. With every passing block, the city's bustle returned in full force, car horns, laughter from a street corner, the scattered melodies of an off-key trumpet player. But beneath all the normal chatter, Elle sensed an extra layer, as though invisible threads tugged at her awareness. She kept picturing that second card, Death, and hearing Laveau's calm voice repeating that time was running out.

"Want to talk about what she said," Tansy asked gently as they turned onto a quieter street. Bright flowers hung from wrought-iron balconies overhead.

Elle stared at the cracks in the sidewalk. "She said I already have the answer. Maybe I'm missing a clue from my grandmother or a memory. I can't lie, Tansy. I feel like there's something I've been ignoring for years. Ruby tried to warn me about the necklace's importance, but I wrote it off like a sweet old lady's superstition."

Tansy checked her phone, as if she might rummage up a lead from one of her contacts. "We can double-check any detail you remember. I can also see if a friend of mine has heard rumors about stolen antiques. New Orleans is small if you know the right people."

Elle curled her hands into loose fists. "All I know is that I have two weeks to figure this out before something horrible solidifies." She hesitated, afraid to say the word doom or closure, as if speaking it made it more certain.

They continued to the next corner, mulling over potential leads. A faint drizzle began to drift from the sky, so Tansy pulled them under the canopy of a small café. After ordering iced coffees, they sat near the open door, letting the warm air swirl in a slow dance with the café's air conditioning.

Tansy studied Elle over the rim of her cup. "Madame Laveau also said something about your grandmother's power."

Elle let out a breath in a rush. "Yes. She implied it's in my blood, which... Ruby was always telling those old stories about magic. Now it haunts me a bit. I never thought it could be real."

Tansy gave a half shrug. "She taught me to have an open mind, but I get why you doubted. You left for Chicago, tried to make everything normal." Concentration crossed her face. "Still, if there is even a hint of truth, Ruby might have left clues in her journals or at her old house."

Elle sipped her coffee, the sweet, milky taste mingling with her anxiety. "I will have to check every nook and cranny because I cannot lose that necklace permanently, Tansy." She felt a lump pushing at the back of her throat. She tightened her grip on the plastic cup. "It is all I have left of Ruby."

Tansy's eyes softened, and she reached across the table to squeeze Elle's hand. They exchanged a moment of unspoken understanding, sharing the ache of Ruby's absence. Then the conversation shifted to practical concerns, canceling the rest of Elle's stolen credit cards, checking online listings for the necklace, maybe scouring pawn shops. Though none of it felt like enough.

That evening, after Tansy retreated to her own place, Elle returned to her hotel room. She unzipped her bag and rummaged for her phone charger, setting it on the nightstand. Her mind buzzed with the day's revelations. She replayed the memory of The Lovers card, knit with the haunting specter of Death, and felt an unsteady swirl in her chest. Maybe Tansy was right, they could methodically trace leads. Yet Madame Laveau's warning felt larger than logic could tame.

By the time she showered and settled into bed, her body was exhausted, but her mind battled sleepless tension. She gave in near midnight when unconsciousness pulled her under.

She dreamed she stood inside a high-ceilinged corridor, lit only by guttering candles that lined the walls. The air smelled of damp stone and old memories. At the far end, she glimpsed the tall silhouette of a man. She recognized him—the detective from the police station, though they had barely exchanged glances. He regarded her with a steady, unreadable gaze, as if he was standing guard over a secret or a passage she was meant to cross. His presence offered an unexpected sense of reassurance. Yet she heard a voice behind her, so familiar that it momentarily paralyzed her. Ruby's voice. Child of fate, it whispered. Child of fate, do you hear me?

Elle tried to turn, tried to find her grandmother's face, but only shifting shadows greeted her. The corridor lengthened, stretching into darkness, and the sound of footsteps echoed from unseen corners. The detective's silhouette stood immovable like a sentinel. She stepped forward, heart pounding, yet the scene warped under her feet.

A ragged cry tore from her lips as the dream dissolved

into a swirl of blackness. She startled awake, her chest tight. Her hotel room lamp glowed faintly beside her, and the clock hinted she had only slept an hour. She pressed a hand to her heart, trying to calm the frantic beat. The phrase from her dream clung to her thoughts.

It begins.

She sat in the dim quiet, the sheets tangled around her. Ruby's words consumed her mind with a dread she could not name. Half asleep, half in panic, she whispered them aloud, testing how they sounded in the real world. The night offered no reply. But she could not shake the sense that something had indeed begun, a current of magic and warning already shaping her fate.

THREE

Elle pressed a shaky hand against the door of the small coffee shop, inhaling the mingled aromas of roasted beans and sugary pastries. The sign on the glass pane promised a warm corner of calm next to the police station, and she told herself she could use the comfort, one decent cup of coffee before braving another round of indifference from officers who had no real interest in her stolen purse. She glanced at her phone. The battery remained high, though the morning's tension felt like it should have drained more than her energy.

Inside, the space was cozy in an unassuming way, low-slung chairs, lingering patrons skimming newspapers or scrolling their phones, a barista busy behind the counter. The hum of saxophone music flowed in from somewhere outside, competing with the hiss of the espresso machine. Elle collected her thoughts and stepped up, trying to smile at the clerk. She ordered a medium roast with room for cream and dug the last few bills from her wallet.

Waiting for the barista to finish, she tried to push away the frustration that had built since sunrise. Her official theft report felt doomed to gather dust. The stolen bag was one thing, but the heirloom necklace kept her tense and sleepless. Her grandmother Ruby's final gift belonged in the family, not in some criminal's hands. She had come to realize that without that piece of her grandmother, she felt fractured, as if a link to past generations had been severed.

The barista slid a cardboard cup across the counter. Elle thanked him and moved aside. She lifted the lid to pour in a tentative stream of cream, stirring absently. A seat in the corner caught her eye, but before she could settle, a tall figure entered, letting a ripple of fresh air swirl inside. At first glance, he looked like any other morning customer, dark hair brushed neatly back, a quiet presence in his posture. Yet there was something about him that made her pause. His gaze, sharply focused beneath steady brows, moved across the shop until it found her.

The detective. She recognized him from a brief glimpse at the police station the previous day. Her heart gave a small lurch of surprise. She had not expected to see him again, not outside the precinct's gloomy corridors. He approached the counter with calm purpose, greeting the barista politely. While he waited for his order, he stepped to the side, just close enough for her to hear him clear his throat in a thoughtful way.

She pressed her lips together and glanced at his reflection in the glass pastry display. He seemed too poised for an ordinary morning off. The quiet set of his jaw indicated all business, but his eyes held a hint of curiosity. She wondered if he had recognized her or if she was imagining the interest in his careful stance.

"Elle Beauregard?" His voice was low and measured.

Her stomach flipped. She turned. "Yes?"

"I'm Detective Mateo Cruz," he said with a nod. "I saw your name in a theft report at the station yesterday. Odd details about a stolen heirloom. I hoped I might cross paths with you."

She found it disquieting that he recalled her so easily. The flutter of nerves in her belly warred with faint relief that at least one detective in the precinct seemed to care. Hugging her coffee cup, she gave a quick nod. "You recognized my name from the file?"

He lifted a modest paper bag from the counter and thanked the barista under his breath. In the shop's cozy lighting, she noticed a faint scar near his eyebrow, a subtle reminder that life as a detective was more than desk work. He moved to a small table near the window and gestured politely for her to join him if she wished. After a moment's hesitation, she followed.

The hum of conversation surrounded them, a benign background of cups clinking and low chatter. Outside, the saxophone tune shifted to a lively crescendo, distracting her for only a moment before Detective Cruz drew her focus again.

He rested one hand lightly on the table, the other wrapped around his coffee. "I saw that you described the necklace in precise detail. You said it had unique filigree work, family significance. The notes in your statement jumped out at me," he studied her face, brow furrowing in quiet concern. "When did you say it went missing?"

"Yesterday morning." She took a small sip of her drink, trying to steady herself. "A thief grabbed my purse on Decatur Street. I tried explaining at the station that it was more than a random trinket, but nobody cared."

She forced a small laugh, though it carried bitterness. The officer who had taken her statement refused to grasp the emotional weight, as if her grandmother's piece was cheap costume jewelry. Detective Cruz did not interrupt. Instead, he nodded once, encouraging her to continue.

With a sigh, she explained, "That necklace was my grandmother's. I lost her not long ago, and it's the last chance to hold something of hers. Losing it felt like losing her all over again. Does that make sense?"

A softness crossed his features. "It does. Family heirlooms can carry a lot of weight."

His calm certainty caught her off guard. Her eyes dropped to her coffee cup, the swirling foam reminding her of the swirl of her thoughts. The rest of the station gave her the runaround, but here was someone listening without belittling or brushing her aside.

"You're not just humoring me?" she asked quietly.He tilted his head. "If it stood out in the report, it's worth looking into. I trust my instincts. Have you got time to walk me through the theft location?"Her tension eased, replaced by gratitude. "Yes. That would be great, actually.""There's a route from here past Jackson Square," he said. "It will not take long to show me where it happened."Clutching her coffee, she followed him outside.

The day was mild, sun cutting through the lingering haze of morning. Saxophone music floated along the sidewalk, merged with the bustle of tourists vying for café seats. Detective Cruz walked with assured steps, scanned the street as though collecting data from every movement around them. She tried to keep pace, disturbed by how her own pulse pounded in time with her footsteps.They wove through narrow roads, passed clusters of visitors snapping photos in front of old statues or sipping iced drinks. When they reached Jackson Square, he paused, his gaze moved over the wrought iron fences and the swirl of artists setting up easels."Which street by the square?" he prompted.Elle gestured to the corner near Café du Monde. "I was right there, looking at a band. I shifted my purse strap to the side, and the next thing I knew, it was gone." Her throat tightened in frustration at the memory. "I ran after the guy, but it was useless."

Detective Cruz listened, scanning the perimeter with a detective's sharp eye. She spotted him quietly noting possible exit routes, alleys, side streets, anywhere a thief might vanish fast. It struck her how different he was from the jaded officers in the station lobby.

They walked along the path the thief had likely taken. Tourists occasionally brushed by, some glancing curiously at the pair. She found herself sharing details she had not admitted before, how she felt a chill the moment it happened, an odd static in the air that afternoon. She confessed that she had felt a flicker of panic beyond ordinary fear, as if something more than theft had happened. He listened intently, though he gave no sign of disbelief.

They circled a corner, the swirl of street performers behind them. Detective Cruz's phone chimed once in his pocket. He ignored it in favor of focusing on Elle. She noticed an unusual heaviness in the atmosphere. The mild sunlight did not match the tingle coursing along her arms. For a moment, she thought a storm might be rolling in, but there were no clouds overhead.

He must have felt something as well. His steps slowed. She heard him exhale sharply before murmuring, "You feel that?"

Her response was a tight nod. The air around them seemed charged. Then her phone's screen flickered. She lifted it, alarmed to see it going dim as though drained. She tapped the power button and expected it to show a low battery icon. Instead, it displayed the same high percentage from earlier.

"That's happening a lot lately," she admitted, voice trembling. "Lights or electronics flicker for no reason. I thought it was just my imagination."

Detective Cruz angled closer. His expression was controlled, yet his eyes mirrored her unease. The moment stretched, a silent question pulsing in the space between them. She wondered if he had experienced odd flickers in other investigations, or if she was inadvertently sounding like a person chasing ghosts. Instead of dismissing her, he studied the phone's dimmed screen with quiet intensity.

A wave of static crackled in the distance. She saw a streetlamp down the road sputter. Then it stabilized. They stood there, tension rolling through them. Jackson Square's airy charm felt overshadowed by something intangible. Elle's heart pounded. She did not know how to explain it, but she sensed Detective Cruz took it seriously.

"All right," he said after one final look around. "I'll make a note about this. You said your phone does it sometimes?"

She nodded. "Every so often. Especially when I'm thinking about my grandmother's necklace." She realized that sounded almost superstitious and added quickly, "I know it's weird."

He simply said, "I've seen odd things in certain cases. Not weird enough to dismiss." His mouth curved into a brief, reassuring hint of a smile.

They made their way back toward the police station area, though they did not enter. Tension eased a fraction, but she could not ignore the buzz under her skin. Detective Cruz bent closer to speak in a quieter voice and explained that he would keep an ear out for any stolen property leads matching her filigree description. As he spoke, she sensed a sincerity that made her chest tighten with unspoken relief.

Her coffee cup had cooled to a lukewarm memory in her hand, but she still cradled it like an anchor. They stopped by the sidewalk near the same coffee shop while the swirl of traffic and passersby bustled around them.

"Thank you," she said, voice hitching on the words she had repeated to uninterested officers. "I appreciate that someone believes me. Or at least doesn't treat me like I'm imagining things."

"I believe you," he answered simply. "I can't guarantee results today, but I'll try." His eyes moved over her face, calm and careful. "Let me know if you notice anything else unusual leading up to the theft or after. Even small details can matter."

She fought an impulse to spill every bizarre moment plaguing her since returning to the city. Instead, she managed a faint nod. Her thoughts raced with half-formed explanations about her grandmother's old stories, about how she had sometimes claimed that New Orleans carried magic in the cracks of its streets. Elle now suspected it was more than a folktale, but she was not ready to voice that to a detective she had just met.

He gave her a business card with neat lettering. Detective Mateo Cruz, with a precinct phone number. She slipped it safely into the pocket of her purse. When he turned to leave, she felt an inexplicable pang, an impulse that she might not see him again. Yet she sensed he would be around. Shaking off her nerves, she thanked him once more, then walked along the sidewalk back to her hotel with an uneasy swirl of thoughts.

The midday sun had grown hotter, pressing on her shoulders as she navigated the French Quarter's narrow streets. She thought about the static charge near the square, the bizarre behavior of her phone's screen, and the detective's steady reaction. At least someone listened, even if he had no immediate answers.

In the hotel's small lobby, she paused in front of the creaking elevator, replaying the memory of Detective Cruz standing with quiet confidence as the air charged around them. She realized she felt not only relief but curiosity toward the man who actually believed her story. There had been a spark beyond logic in the way he listened. It was faint, more like possibility than certainty, but it left her wanting to know more about him.

Riding the elevator up, she could almost taste her own conflicted emotions. Part of her wanted to keep things simple, just find the heirloom and leave. But that plan no longer felt so straightforward. If the city truly pulsed with hidden forces, maybe she needed more than official channels or her own stubborn hope. The sense of something bigger happening refused to fade.

When she reached her small room, she dropped onto the stiff bed and closed her eyes. She could not ignore her fluttering pulse. Detective Mateo Cruz believed her. That single fact, small as it might be, steadied her in a way she had not expected. For the first time since the theft, she felt less alone. She set her phone on the nightstand, half expecting another glitch, but all remained quiet. Warm air from the aged vent blew across the room, ruffling a stray piece of paper on the bedside.

Exhaling slowly, she told herself she would not let odd static or a reluctant precinct deter her. She had a new ally, maybe not a friend yet, but at least someone inclined to help. She stared at the ceiling, thinking about their short walk near Jackson Square. Her cheeks flared with a faint heat that had nothing to do with the sweltering weather. She told herself that she was only grateful, that curiosity was natural. Yet the memory of his careful gaze lingered along with the memory of that unspoken hum in the air.

For now, she had no plan beyond waiting for any lead or clue. She had picked up a detective's business card and a fragile sense of hope. With those in hand, she believed tomorrow might reveal new answers. Maybe she could salvage her grandmother's legacy after all. Hugging her arms around herself, she let the swirl of coffee-scented warmth from earlier fill her mind, holding on to the idea that she was not entirely alone in her search.

FOUR

Elle arrived at Jackson Square just after midmorning, the sun already heavy in the sky. Heat radiated from the pavement beneath her sandals, and she silently scolded herself for wearing jeans on such a sweltering day. She paused by the old wrought-iron gates, adjusting the lightweight bag slung over her shoulder. Every inch of her muscles seemed poised, tingling with anticipation. She had arranged to meet Detective Mateo Cruz here, and the memory of his quiet intensity from the day before still echoed in her mind.

She took a slow breath, keenly aware that this bustling part of New Orleans had once been the scene of her purse theft, an event that for most people would remain just a random street crime. For her, it had opened new questions she never thought she would ask. Standing so close to where she had been robbed made her pulse flutter with a mix of tension and longing for answers. Tourists ambled past in sunhats and paused to snap pictures of the cathedral and the horse-drawn carriages. Jackson Square vibrated with life, but she felt her own thread of anxiety weaving through the crowd.

Across the street, she spotted Mateo. He wore a short-sleeve collared shirt in a deep gray that emphasized his lean frame. His posture remained alert yet unhurried, as though searching for suspicious details even on an ordinary morning. She lifted a hand to catch his eye. When he saw her, he gave the barest nod and crossed toward her with firm steps. The heat made the air shimmer around them, and her heart gave a small, traitorous leap.

"I see you found the place," she said, forcing a brief smile. Her voice came out steadier than she expected.

"I did," he replied, glancing at the gates and then back at her. "It's quite a location. Busy enough that a thief could vanish in seconds."

She swallowed, recalling the panic of that instant when her bag disappeared. "Exactly. One moment I was watching the street performers, the next my purse was gone." She gestured farther north, beyond the swirl of artists. "I was standing right over there, near those benches. I'd stopped because someone started playing this lively trumpet piece. Then everything blurred."

He inclined his head. "Show me as precisely as you can." They walked side by side along the iron fence, weaving around a trio of street musicians warming up for the midday crowds. Elle led him to an open space by a bench painted a vivid turquoise. Memories seized her, the music, her own startled cry, and the thudding of her heart as she realized her heirloom necklace was inside the stolen purse.She cleared her throat and pointed. "I was just behind this bench. There was a small band playing. The suspect must have stood nearby, waiting for me to get distracted."Mateo crouched for a moment, brushing his fingertips across a faint scuff mark on the concrete. A breeze kicked up, hot and sticky. He stood and rested his hand on his hip, near the badge clipped to his belt. "You chased him, right? Which direction?"She turned, looking at her shoulder. "He ran down the sidewalk toward that cafe's awning, then darted into a side street. I tried to follow, but with so many people around, I lost him."His eyes narrowed thoughtfully. "Side street. Could be Chartres or one of the smaller alleys between shops." He paused, letting the chaotic swirl of the square fill the silence. "You mentioned the necklace was in your purse, and it's significant to you. I'd like to hear more, not just that it belonged to your grandmother, but anything that stands out. Anything unusual."

Her stomach knotted. She still was not sure how much to reveal about the strange vibrations she felt whenever she wore it. The idea of telling a police detective that the filigree necklace might have a supernatural aura made her palms sweat more than the heat already did. Yet something about Mateo's quiet readiness encouraged her to speak. She remembered how seriously he had taken her story the day before, how he seemed less skeptical than she expected.

She exhaled and folded her arms lightly. "It meant a lot to Ruby, my grandmother. She called it a piece of our family history. Whenever I asked why, she said it was more than just an heirloom, but she never explained it in simple terms."

He studied her with intent. "Are we talking about sentimental value or something else? You mentioned you felt different when you wore it."

She hesitated, then nodded. "I am not saying it is magic or anything like that." Her voice wavered, betraying her uncertainty. "But it carries weight. A kind of I do not know. Sometimes I think about it like an emotional presence. Maybe I was just caught up in her stories. I cannot tell anymore."

Mateo tilted his head and did not dismiss the possibility. "Family legacies can be powerful." His tone stayed neutral, but she sensed the curiosity churning behind his eyes.

A sheen of perspiration beaded along her hairline. The sun pressed down without mercy, making the air heavy. Despite the discomfort, an undercurrent of tension hummed between them. Every time he spoke, she felt heightened awareness through her body.

She cleared her throat. "Well, that is all I know, just that I cannot lose it. If you find anything in your investigations that gives even the slightest clue about who took it or why, I would appreciate it."

"I'm trying," he said quietly. "The suspect you described could match a few petty thieves who haunt the Quarter. We'll keep checking. But something about your details about the necklace stands out to me. This might tie into a pattern of odd property crimes." He glanced beyond her shoulder, where tourists wandered in bright clusters. "I've had a few open cases that defy easy explanation."

He let the words settle, then shifted his weight. It felt too warm, too quietly charged. Elle swallowed again and blinked away the sudden dryness in her throat.

Before either could speak, a familiar voice called out from behind the bench. "Elle! There you are, good grief, I've been trudging around in this heat trying to find you. You promised me a beignet run after this, remember?"

Tansy bounded into view, wearing a sundress splashed with gigantic pink flowers. She waved enthusiastically at Elle, then flashed a friendly grin at Mateo. "Oh, hey, Detective. The hot cop is here." She winked at Elle, who felt her cheeks blaze in mortification.

Mateo went rigid for a split second before a slow, almost self-conscious smile curved his mouth. "Morning, Tansy."

"Morning," Tansy chirped as she bustled closer. She tossed her hair behind her shoulders, entirely unbothered by the sweat that glistened on her brow. "Elle told me you're trying to help find that stolen purse." She leveled him with an assessing stare. "And I appreciate that, detective. Because that necklace is special to our family."

Elle shot her cousin a warning look, silently pleading that Tansy not spill every weird hunch or rumor. But Tansy only lifted her eyebrows in a knowing way and gestured at the bench. "So, are we done with the tour? I'm cooking alive out here."

As if in response, an overhead streetlamp flickered, its bulb humming. All three of them looked at it. Another sputtering flash followed. Then the lamp shattered in a sudden burst, raining tiny shards onto the sidewalk. Tourists gasped and stumbled backward, shielding their faces. Someone let out a high-pitched squeak and grabbed a friend's shoulder for balance.

Elle's stomach plummeted. She stepped back, scanning for any sign that a stray baseball or rock could have caused this. There was nothing obvious, just the swirling midmorning heat and a faint static charge on the breeze.

Mateo exhaled sharply and moved in front of the two women as if to block them from any danger. Tiny fragments of glass dotted the ground. Tansy's eyes widened. She stayed close to Elle, hooking an arm around her waist, while Mateo reached for his phone, likely planning to report the incident.

"That is not normal," Tansy muttered, glancing between them. "This day is too hot, and that lamp just decided to explode?"

A security guard from a nearby building arrived and peered upward with baffled eyes. He started to usher people away from the hazard. Voices hummed, bustling and uncertain. Elle tried not to tremble, but a wild rush of adrenaline streaked through her chest. She and Tansy exchanged uneasy glances.

Mateo turned back, concern shadowing his features. "Either that bulb was faulty, or something triggered a surge." His words were calm, but his stiff posture revealed his apprehension. She saw the question in his gaze. He must have been thinking about the phone flickers and static charges near her in the past days.

Tansy pressed her lips together. "It is freaky, right?" She lowered her tone so only Elle and Mateo heard. "Maybe another sign of weird stuff happening around here, because lamps do not just blow up on a cloudless day."

Elle's pulse continued to pound. She tossed an anxious look at Mateo. "I, we should get out of the street. Maybe find somewhere cooler."

He nodded, exhaling a measured breath. "Agreed. I can file a quick note with the city to check the wiring. They might have to replace the lamp."

While Mateo stepped over to the security guard, Tansy leaned closer to Elle. "You told him about the necklace, right? About how it might be special?"

"As much as I could," Elle murmured. "I figure letting him know the basics is enough for now." She swept a hand over her forehead, wiping away sweat. "This heat is intense."

"Or maybe you are tense around him," Tansy teased, though her tone held genuine worry too. "You cannot hide that you are, I do not know, intrigued by him. Even if your necklace drama is overshadowing everything else."

Elle forced a laugh, but it sounded hollow in her own ears. "It is complicated. We barely know each other."

Tansy patted her arm. "Barely knowing each other has not stopped him from taking your case personally. I am saying, keep your eyes open." Then she turned and waved as Mateo returned.

They regrouped near the iron fence again, cautious of the shattered lamp overhead. She spotted a city worker arriving, presumably to cordon off the area. Tourists scattered, though a few lingered to take photos of the broken fixture, as if this small catastrophe was another souvenir of their New Orleans visit.

Mateo readjusted his collar, a hint of sweat darkening the fabric near his neckline. "I explained what happened. They will handle it from here." He paused, taking in the tension lining Elle's face. "You both all right?"

"I am startled," Elle admitted. "Everything feels like it is hitting at once. The theft, the odd flickers, and now this."

Tansy slipped a supportive arm through Elle's. "I vote we leave this patch of sidewalk behind us before anything else happens. Coffee might help."

Elle nodded, though part of her wanted a moment alone to sort through the nagging fear. The coincidence of small electronics or lights acting strangely around her had grown too frequent to dismiss. Mateo's presence, while comforting, also made her heart race in a way that felt suspiciously like attraction. She did not think the city's electrical grid was the only thing sparking around them.

They strolled back toward the main square. Street performers resumed their songs, almost as if the lamp incident had never happened. Tansy hopped ahead to check the posted schedules for local concerts, offering them a modicum of privacy. Elle noticed how Mateo kept glancing at her, concern softening the lines of his face.

She cleared her throat, speaking quietly. "Thanks for taking the time to come out here. I appreciate you following up, even in this unbearable heat."

He gave a slight shrug. "It's my job, but it's also your peace of mind. If there's anything bigger going on, I want to figure it out." His gaze locked with hers, and she felt the warmth of it ripple along her skin, a different kind of heat altogether. "Let me know if you notice anything else or if you remember details from your grandmother about the necklace."

She managed to steady her breathing enough to answer. "I will. I promise."

Tansy returned, a bright smile on her face. "All right, coffee or iced tea? Because I personally feel like I'm going to melt in about thirty seconds."

Mateo lifted his wrist to check the time. "I should head back to file a couple of reports. You two go ahead. I'll call you if I get any leads."

Elle's disappointment flared, surprising her with its intensity, but she managed a neutral nod. "Sounds good."

They all moved a bit closer to the fence, making room for a family laden with shopping bags to pass by. Tansy fiddled with her dress strap. Mateo shifted from one foot to the other, then extended a quick handshake to Tansy, who shook his hand with playful exuberance. Finally, he turned to Elle, offering a nod instead of a handshake. It was almost more intimate than contact might have been, given the penetrating look in his eyes.

She realized she was holding her breath. Something between them made her feel unsteady. He said a quiet goodbye, then walked away, weaving through the groups of onlookers. For a long moment, she watched him go, absorbing the flutter that remained in her chest.

Tansy didn't speak until he was out of earshot. "So. That man is definitely smitten."

Elle shot her a dubious look. "He's just being thorough. And I'd like to focus on the stolen necklace, not romances."

"If you say so," Tansy teased, slipping an arm around Elle's shoulders. "Now let's get iced coffee before we burst into flames."

They wandered away from Jackson Square, the heat still wrapping them like a cloak. On any other day, Elle might have laughed at Tansy's commentary and dismissed the shattered streetlamp as an unlucky fluke. But she couldn't ignore the gnawing sense that something bigger was unfolding. The flickers, the eerie static, and the way her grandmother's name seemed to hover in her thoughts all suggested that fate was stepping in and not subtly.

They navigated the sidewalks in silence for a while, each lost in private wondering. Elle kept revisiting the slow burn in Mateo's gaze, the watchful concentration he had worn, and the crackle that lingered every time he stood too close. She sensed that the city's restless energy was binding them in ways she did not fully comprehend.

When she and Tansy finally parted ways near a café, Elle drifted toward her next errand, though her mind lingered on the detective's gentle intensity. If random streetlamps were shattering and her phone kept glitching, she had to face the possibility that this was far beyond normal. Whether it involved the stolen heirloom, her grandmother's half-whispered stories, or some brand of supernatural quirk, she could no longer pretend it was all coincidence. A chill slid through her despite the oppressive heat.

She moved deeper into the French Quarter, sidestepping a group of tourists, her thoughts circling around what might happen next. She wondered if she was ready to accept that real magic laced the city. With every spare breath, she recalled the spark in Mateo's dark eyes, so at odds with his calm demeanor. That memory tugged at her composure, reminding her that some storms gathered without warning, fueled by something more potent than the summer sun. And in the smoldering quiet that lingered after he left, she realized she could not undo the flustered warmth that bloomed whenever Detective Mateo Cruz looked her way.

CHAPTER

FIVE

Elle pressed the side of her face against the pillow, half-wishing she could melt into the mattress instead of wrestling with restless thoughts for another hour. The small bedside clock announced it was well past midnight, yet her mind refused to settle. She had kicked off her sheets in frustration, leaving her legs exposed to the humid air. The overhead ceiling fan circled, offering little relief. A line of sweat trickled down her temple, and she wiped it away with a sigh.

She recognized the knot of tension in her stomach. It felt like a coil drawn too tight, ready to snap if a single worry tugged too hard. Each time she closed her eyes, she pictured her grandmother's radiant smile and the delicate filigree necklace that had once been in Ruby's possession. She could still recall its intricate metal vines and how it sometimes warmed mysteriously under her touch. Now, even though she had encountered Detective Mateo Cruz and a somewhat cooperative police department, she felt no closer to retrieving that precious heirloom or understanding the energy that seemed to swirl through the city.

For a moment, she considered rising from bed and pacing around the cramped hotel room. Perhaps a drink of water would calm her. The old wooden floor creaked whenever she shifted her weight, though, threatening to break the fragile silence. Despite the city's usual nighttime hum, she sensed something different tonight, as if the world expected something to happen. With a sluggish blink, she forced her eyelids shut again, determined to court even a fragment of sleep.

Sleep did not come quietly. It arrived in flickers, an odd swirl of color at the edge of her mind, and then darkness. Her awareness wavered as she drifted, the soft hum of the fan fading into nothingness.

Eventually, a dream took shape.

She found herself standing at the edge of the French Quarter, though the streets were transformed into something ghostly. Every lamp cast a pale glow like the last ember of a dying fire. The air smelled of old incense, thick with a metallic hint she could not name. When she started to walk, her footsteps rang hollow against the stone, echoing louder than they should. Not a single tourist or street performer roamed these roads. No trace of life, save for a slow jazz melody that seemed to waft from some unseen corner.

In the dream, she turned onto a street lined with wrought-iron balconies. The shadows twisted at the corners of her vision. A faint shape appeared on one of the balconies above. As she looked closer, she recognized her grandmother's outline. Ruby's familiar silhouette stood beneath a gaslit lantern. The older woman's arms rested on the railing, and her chin tilted up as if she surveyed the entire Quarter below. Elle felt a sudden pulse of longing. She missed that voice. She missed the smell of lavender that always clung to Ruby's sweaters.

"Grandma," she called, voice trembling. The dream responded with a hollow echo. She tried again. Ruby turned her head and met Elle's gaze. Her lips moved, forming words Elle could not hear. A pang of sorrow tugged in her chest, and she found herself reaching a hand upward, desperate to glean any clue from Ruby's silent warning. The more she focused, the more the city blurred, as though it refused to let her hold on to the image.

One chord in the unseen jazz tune swelled, then fractured into discord. A swirl of red light flared from the corner of her eye. She turned, heart skittering in her chest, and saw Detective Mateo Cruz standing across the street. In his hands, he held the filigree necklace. The pendant glowed the color of embers, casting an unsettling light across his face. His expression looked conflicted. He stepped forward, holding the necklace out as though he wanted her to take it.

She licked her lips, uncertain. Every warning bell in her mind told her this was a dream, that nothing here was real, yet her emotions felt painfully raw. Mateo's eyes showed a mixture of concern and urgency, and she tried to speak. Before she could call to him, a sharp hiss filled the silence. Blood-red sparks crackled around the pendant, and she felt a surge of heat brush her cheek.

"Mateo," she whispered, voice tight with dread. He offered no reply. Instead, he lifted the necklace higher. The filigree glowed so bright that she had to look away. The red radiance morphed into the swirling shape of a fleur-de-lis. It expanded and dissolved the dream's murky corners until the sky itself bore that same symbol, a fiery brand searing across the blackness.

Elle's heart pounded as she stumbled backward. The city's buildings swayed like illusions in the distance. The swirl of the fleur-de-lis pulsed overhead, and somewhere beyond it, she could still see Ruby's silent warning on the balcony. A sensation like static prickled from her toes to her scalp, urging her to wake up, to do something, but she could not move. The dream pinned her in place and forged the memory of that symbol into her mind.

A moment later, she ripped free of the dream. She woke in a full-body jolt, drenched in sweat. Her lungs dragged in air as if she had sprinted a mile. The hotel room was dark aside from a faint stripe of light under the door, yet her vision still glowed with the afterimage of that crimson fleur-de-lis. Her pulse thundered, and her skin felt clammy. She swallowed and tried to regulate her breathing.

She fumbled for the bedside lamp while her heart rattled against her ribs. The small lamp clicked on and illuminated the cramped walls and the battered suitcase leaning in the corner. For a moment, the ordinary sight of her surroundings steadied her. She pressed a hand to her chest and struggled to slow her heart. Her entire body was shaking. The memories of Ruby, of that jazz tune, and of Mateo holding the ominous necklace refused to fade.

She sat up, pushing damp hair off her forehead. Something about the room felt off. A new sense of tension sizzled in the air. She scanned the shadows, half convinced the dream might have spilled into reality. Then her gaze snagged on the windowsill. A small shape on the peeling paint drew her attention. At first, she thought it was a trick of the lamp's light on chipped wood. But as she squinted closer, she realized it was blackened, singed into the paint itself.

Her breath caught. The mark resembled a tiny fleur-de-lis, the same shape she had just seen blazing in her dream's sky. She swung her legs over the side of the bed and stood, ignoring the trembling in her knees. The floorboards squeaked underfoot. In three steps, she reached the window and trailed her fingertips over the burnt spot. The texture around it flaked away at her touch, leaving a delicate scorch pattern that had crisp edges. That shape had not existed when she went to bed.

A cold ripple coursed down her spine. She pressed her lips together, grappling with both fear and a strange excitement, as if the city itself were playing some private game with her. First her phone flickered. Then the streetlamp shattered near Tansy and Mateo. Now this. The logical part of her mind demanded an explanation, but no rational answer arrived. This weird mark did more than unnerve her. It confirmed her suspicion that the dream was not just dreamscape nonsense.

She turned away from the window and let out a shaky

breath. She needed Tansy. Even if Tansy did not have all the answers, at least she would not dismiss this as a coincidence. She patted around for her phone, found it half-buried in the twisted sheets, and unlocked it. It was barely a few minutes past three in the morning. Tansy was likely asleep or out with friends. Still, Elle could not contain the sudden crushing need to talk to someone.

With trembling fingers, she typed a frantic text.

> Tansy, something happened. The strangest dream. Then I woke up to a fleur-de-lis burn on the windowsill. Please call me.

She hit send, but the energy buzzing in her chest refused to settle.

She shot off another wave of messages.

> Are you up?
>
> This is important.
>
> I'm losing my mind.
>
> Tell me you're home.
>
> I can't do this alone.

When no immediate response arrived, she felt the hollowness of the moment pierce her. She set the phone aside, pressing her palms to her eyes. A swirl of exhaustion swamped her, making her dizzy in its intensity. She yearned for Tansy's warm, confident presence, but she also felt uncertain how she would even explain the dream.

She pictured how Tansy might raise her brows and insist they call Madame Laveau or search through another one of Ruby's half-finished spellbooks in an attempt to interpret the sign.

A faint hum from the hallway startled her. She realized it was another guest walking by, likely returning from a late night venture, their footsteps fading into silence. The normalcy of it all contrasted so starkly with what she had witnessed that she felt tears prick at her eyes.

She knelt by the windowsill and examined the scorched mark more carefully. It was no larger than the palm of her hand, but its edges were precise, curved in the right way to form the fleur-de-lis tip. There was no ash or soot around it, as if it had been burned with pinpoint heat. She searched her brain for any rational scenario, a hidden candle, a bizarre electrical arc, but nothing logical explained a perfect brand, especially not one that appeared right after she dreamed of it.

Her pulse refused to slow, each beat a reminder that she was alone in this surreal state. The city streets below were silent, though she knew bars might still remain open for the stragglers. She thought about stepping outside, perhaps the night air would help, but the idea of wandering the Quarter in her sweaty pajamas felt foolish. A flash of memory from her dream pulled her thoughts back. She wondered if the illusions of Ruby and Mateo carried coded messages. Ruby's parted lips had formed words she could not hear, yet she sensed the urgency. Mateo had seemed torn, holding the glowing necklace as though it hurt him to touch it.

She ran her hand over her face. The ring of pressure around her temples pounded, an ache that demanded relief. She turned off the lamp and returned the room to shadow. Nothing in the darkness changed the silhouette burned into the windowsill. Her phone stayed silent, Tansy's usual flurry of texts withheld by the hour. If Tansy had her phone muted, there would be no immediate rescue from confusion.

Elle considered contacting Mateo. The idea warmed something in her chest, though it made her heart clench with hesitation. She pictured how he might react, with concern, perhaps heading straight here if he believed she was in danger. She pressed her lips together and imagined the low timbre of his voice, the gentle steadiness he showed when she first told him about the heirloom. Yet part of her balked. She was not sure how to admit the details of this dream, how to describe the fleur-de-lis scar left behind. She had no desire to confirm that the city's strangeness followed her even into slumber. She could not bear the risk that he might decide she was an over-imaginative out-of-towner, disturbing him in the middle of the night with something he could not fix.

With a heavy sigh, she set her phone on the small bedside table. She crawled back into bed and fought the tremor in her limbs. She longed to toss all logic away, to throw open the window and gasp out her frustration into the quiet city night. But she felt pinned in place by a silent vow to handle this, or at least to survive it until morning, when Tansy might respond.

CHAPTER

SIX

Elle jolted awake to the faint whir of a passing tour bus below her window. Sunlight looked timid as it slipped around the edges of the curtains. Blinking groggily, she pressed a hand to her temple, half expecting to feel the same heavy anxiety that had clung to her all week, but she found it replaced by an uneasy stillness. The hotel room's air conditioner hummed, stirring the stale smell of last night's leftover coffee, and her heart lurched with the memory of the dream that had kept her tossing until the early hours.

She rose from the bed and rubbed her arms briskly. She was still in the T-shirt and shorts she had slept in, if that restless fit of tossing could be called sleeping at all. The battered digital clock on the nightstand read 7:08 AM. Not exactly early, but she had been too anxious to rest properly. There was no sign of a forced entry into her room, yet she could not shake a prickling sense of intrusion.

Crossing to the door, she flipped the lock's latch to confirm it was still engaged. The brass chain dangled where she had set it last night before dozing off. There had been no beep from the electronic lock, no jostle of the handle, no clicks aside from her own.

Unease thrummed in her, prompting her to double-check. She swung the door open slightly and blinked at the broad hallway. A couple carrying gift bags from the local shops strolled by, giving her a friendly nod. She forced a quick smile in return. Then, slipping on a pair of sandals, she stepped out and marched straight down to the front desk.

At the desk, a young clerk with bright orange nails greeted her with a polite smile. "Good morning, Miss Beauregard. Everything all right?"

She braced her arms on the tall counter. "I hope so. Can you tell me if anyone has accessed my room overnight? I mean the key logs. This place uses electronic keycards, right?"

Concern flickered in the clerk's eyes. "We do. Is something missing?"

Elle hesitated, wrestling with how to phrase it. "Not exactly. I just... I heard something strange. I wanted to be sure my door was secure." She didn't dare mention specifically what she feared. The clerk typed in a few commands, then studied the screen with a faint frown.

"I'm seeing your own name from check-in yesterday, but no other entries are logged for your room. No housekeeping requests, no staff visits—not since you arrived."

Elle exhaled. Her arms still tingled, as if expecting to

catch the culprit red-handed. "You're sure nobody swiped a keycard or a master pass?"

The clerk shook her head. "We keep a record for all usage, and we haven't had any anomalies." She gave a soft laugh, probably hoping to soothe. "I promise, we'd see if someone snuck in."

"Right," Elle murmured. "Thank you."

She walked back to the elevator, forcibly steadying her breathing. If no one had broken in, then why had dread tightened her chest the moment she woke up? Her mind darted to the weird flickers that had followed her around the city—lights shorting out, that streetlamp exploding near Tansy, the phone battery glitching. But those had all been public. This was private. Her safe space.

The elevator doors slid open on her floor, and she stepped through them into the corridor. Something made the back of her neck prickle. She thought she heard distant footsteps, but they faded into the next hallway.

Returning to her door, she ran a palm over the wood, then turned the handle. Inside, the lamp was still off, and the glow of morning lit everything in a soft wash. Her pulse thudded in tune with the air conditioner's dull drone. She kicked her sandals to the corner and slipped deeper into the room.

She froze at once. Propped neatly on the center of her pillow was the filigree necklace, her stolen heirloom, gleaming in the early sunlight.

Her breath hitched, mind blanking as she stared. The item she had been chasing was here, casually perched among rumpled sheets. It lay with its chain draped in a small coil, as if waiting for her to pick it up.

Cautiously, she stepped closer. A flood of conflicting emotions hit her, rage at whoever had stolen it, relief at seeing it intact, and something colder, more unnerving, a whisper of the unknown presence that had brazenly placed it there. She dared not touch it yet, certain it might vanish if she blinked too hard.

A slip of folded paper lay partially tucked beneath the pendant. Hands trembling, she grabbed it and read the words, scrawled in a sharp, almost impatient script: You weren't ready. Try again.

Her mouth went dry. She read it a second and third time, mind reeling.

"You weren't ready for what?" she whispered, scanning the empty room. Nobody lurked in the corners. Nobody hid under the bed. She pressed the back of her hand to her lips, fighting the urge to call the police. Or Tansy.

But Tansy would be her first choice. She scrolled through her phone contacts with shaking fingers, then tapped Tansy's name.

Her cousin picked up on the second ring. "I am ahead of schedule today," Tansy said, voice bright. "I figured you would sleep in after that dream fiasco. Are you good?"

Elle forced words out. "I, Tans, the necklace. It's back."

A stammer of shock on the other end. "Back? Where? Who found it?"

"In my room. My locked room." She almost choked on dread. "Tansy, it was on my pillow when I got back from talking to the front desk. And there is a note. Something is wrong."

Silence, then Tansy said, "I am coming over. Right now."

Elle unlocked the door for her cousin and hovered by the pillow, staring at the delicate metal curve of the pendant. She remembered the first time she had put it on after her grandmother's funeral, its presence had felt so familiar, a last connection to Ruby. The day it was stolen, she had been heartsick, sure she had lost that final piece of memory forever.

Seconds later, Tansy burst into the room, wearing a floral sundress twisted slightly sideways, as if she had scrambled into it in a hurry. "Holy smokes," she whispered, her gaze immediately drawn to the bed. "Elle. That is definitely the same filigree, right?"

Elle swallowed. "It is the same. Down to the tiny scratch near the clasp."

Tansy hesitated, then gingerly picked up the folded note from where Elle had dropped it. Her eyes grew wide at the message. "You were not ready. This is bizarre. It could be a threat or a twisted apology. Or maybe Grandma's spirit forced someone to bring it back!"

"Tans, you cannot jump straight to magical theories," Elle said. But her own practical brain was faltering because no normal explanation made sense.

Her cousin slumped onto the edge of the bed. "Should we call the cops? Or maybe Detective Cruz? He was the only one taking your theft seriously."

Elle did not answer right away, uncertain if she had

the energy to file a new police report. She felt as though she was teetering on the threshold of the unknown. Part of her wanted to fling the necklace out the window and pretend none of this was happening, but the deeper part remembered that jolt of recognition she had felt every time she held it.

Tansy's phone buzzed a moment later. She scooped it up. "Speak of the devil." Her eyes darted to Elle. "It is actually from him, Mateo. He says something about a new witness statement regarding a figure who might have your purse. He is down in the hotel lobby."

Elle's heart clenched, uncertain whether to be relieved or more agitated. "He is here?"

"Well, he texted me first. He probably guessed you would be creeped out by all this." Tansy stood, smoothing her dress. "Maybe we can show him the note."

Elle gripped the necklace's chain between her fingertips. A rush of warmth skittered across her palm. She remembered how the detective's presence had grounded her more than once. But telling him about a phantom intruder who left zero keycard trace felt like stepping into a world too bizarre for standard police protocol.

"All right," she said breathlessly. "Let's talk to him."

They tucked the slip of paper into Elle's back pocket, though Tansy insisted on taking pictures of it with her phone first. Then, with a last wary look at the bed, Elle carefully slid the necklace into a cloth pouch she used for jewelry, not ready to wear it. A light sweat beaded along her forehead as they moved into the hallway.

Downstairs, the lobby bustled with morning energy.

Tourists milled around, some hauling suitcases to the front door, others picking up complimentary pastries from a side table. Smooth jazz played overhead, though Elle registered it only dimly.

In the far corner near a potted fern, Mateo Cruz stood scanning the crowd. He wore dark jeans and a short-sleeved button-up that highlighted the lean angles of his frame. The sight of him sent a swirl of conflicting emotions through Elle, relief, curiosity, and that ever-present spark of attraction she had been trying to ignore.

He spotted them and gave a quick nod. His expression tightened with concern as they crossed the tiled floor. A white folder rested under his arm, presumably the new witness statement.

"Morning," he said quietly, looking first at Tansy, then at Elle. "I hate to barge in, but I got a lead I wanted to share. And I thought you might prefer we speak in person."

Elle swallowed. "Thanks for coming." Her brain buzzed with how to mention the necklace. The stolen item that had reappeared like a ghost.

Tansy, never one to stall, blurted, "We have news, too. The necklace, Elle's necklace, some creep left it on her pillow this morning."

Mateo's eyes locked onto Elle, a flash of alarm crossing his face. "Wait, they returned it? How?"

"No clue," Elle replied. "No record of keycard entry. No forced door. But it was definitely in my room." Her voice wavered, and she caught the startled glance of an older tourist passing by. Lowering her tone, she added, "There was a note. It said, You weren't ready. Try again."

His expression darkened. "Did you handle it with gloves, or," He shook his head, apparently realizing that might sound too rigid. "Look, I don't want to treat your personal items like evidence, but we should be careful if we're dealing with someone who left you a borderline threatening message."

The subtle hum of tension in the air crackled, as though the overhead lights might flicker at any second. She caught Tansy's watchful gaze flicking between them.

Elle found her hand drifting toward the cloth pouch in her pocket, drawn by the necklace's weight. "I took photos of everything. The note, the arrangement on the pillow. But like I said, no sign of forced entry."

Mateo gently placed a hand on her shoulder, that same quiet steadiness he carried everywhere. A spark of static prickled where his palm touched her. Her breath caught, and a wave of heat that wasn't entirely from embarrassment rippled through her.

"You're shaking," he observed softly, his voice barely above a murmur.

She forced a swallow. "I'm just tired and angry and confused."

He nodded, letting his hand linger a moment longer than felt strictly professional. The static charge dissipated into a soft warmth that pooled in Elle's stomach, leaving her both comforted and off balance.

"Maybe we should sit down?" Tansy gestured at the lounge area near the window, though her tone hinted she might vanish soon if it helped Elle and Mateo speak privately.

Mateo lifted the folder he carried. "I have a statement from one of the Quarter's late night servers who apparently saw someone rummaging through a purse that might match yours. This witness said the suspect kept muttering about 'not the right time.' I wanted to confirm details with you, but first I want to understand this new development."

He motioned slightly toward her pocket. Elle realized he had guessed that was where the note or necklace currently resided. She and Tansy exchanged a glance, uncertain how to proceed.

The lounge chairs, upholstered in a maroon pattern, clustered beside a stand of brochures advertising local tours. Tansy pulled out one seat, while Elle sank into another, relief flooding her limbs. She still gripped the little cloth pouch in one sweaty hand.

Mateo settled on the chair across from them, posture alert but not rigid. He eyed the leftover space on the couch next to Elle, as though debating if he should move closer.

"All right," he said, exhaling quietly. "Would you mind telling me everything? Start from when you woke up."

Snippets tumbled out of her, the hum of the street outside her window, how she had found nothing suspicious in the keycard log, and the exact scene that greeted her returning to the room. She tried to keep her voice calm, though it quivered on occasion. The presence of Tansy, occasionally squeezing her arm in solidarity, steadied her enough to form coherent sentences.

When she finished, Mateo rubbed his jaw, brow furrowed. "So no sign of forced entry, no lapses in staff accountability. That suggests either someone with inside access who can override logs, or something else," He paused, searching for polite phrasing. "Something unexplainable."

Elle noted his deliberate choice of words. He had witnessed enough oddities with her already that the notion of "unexplainable" didn't spook him as much as it might another officer.

"Yeah," Tansy said. "We thought maybe we'd show you the note. I took pictures. Or we can let you see the original."

He extended a hand, but before Tansy could move, Elle fished the note from her pocket. Carefully, she flattened it onto the small coffee table in front of them. The scrawled words stared back, mocking her: You weren't ready. Try again.

Mateo's lips thinned as he read it. The hum of early morning footsteps continued behind them in the lobby, but the three of them felt sealed off by the tension.

"Could be a power trip," he said after a moment. "A way to rattle you. Or it might indicate that they were after something in your purse besides money, like the necklace. Maybe they realized it wasn't as easy to handle as they thought."

Elle swallowed, remembering how the necklace sometimes pulsed with a strange heat. "That might be it. It never felt normal, even to me."

"Your grandmother's necklace was special, right?"

Tansy put in. "She always told us it carried family significance."

Mateo studied Elle carefully. "If the piece has more than mere sentimental importance, whoever stole it might have realized they bit off something they could not chew. Maybe they recognized how attached you were and left it here as some twisted courtesy."

Elle's voice wobbled with the swirl of relief and dread. "They had to break into my room, though. How? Are the doors rigged or did they pick a lock that leaves no trace?"

He let out a breath. "As a detective, I have seen skilled thieves bypass locks, but it is rare to leave zero evidence, unless the person had a hidden pass. Or as we have considered, it could be something else." His eyes flicked to Tansy, then returned to Elle. "I am not dismissing unusual possibilities, not anymore."

Elle exhaled, grateful and scared at once. She needed him to believe, but that belief also forced her to acknowledge that the city's strangeness might be bigger than casual crooks.

A moment of silence settled until Tansy stood abruptly. "I am going to check out that little gift store in the lobby, grab some water maybe. You two can chat."

SEVEN

Elle stood in the quiet side corridor of the hotel, eyeing the filigree necklace that glimmered softly in her palm. She felt wary about placing it around her neck again. The events of the past day still clung to her, raw and unsettling. Despite the airy hum of conversations drifting from the lobby, her small corner seemed distanced from all normalcy. Tansy and Mateo waited only a few steps behind her, exchanging murmured concerns while she worked up the nerve to secure the clasp.

She turned the necklace between her fingers and noticed a faint warmth against her skin. The metal felt heavier now, though it looked delicate as ever. A leaf-shaped swirl caught the overhead light and reflected tiny pinpricks onto the wall.

"You sure you want to wear it right here?" Tansy asked, arms folded over a casual sundress covered in bright poppies. Although her tone carried a teasing lilt, her gaze held genuine worry. "After what happened with it being stolen and returned, maybe we should store it somewhere safe."

Elle scanned Tansy's anxious expression. Her cousin had witnessed the note, the strange reappearance on Elle's pillow, and all the unanswered questions swirling around them. But Elle could not bear the idea of tucking the necklace away again without knowing whether that would invite the next thief or the next bizarre occurrence. She exhaled and felt tension purl through her shoulders.

"I need to keep an eye on it," she said. "If I hide it, I might lose track of it again. Besides, maybe wearing it means I can sense if something is wrong."

Mateo stepped up quietly, his dark gaze reflecting a calm concern that made Elle's pulse jump. He had tried earlier to question the hotel staff about suspicious visitors, but nobody found clues about who might have gained entry to her room in the early morning. In the end, all they had was the necklace and a mystery.

"We can be careful," he said, voice low. "We will keep watch. If you get dizzy or feel anything strange, tell us right away."

Elle offered a small nod of acknowledgment. She realized that after everything, she trusted him more than she would have expected a few days ago. He made her feel like they had a plan, even if they were improvising. She brushed her thumb over the necklace's chain and bit her lower lip.

"All right," she whispered. "I'm putting it on."

Tansy reached out in an instinctive show of support, resting one hand on Elle's forearm while Mateo took a small step closer, protective. The corridor smelled faintly of fresh paint and cleaning solution, a sharp contrast to the stale sense of magic that still clung to the filigree. Gently, Elle lifted the chain and brought it around her neck. She forced slow, calm breaths and ignored the sudden flutter in her chest. The clasp gave a tiny click as she fastened it. She lowered her hands, the pendant resting lightly against her collarbone.

The effect was instant. Heat jolted through Elle's body like a sudden, powerful wave of vertigo that threatened to upset her balance. She managed to gasp out a startled breath before her vision blurred. Everything around her dipped and swayed. The corridor's patterned wallpaper melted into hazy shapes. Blood roared in her ears.

"Elle?" Tansy's voice floated from somewhere above water, muffled by the pulse pounding in Elle's temples.

Elle tried to steady herself, but her knees buckled. As she began to collapse, she felt a pair of strong arms encircle her waist from behind, keeping her upright. Through dim flashes, she recognized Mateo's scent of soap and faint cologne. Her head lolled against his shoulder, and she felt the rapid thud of his heartbeat. His concern pulsed through the contact, an anchor for her rattled senses.

The heat turned prickly. Every nerve in her body tingled as though pinned by static. Her mouth felt thick and unresponsive, yet a strange whisper slipped from her lips. It was a string of words she did not recognize, unspooling in a softness that made little sense in her own mind. She heard them reverberate in her ears, as though they were coming from someone else. Tansy's startled gasp indicated that she too heard the unfamiliar language.

"Hold on," Mateo urged. "Elle, you're okay. We have you."

He pressed a hand against her stomach, keeping her upright, then swept his other arm fully behind her back. She felt the corridor's cool air vanish, replaced by the press of his warm shoulder. The floor slipped away. Mateo lifted her into his arms. She tried to lift her lids, but the overhead light only aggravated the spinning sensation in her head.

"Is she, oh my god, is she fainting?" Tansy's voice pitched higher, underscoring her alarm.

Elle wanted to assure them she was fine, or at least that this was not as dangerous as it felt. But the swirl of dizziness tightened, yanking her deeper into a half-conscious haze. She heard footsteps echo across the tile, felt Tansy's fluttering hand at her wrist, and then heard a door squeak open. Distantly, she realized Mateo had carried her into some kind of back office or staff room. The scents of coffee and disinfectant drifted by. Storage boxes rustled when Tansy brushed past them.

Mateo lowered Elle onto a small couch, the cushions squeaking beneath her weight. She blinked at him, her vision slowly returning to clarity. Her chest heaved as she gulped oxygen, though her limbs still trembled with leftover shock. Every muscle tingled. She sensed Tansy looming near, uncertain whether to call an ambulance or wave a bundle of sage to ward off unwelcome forces.

"Take it slowly," Mateo said, kneeling beside the couch. "Breathe in and out."

His voice contained that same quiet steadiness she had come to rely on. She obeyed, forcing her lungs to draw measured air. Tansy crouched at the other side, rummaging through her purse. She mumbled something breathless about water bottles and electrolyte packets, muttering that she should have brought snacks for nerve-wracking days like this.

Lights glowed overhead, a single harsh fluorescent that made the tiny office feel claustrophobic. Elle shut her eyes again. Her head throbbed. Yet beneath the discomfort, she became aware of a new undercurrent surging through her bloodstream. It was as if the chain around her neck channeled some hidden reservoir of energy, making her limbs buzz with renewed strength. The sensation reminded her of hearing a faint electrical hum from a distant power line, only that hum now lived inside her.

"Elle?" Tansy pressed a slightly chilled water bottle to her palm. "Can you talk?"

"I'm okay," Elle managed, voice thin. She tested her muscles, found them stable enough to sit up. Her dizzy spell had passed as quickly as it arrived. The rapid change startled her almost more than the fainting itself.

Mateo continued to watch her closely, one hand still resting gently on her shoulder. A spark of warmth eddied through that contact point, a tingling synergy that radiated from his fingertips. She swallowed and tried to ignore the quickening of her pulse. Her confusion gnawed at her. Was that feeling purely magical or something else?

"That was terrifying," Tansy said, exhaling in relief. She unscrewed the water bottle cap and offered it. "You just crumpled. I thought we lost you for a second."

Elle accepted a sip. The water tasted metallic on her tongue, though she suspected that was simply her rattled nerves playing tricks. "Thanks," she whispered. "I don't know what happened. The second I fastened the necklace, everything tilted. I heard myself speaking nonsense words."

Tansy hissed softly. "Nonsense words? Well, they sure sounded like a chant to me. No clue what language, though. Sounded old."

Elle set aside the water bottle and lifted her hand to the filigree pendant. It rested against her skin without apparent heat now, as though the initial surge had subsided. She felt uneasy recalling that wave of disorientation. But her body no longer felt drained. Instead, she felt alert, almost invigorated. Her fingers curled against the charm, testing it. No searing pain or glow.

Mateo looked at Tansy. "I'll get more help if we need it," he said firmly. "But she's breathing fine now."

"No ambulance," Elle insisted. "I feel normal again. I promise."

"Nobody else calls that normal," Tansy said, though her teasing tone slipped in. "But you're not collapsed on the floor, so that's progress."

Elle's cheeks warmed. She must have looked ridiculous moments earlier, limp and mumbling. The closeness of Mateo's gaze made it difficult to maintain her composure. She noticed how he lingered, hand still braced gently on her shoulder, as though half expecting her to topple again. The tension that sparked through the air upheld the sense that something larger than a fainting spell had just taken place.

"I mean it," Elle murmured, tapping her chest. "I feel stronger?"

"Stronger?" Tansy echoed. "You basically blacked out."

"But the second it ended, I got this rush of clarity." Elle tested her legs, shifting on the couch. "I'm not shaky. Look, my hands are steady."

She raised her palms for Tansy and Mateo to see. No tremor betrayed her. Instead, a faint tingle continued coursing up her arms, as if residual magic circulated beneath her skin.

Mateo's brows knit. "Strangely, you look more awake than you did before. Almost glowing." He studied her, as though verifying she was not about to faint again. Then his mouth relaxed into a measured half-smile of relief. "I guess that's a good sign."

Elle recognized the swirl of complicated feelings behind his calm words. His job was to remain logical, keep people safe, file reports. None of this was textbook procedure. Yet, he had carried her without hesitation. She felt the subtle shift in her chest at that realization. The intangible perimeter she always kept around herself had cracked months ago, letting New Orleans' swirling magic seep into her life. And Mateo had walked right into that swirl, bracing her shoulders so she would not drown in it.

She cleared her throat, trying to lighten the mood. "I

suppose next time, I should sit before I randomly clasp weird, possibly cursed objects around my neck."

Tansy let out a thin laugh and plopped onto the floor, crossing her legs. "I'd vote yes on that plan." Her expression flashed with curiosity. "But do you have any idea what you said? The language sounded archaic, a bit melodic. Do you remember any part of it?"

Elle closed her eyes, trying to coax the memory from her disoriented mind. She recalled the words stretching like ribbons, but she could not pinpoint them. "Not exactly," she admitted. "It was more like a feeling than speech. Like a reflex I had no control over."

Mateo shifted closer, attention sharpened. "That might be important. Maybe your grandmother left more in that necklace than just memories." He offered a wry, thoughtful look. "Though it's possible that was your own power reacting."

Elle's eyes moved to the pendant again. Each curve and swirl of the filigree seemed more detailed than before. She jostled it slightly, but the metal did not react. "All I know is I had zero time to prepare," she said quietly. "It threw me into darkness, then spat me back out feeling wired. Like a jolt of adrenaline but also something deeper."

At that, Tansy's phone buzzed from inside her purse. She fished it out, gave the screen a quick glance, and shook her head. "Just a spam text." She rose to her feet, dusting herself off with quick, restless motions. "So, am I the only one who wants some fresh air? This office feels stuffy and I'm worried if I breathe wrong, I will upset another wave of magical nonsense."

Mateo let go of Elle's shoulder, but he stayed kneeling next to the couch, searching her expression. "How about you? Are you steady enough to move around?"

She rolled her shoulders, testing each vertebra for any sign of dizziness. Nothing. If anything, she felt downright unshaken, little sparks of energy still hummed in her muscles. "I think so," she said. "I'd rather not hide in here. Let's find a place with open windows, maybe that small lounge near the courtyard. I need to figure out if this 'surge' is going to happen again."

They helped her stand, though her body barely required assistance. She walked on her own, only occasionally glancing back to see Mateo behind her, watchful. Tansy pushed open the office door, and the corridor's gentle lighting enveloped them again.

As they made their way through a short hallway, a pair of housekeeping staff members passed, glancing curiously at Elle. She realized she must look rattled, though she tried to maintain her composure. She sensed the necklace shift with each breath, and now that she was more alert, its presence pressed on her collarbone with a calm, comforting heat rather than the fierce blast from earlier.

The lounge at the end of the corridor was empty, its doors propped open to let in a mild cross-breeze. Large windows overlooked a narrow courtyard where potted ferns swayed. Elle's steps slowed as they entered. She scanned the plush chairs organized in a semicircle around a low table. The place smelled faintly of lemon polish and coffee beans. She chose one of the chairs and lowered herself into it.

Tansy grabbed another seat and released a breath. "Okay, crisis averted for now."

Mateo took the chair beside hers and turned to face Elle. She found herself hyperaware of the space between them, just a few inches. She cleared her throat, color creeping into her cheeks.

"Let's talk it through," he said. "We have a stolen necklace that reappeared out of nowhere. It triggers a massive surge of energy the moment you put it on. You speak some unknown words. Then you bounce back stronger than before. That's not typical." The corner of his mouth crooked with irony.

Elle lifted her chin, forcing a tiny smile of her own. "You're telling me. I'm living it." She paused, shoulders relaxing as she let out a slow breath. "It might be that my grandmother really did enchant this piece with something bigger than I ever understood. Maybe it's trying to wake up some part of me."

Tansy's eyebrows rose. "Or it's giving you hints about what it did for Ruby all those years."

Mateo studied Elle's profile, a thoughtful crease across his forehead. "No matter how it works, we need to be cautious. If it knocks you out like that in public, we risk scaring a lot of people. Or worse, we risk you getting hurt if the surge comes mid-street."

Elle realized they all shared the same unspoken question, would it happen again, and would it be worse next time? The lounge's quiet ambiance pressed around them, wrapping them in a moment of collective reflection. Outside, the wind rustled the courtyard's ferns, and the mild click of a distant door reminded her the world carried on, oblivious to their predicament.

Eventually, Tansy rubbed her temples. "I need coffee or something to calm my nerves. I think they have a small station near the front desk. Anybody else?"

Mateo gestured for her to go ahead. His concerned gaze lingered on Elle, who felt another wave of warmth spread beneath her ribcage. She realized that the day's confusion paired with the subtle current pulsing through her limbs had left her yearning for calm. But she also felt reluctant to break away from Mateo's steady presence.

"I'm good," she told Tansy. "Go get your coffee. Take a few minutes."

Tansy popped to her feet with a sharp nod. "All right. I'll be right back." She tossed them a look, something between protective curiosity and approval, then slipped out.

When she was gone, everything felt deeper. Elle turned toward Mateo, half embarrassed by the intensity of her own relief in being alone with him. A swirl of memories surfaced, the stolen purse, the strange flicker of static the first time their arms brushed, the glint in his eyes whenever he tried to reassure her. He might be the only person so far who believed her when she insisted something supernatural was circling her life.

He reached for her hand, pausing an inch away as if waiting for silent permission. She nodded slightly, and he clasped her fingers. A small spark of current jumped between their palms, not painful, but enough for them both to notice. She felt her heart spike in response. That same electric intensity had erupted earlier when he caught her before she fell. This time, it did not scare her. It felt almost comforting.

"Do you actually feel better now?" he asked, voice gentle.

She brushed her thumb across the lines of his knuckles, testing the surprising comfort in that contact. "Yes," she said. "It's weird, but I do. In fact, I feel like I could sprint across the Quarter."

He inclined his head in a slow acknowledgment. "That's good to hear, but let's not test your body too hard right away."

She smiled, letting the warmth of his gentle teasing settle in her chest. They spent another moment in silence. She sensed the necklace's energy thrumming. Yet no dizziness accompanied its pulse, only a mild awareness that she was no longer just Elle Beauregard, the woman who flew down from Chicago to settle her grandmother's affairs. She was more.Gently, Mateo gave her hand a reassuring squeeze. "I'm glad you're safe. I worried when I saw you go pale."

His confession stirred an ache of gratitude in her. "Thank you for catching me," she murmured. "I would have cracked my head on the tile if not for you."

A hint of emotion passed over his face before he cleared his throat, as though dismissing praise he did not think he deserved. "Anyone would have done the same."

"I'm not sure 'anyone' would have," she countered

softly. "There's something about you that makes me feel protected."

He looked at her then, the quiet sincerity in his eyes sending that now-familiar rush of static through her veins. For a charged heartbeat, neither spoke. She felt her pulse throb in her ears and felt how the necklace's heat matched her own blooming flush. The city's swirl of magic, the hotel's subdued air conditioning, the hum of traffic outside all seemed to fade, leaving only the question of how to proceed.

EIGHT

Elle stepped into the heat of the afternoon, feeling as though the New Orleans humidity reached out with invisible hands to grip her neck. Her lungs constricted as she drew in a shallow breath, struggling to adjust after the air conditioned chill of the back office. Outside, the narrow side street behind the hotel was filled with the clamor of distant horns and a rumble of passing carriages. Tansy fanned herself with a playful flourish, though her worried expression never wavered. Next to her, Detective Mateo Cruz wore concern openly in his dark eyes, his squared shoulders suggesting he was ready for any new surprise the day might offer.

They formed an uneasy trio just outside the hotel's rear entrance, not quite sure how to proceed. Elle's hand darted to the filigree necklace resting above her collarbone, tiny beads of moisture prickling where metal met her skin. She was all too aware of the heat radiating from it, as if it possessed a pulse of its own. Though it no longer buzzed with the fierce energy that had nearly toppled her earlier, she could not dismiss the memory of collapsing into Mateo's arms in a surge of dizziness and power.

Tansy ran a hand over her forehead and brushed away strands of hair that clung to her temples. She looked from the necklace to Elle's face. "So," she said, voice pitched high with worry, "are we going to talk about how this thing nearly knocked you unconscious? Or how every time you so much as blink these days, weird stuff happens?"

Elle let out a slow breath. "I wish I had a good explanation. The necklace returns, then my head spins with these energy surges." She swallowed past the dryness in her throat. "I don't know what to do. I know I can't keep pretending everything is fine."

Mateo's gaze moved to the filigree pendant. He stepped closer, his presence comforting yet charged with an undercurrent of tension that made Elle's stomach flip. The invisible static between them, which she had first dismissed as an odd coincidence, now felt deliberate. Something about his proximity sent little sparks across her awareness, as though the city's magic recognized him as part of her story.

Tansy pressed her fists to her hips and looked between Elle and Mateo. "We need answers. Whether that means talking to some local witches or hauling your butt to the ER, I don't care. But I'm not letting you walk around with a ticking supernatural bomb on your chest."

Elle nodded and rubbed a knuckle over the throbbing spot near her temple. She hated feeling helpless. Only days ago, she had convinced herself she could navigate these bizarre occurrences alone if she stayed calm. Today, that fragile image of self-sufficiency had broken. "I think we should see Madame Laveau," she said, voice unexpectedly firm. "She might not tell me everything, but at least she knows more about these psychic phenomena than I do, or than any normal doctor would."

Tansy nodded vigorously. "Great. Then let's go before you pass out again." She directed a pointed look at Mateo, who gave a small nod of agreement. He might have been off duty, but he carried himself like a man ready to step in front of danger. A wave of gratitude warmed Elle's cheeks.

They set off through the French Quarter, weaving among the smattering of mid afternoon foot traffic. Tourists clutched paper sacks of pralines, pressing them to sweaty cheeks in the hope of relief. Street performers lined the sidewalks, saxophones releasing jazzy undertones that seemed to swirl beneath the hum of conversation. The wrought iron balconies overhead provided thin shadows across their path. Each time the group trudged around a corner, the thick haze of summertime air clung more tightly to their skin.

Elle often felt Mateo's presence behind her, a silent guardian who kept a careful watch on any worrisome shift in her stride. She tried not to dwell on the magnetism that flared whenever she sensed his gaze, but it was impossible to ignore the way her pulse kicked up each time he leaned in to ask if she was okay. She murmured a few acknowledgments and tried to keep her tone brisk and unaffected.

Tansy, walking just a step ahead, rattled off theories like she always did when anxious. "What if it's Grandma

Ruby's spirit, amping up your abilities? Or maybe some residue from that streetlamp fiasco the other night. Or," she glanced over her shoulder with a hint of humor, "maybe you're just lovesick or something."

Elle's cheeks flushed hotter than the New Orleans sun. She pretended not to notice the amused tilt of Mateo's lips. "I'm fine," she lied. "I just feel this weird friction in the air, like something wants to either protect me or consume me." She shook her head and wished she could articulate it better than that. "I'm done ignoring it. We see Laveau, get some real answers, and hope she knows how to keep me from blacking out again."

They reached the entrance to Madame Laveau's shop on Royal Street. Elle could smell the incense before she glimpsed the interior, a unique blend of sandalwood and something spicy that perked her senses. Overhead, a wind chime made of small bones rattled in the sudden breeze. The shop's front was draped with thick purple curtains, parted just enough to reveal the inviting glow of candlelight inside. Painted letters on the door read: Readings, Charms, and Spirit Guidance.

Elle paused on the threshold, mindful of the swirling energy inside. Sometimes, stepping into Madame Laveau's domain felt like crossing into another realm. She swallowed any lingering reluctance and opened the door. The bell above it jingled, and a gust of much cooler air hit her sweaty face, sending a pleasant chill across the back of her neck.

The interior was dimly lit, every surface draped with velvet or piled with crystals that gleamed in candlelight.

Shelves showcased jars of herbs, shimmering pendulums, and tarnished mirrors. At the center of it all stood Madame Laveau herself, her regal posture evident even in silhouette. She wore a loose black shawl, embroidered with gold thread, over a dark dress that accentuated her ageless features. Her attention snapped toward them the instant they stepped in.

Without speaking, she lifted one hand, a gesture that urged them to stay quiet. She studied Elle with discerning eyes, shifting her focus from Elle's face to the necklace glinting against her collarbone. At that moment, every candle grew brighter. Flames leaped as though greeted by a sudden gust, though the air in the shop felt still.

"So, it has awoken," Madame Laveau said softly, stepping closer until she was within arm's reach of Elle. She pressed her palms together beneath her chin, as though observing a sacred artifact. "That filigree was meant to lie dormant until you were ready."

Elle's mouth felt dry. She managed a small nod, ignoring Tansy's sideways stare urging her to speak. "I guess I wasn't ready at all," Elle said. "It showed up in my locked room. It's been burning hot, making me feel like I'm going to faint."

Madame Laveau's lips parted in a thoughtful sigh. Her eyes, an indefinable gray, hinted at centuries of knowledge locked behind them. "Your grandmother believed you would inherit her gift in time," she said. "She expected you to discover your power under quieter circumstances, but fate is rarely gentle."

Tansy rested a hand on Elle's shoulder. "So you are

saying Ruby wanted to pass down all of this weird energy, that she planned for it?" Her voice faltered on the last words, betraying her lingering hope that maybe none of this was real.

Madame Laveau turned her gaze on Tansy and Mateo, nodding once in greeting. Then her attention returned to Elle. "Your grandmother sharpened that necklace with her own blood magic, ensuring it would respond strongly to your lineage. She tried to keep it contained, but if your emotional state flares, you can expect the energy to spike as well."

Mateo cleared his throat, stepping forward enough that Elle caught the faint brush of his arm against hers. That small contact sent a ripple of warmth down her side. "What kind of energy are we dealing with?" he asked. "Elle nearly passed out earlier. Is it dangerous?"

"The danger depends on how it is handled," the psychic replied, eyes flicking to Elle's anxious features. "The slightest emotional surge, be it fear or anger or even attraction, can trigger a reaction." She paused, letting the weight of her words sink in. Then her expression grew more sympathetic. "But you hold the final say in how this power is shaped."

Elle's stomach twisted. Her chest felt hot, as if her own breath scalded her from the inside. She remembered how the flickers of magic spiked when she grew nervous in Mateo's presence. Another wave of panic built at the thought that her own body might be a ticking bomb of raw magic. "I'm not in the mood to carry some big super-natural legacy," she blurted. Her hands balled into fists at her sides. "I just want to figure out how to live without being afraid."

A faint rustle came from behind one of the shelves. A cluster of crystals, each perched on a small display stand, clattered ominously. Elle felt something coil in her gut, a tension that crackled up her spine. Her heart pounded as an invisible wind seemed to swirl around her ankles, tugging at the hem of her shirt. Before she could step away, an invisible jolt burst outward like a mini shock-wave. The crystals, once neatly arranged, toppled from their display. A few scattered to the floor, clinking against the polished wood.

Tansy gasped and hurried forward, dropping to one knee to gather them. Madame Laveau raised a hand to halt Tansy and slowly knelt to pick up the nearest piece. A chunk of rose quartz rolled across the floor until it bumped the shop's counter. The psychic aimed a measured glance at Elle, lips pressed into a line.

Elle's cheeks flamed with embarrassment. She had not intentionally summoned any wind. She had only felt her frustration and worry churn inside her. "I'm sorry," she stammered. "I didn't mean to do that." Her voice trembled with disbelief as she looked askance at Tansy, then at Mateo.

Mateo's eyes softened, reflecting a quiet concern that tightened the space around Elle's heart. Tansy hovered protectively, though it was clear she was just as shaken. This was proof, as if they needed more. Elle's power was responding to her every emotion, whether she liked it or not.

Madame Laveau exhaled, turning the rose quartz between her fingers. "You see now," she said in a calm voice, "why your grandmother tried to guide you slowly. That necklace magnifies your feelings in unpredictable ways. The more you deny it, the stronger the backlash."

Elle rubbed her wrists as if trying to rid herself of static. "It isn't fair," she whispered, sounding petulant even to her own ears. She didn't enjoy feeling like a child faced with an impossible task.

"There is no fairness in the old ways," Madame Laveau said. "Only acceptance, understanding, and discipline. If you continue to fight this, the eruptions will keep happening."

With a slow nod, Elle felt her throat tighten. A thousand questions roared in her mind. How was she supposed to control power she barely believed in until a few days ago? Could she risk trusting an ability that had already proven dangerous? And how was she supposed to handle the growing spark that flared whenever Mateo stood close, if even the faintest emotional flutter could release another surge?

Madame Laveau stood clutching the rose quartz. She carefully placed the crystal on the countertop. Then she bent down for the other fallen pieces, collecting them in quiet deliberation. Tansy edged nearer, pressing a comforting hand to Elle's back, her expression torn between awe and fear. In the corner, Mateo shifted his weight, the subtle tension in his posture betraying how unsettled he felt, though he tried to mask it for her sake.

A quiet fell over the shop, broken only by the slight

scrape of gems against the polished floor as Madame Laveau gathered them. The incense smoke drifted lazily overhead, refusing to stir despite the gust that had just rattled the stands. It was as if the entire room recognized that a line had been crossed, that Elle could never again dismiss the possibility of her magic or hide behind doubt.

Madame Laveau finished rearranging the crystals and looked once more at Elle. "The truths you fear are already stirring inside you," her tone was neither cruel nor unkind, merely matter-of-fact. "Whether you like it or not, child, there is no turning back."

A prickling sense of finality crawled under Elle's skin. Part of her wanted to run from the shop and pretend none of this was real. Yet the more rational part of her realized that she and her power were already entwined. Reality would not let her revert to normal. The slip of paper she had found with the returned necklace, You weren't ready. Try again, echoed in her mind.

Madame Laveau began to clean up the area, wiping away imaginary dust and resetting the stands. The silence was deafening, magnifying every heartbeat in Elle's ears. Tansy rose with the last crystal cupped in her hands and passed it to the psychic. The two women exchanged a look of faint solidarity, though both seemed uncertain how to proceed.

Slowly, Elle gazed at Mateo, noticing how his stance tensed in quiet vigilance. He offered her a look of encouragement, though she saw unspoken questions warring behind his eyes. Tansy hovered at Elle's side, lips slightly parted, as though one breath away from unleashing more anxious words. A candle light reflected across the glass cases, and it struck Elle that she was standing at a precipice she never asked for.

She had hoped Madame Laveau might wave a hand and rid her of this burden, or at least offer a gentle pathway to keep it under control. Instead, she now understood that tackling the power inside her was the only way forward.

As Madame Laveau's slender fingers set the final crystal onto its perch, Tansy bit her lip. Her eyes darted to Mateo, then to Elle, her steady presence an anchor. Mateo exhaled, nearly silent, but Elle felt the subtle shift in his posture. He was ready to protect her from anything, even if the threat was coming from within her own soul.

Madame Laveau's words about unstoppable ancestral power lingered in the charged air. Elle recognized the quiet dread in Tansy's expression, matched by the unwavering concern in Mateo's relaxed stance. Yet she also sensed a spark of possibility in her own chest, a faint glimmer that maybe she could harness this magic her grandmother had nurtured. Perhaps, as frightening as it was, this was the path she had been meant to walk all along.

The psychic finished tidying the fallen crystals and turned to present them with a serene nod. She did not speak yet. She simply studied them, Elle, Tansy, and Mateo, before returning behind the counter. Tansy and Mateo exchanged a look that radiated equal parts alarm and understanding, as though they realized this was the moment no one could undo.

Watching them, Elle's heart pounded. A sense of finality pressed down on her shoulders, and a swirl of emotions rattled in her chest. There were no illusions about the next step being easy. Still, she reminded herself, she had survived everything thus far. Despite the fear lodged in her throat, she was here, standing in the midst of candles and swirling incense, holding onto a power she never thought she would claim.

She pressed a hand over the filigree pendant and closed her eyes, inhaling the smoky air. An uncertain road lay ahead, but backing out was no longer an option.

As Madame Laveau resumed her quiet work, Tansy and Mateo shared a worried glance. Elle felt that shared concern pierce her defenses, and she knew she had stepped beyond the threshold of safety. Something powerful had awakened inside her, and nothing in her life would remain the same.

NINE

Elle paused at the edge of her grandmother's shotgun house, struck by how small it looked compared to her recollections. Boards stretched close together in a slender layout, the wood worn smooth by time and New Orleans humidity. Magnolias loomed overhead, their waxy leaves filtering the afternoon light. Petals drifted lazily in the moist air, leaving flecks of white against the peeling paint.

Tansy stood beside her, jingling a brass key in her palm. "Feels like ages since we've been inside," she murmured. She tilted her head, giving Elle a reassuring look. "You ready?"

Elle nodded, though her stomach knotted with trepidation. Entering Ruby's house felt like opening an old diary she had avoided for too long. She had grown up rummaging through every corner of this place, but something about returning now after everything that had happened with the necklace and the sense of swirling magic in the Quarter made her feel as though she was stepping into uncharted territory.

Tansy pushed the key into the lock. Metal scraped, then gave way. With a gentle shove, the door swung open. A wave of dusty warmth drifted out along with a faint odor of lavender perfume. Ruby's favorite floral scent lingered so clearly that Elle's chest tightened the moment it hit her senses.

They stepped into the narrow living room where crocheted blankets lay folded across a faded loveseat. Stacks of old newspapers sat in a neat column against the wall, showing Ruby's habit of collecting local stories and reading them at her leisure. On the far side of the room, mason jars of dried herbs lined a crooked shelf, each labeled in Ruby's distinctive handwriting.

Rosemary, Thyme, Mugwort, Basil.

The curling script overwhelmed Elle with memories of watching her grandmother scribble incantations on scrap paper, never letting her granddaughter see too much detail.

Despite the musty smell and stale air, it felt like a home she still recognized. Sunlight drifted through the narrow windows, illuminating floating motes of dust. Every corner carried familiarity, and yet a new tension rippled under Elle's skin. The city's magic had found its way into her blood, and now even these comforting old spaces felt charged with possibility.

"You take the living room," Tansy said softly, easing

her purse down on a side table. "I'll start in Ruby's bedroom, see if anything stands out. We are looking for more notes about spells, right?"

Elle let out a tight exhale. "Spells, wards, anything that could explain why everything feels so potent." She still remembered how she nearly collapsed days ago when the heirloom necklace flared around her neck. The sense of hidden power had only grown stronger since. If her grandmother's journals or half-finished instructions could shed light on how to control that power, Elle was determined to find them.

Tansy stepped gingerly toward the bedroom hallway and disappeared from sight. Elle nudged aside a footstool and crouched next to a stack of battered boxes by the living room window. She pulled the first box open. It was stuffed with old photo frames and personal trinkets, wooden earrings, Mardi Gras beads, even a faded beignet recipe penned on an index card. A pang of warmth tugged at her heart. She recognized Ruby's broad loops of handwriting.

She placed the items aside with a soft smile, thinking of the countless days she spent watching Ruby cook. She could almost hear Ruby's lilting voice chiding her for measuring sugar improperly, insisting that love mattered as much as exact teaspoons. In the second box, she discovered loose pages filled with scribbled lines referencing *Thinner Veils* and *Full Moon Preparations,* though no single page offered more than scattered glimpses of methods or ingredients. The words read like half-started spells, as though Ruby had jotted them down in a hurry without finishing.

Elle's pulse quickened when she realized the scope of her grandmother's planning. Ruby must have intended to pass along more than just an heirloom. Maybe she had every intention to teach Elle properly, real lessons about wards and protection. The knowledge that she had run short on time hurt more than Elle expected. A lump rose in her throat.

"Find anything fun?" Tansy's voice fluttered from the hallway.

Elle set the scattered notes aside. "Just bits and pieces so far." She rose and stepped to meet her cousin near the kitchen. Tansy clutched a small, worn journal with a russet cover and a frayed spine. A triumphant grin lit her features.

"You want clarity?" Tansy asked, wiggling the little book. "This might be it."

Elle took the journal and flipped through the pages. The handwriting shifted from Ruby's typically flowing style into cramped lines that squeezed between the edges. She recognized the loop of letters though, there was no doubt it belonged to her grandmother. Page after page mentioned simple spells, easy wards for doorways, love charms that required minimal components, and potions for easing headaches. In the middle, she found a rough outline for something called *Beginner's Levitation.*

Her eyes skimmed the page. "So, she wrote instructions for lifting small objects, sugar cubes, wooden spoons, that kind of thing."

Tansy giggled. "Ruby probably intended to give you practice sessions. How else are you supposed to move on to bigger spells?"

Elle brushed her thumb over the cracked spine. "The margins are full of scribbles." Some resembled check marks, others looked like half-forgotten musings about focusing one's breathing. A curious ache formed in Elle's chest. Ruby had likely planned to guide her step by step. There were question marks next to certain ingredients, as if her grandmother was still deciding which herbs to use.

Tansy tapped the page. "Look here. She wrote, *Remember emotional alignment is key. Calm, centered energy lifts the cube. Fear or anger can cause the spell to misfire.* If that's not a warning, I don't know what is."

Elle chewed her lip, remembering just how disruptive her heightened emotions had been lately. Maybe practicing a small-scale spell would help her feel in control. "Let's test it," she said, trying to sound confident. "A sugar cube is harmless enough."

They carried the journal to the kitchen. The linoleum floor squeaked underfoot. Light from the window above the sink cast angled shadows on the counter. A row of chipped mugs sat in a dish rack, the remnants of a life paused rather than finished. Elle took a small sugar bowl from a shelf and placed a single cube on the table. She inhaled, searching for calm.

"All right," she murmured, scanning the handwritten instructions. "Hold the cube in your mind. Picture it rising gently. Steady breathing."

Tansy stood a step back, half-hugging herself. "You got this," she whispered.

Elle forced a measured inhale, then let the air slip from her lungs. She focused on the sugar cube. She pictured it drifting into the air, slow and graceful, just as the journal suggested. She willed her churning anxiety to settle. The corners of her vision tightened as she concentrated on that solitary piece of sugar.

A faint flicker of warmth pulsed along her arms. For a heartbeat, she felt possibility coil in her muscles. The sugar cube wobbled. She gasped, eyes going wide as it rose half an inch. Tansy cheered behind her, but the sudden excitement jarred Elle's concentration. The sugar cube dropped with a dull thud. Elle tried again, chest buzzing with adrenaline. She wanted to succeed.

This time, the energy inside her spiked abruptly. The cube shot upward, but it did not simply hover. It rocketed off the table, bumping into a spoon lying near an old coffee tin. The spoon launched like a tiny projectile, spinning across the kitchen in a wild arc. Tansy yelped and ducked. The metal spoon slammed into a cabinet door with a sharp clang and clattered to the floor.

Heart pounding, Elle rushed up to Tansy, eyes wide. "Oh my god, are you okay?" She could barely believe what she had seen. A sugar cube had unleashed that much force?

Tansy peered from behind her arms, cheeks flushed. "I'm fine. That spoon nearly gave me a concussion, though." Her voice sounded shaky, but a laugh broke free as she glanced at Elle's horrified expression. "Well, at least we know the spell works."

Elle exhaled a staggering breath, trying to calm her racing heart. Her hands trembled, and an unsettling combination of awe and fear lashed through her. "What if I had aimed at you instead of the cabinet? That was intense." She crouched and picked up the spoon from the floor. Its handle bore a slight dent where it had struck the cabinet.

Tansy pressed a comforting hand to Elle's shoulder. "You were eager. Ruby wrote that emotions can trigger bigger surges." She squeezed gently. "You just proved you have real power. You're not imagining it, and it's not all going to be neat or tidy."

Elle puffed out a slow breath and placed the dented spoon on the table. Her heart still thundered. "Yeah, maybe I should hold off on trying anything bigger until I learn how to keep from launching half the kitchen into orbit." A nervous giggle escaped her. "That's stronger than I expected."

They shared an unsteady moment of laughter, though Elle's mind spun with implications. She had tried a harmless, low-level spell and nearly caused a minor disaster. The power surging inside her was no joke. This was not just a vague sense of magic she could ignore or dismiss. It was real, tangible, and potentially dangerous if she lost focus.

Tansy led her back to the living room. "Let's take a break from flinging utensils," she teased, casting a wary glance at the hallway as if ensuring no other items were floating in stealth. In more subdued tones, she added, "We can keep reading through Ruby's notes and maybe figure out a way to stabilize your energy."

Elle nodded, still shaken. She passed a hand over her forehead, wiping away a slight sheen of sweat. The reality of conjuring raw magic, no matter how accidental, sent her adrenaline spiking in a confusing mix of exhilaration and dread. A part of her had always assumed that such feats belonged in stories. Now, it was her life.

They spent the rest of the afternoon sifting through boxes and scanning Ruby's scribbles. Most entries offered glimpses of spells for household charms, mild potions to settle upset stomachs, or protective wards fashioned from everyday objects. But none provided a straightforward guide to controlling large surges of power.

When the glow of dusk seeped in, creating a haze of orange light across the floor, Tansy and Elle decided to leave the rummaged boxes in the living room and settle for the night. The house had only one bedroom, and they agreed to share Ruby's old bed to avoid the dusty couch.

With the air conditioner long dead, they cracked a window and let the hum of crickets seep inside. Shadows danced along the walls, shaped by headlights passing outside.

Elle placed the worn journal on the nightstand. She lay next to Tansy under a thin sheet, the heat of the night pressing down on them both. The scent of lavender perfume still lingered in the corners of the room, nudged by the soft breeze. Maybe it was only in Elle's imagination, but the flowery aroma felt deliberate, as if Ruby was watching.

Tansy propped herself on an elbow. "I miss her," she said quietly, voice carrying a tremor that mirrored the sadness in Elle's chest. "Everything in this place reminds me of how she used to call us over for dinner and make us test the weird herbal concoctions she swore would cure anything." Tears formed in Tansy's eyes, reflecting the faint glow of the streetlamp outside. "I keep waiting for her to bustle through the door with her unstoppable energy."

Elle's throat tightened. She folded her hands near her chin and stared at the ceiling. A swirl of memories flooded her mind, Ruby's boisterous laugh, the way she snapped her fingers in the kitchen to conjure the perfect cameo of sweet scents, the unwavering love that always comforted Elle no matter how tough life felt. She had never realized how deeply her grandmother's magic intertwined with her daily warmth.

"Sometimes I think I will turn around and see her in the next room," Elle whispered. "My biggest regret is not asking questions sooner. I spent years away, convinced I had all the time in the world to learn about her secrets and the heritage she carried." She swallowed against the ache in her throat. "Now I am fumbling through these spells like an impatient student with no teacher."

Tansy sniffled and brushed away a tear. "She would be proud to see you trying. Do not let guilt bury you. We all assumed she would be here to guide us. She told me once," Tansy paused to clear her throat, "she said you were special, that you had a spark she had never seen before. She was certain you would embrace it when you were ready."

A surge of emotion rushed through Elle. Doubt mingled with longing as she thought about Ruby's unwavering faith. "It feels unfair," she admitted, voice trembling. "I did not ask for these powers to get so out of control. I did not want to worry about spoons flying across the room or everything else."

Tansy reached for her hand under the thin sheets. "I know. But sometimes life picks us, not the other way around."

The quiet rumble of traffic drifted in from the street. Someone laughed far off, a reminder that the city continued bustling into the night. For Elle, it felt like the world had momentarily shrunk to this bedroom and the gentle heartbreak they shared.

"I remember the day you left for college," Tansy continued, voice subdued. "Ruby said not to fret, that one day you'd come home for good reason. She didn't elaborate, but I saw the tears in her eyes. She wanted you to find your own path first." Tansy squeezed Elle's fingers. "Whatever upended way it happened, you're here now, and her magic is literally humming in your veins."

Elle closed her eyes. She pictured the sugar cube leaping off the table, the raw adrenaline that left her trembling. She had never asked for the kind of power that could fling a spoon across a kitchen. Yet she felt an odd undercurrent of responsibility, as if the city's magical pulse recognized Ruby's descendant and demanded her acceptance.

They lay there, only the rise and fall of their breaths marking the passage of time. Night wore on, the house filling with memories of those who had walked its halls. Finally, Tansy sniffled again and placed her other hand over Elle's.

"Elle," she said, her face glimmering with both sadness and a stubborn hope. "Believe this belongs to you. Ruby passed it down for a reason. Whether it's big or terrifying or complicated, it's yours. You have to keep going. Promise me you won't hide from it."

A tear slipped down Elle's cheek. She thought of the worn journal, of her shaky attempt at levitation, and of how Ruby had probably planned so meticulously. The legacy was indeed frightening, but it was also a piece of herself she could no longer deny. She laced her fingers through Tansy's.

"I promise," she whispered, voice unsteady yet resolute. "I'll do my best. We'll figure it out, one spoon and one spell at a time."

Tansy offered a shaky laugh, and for a moment, the deep sorrow that clung to the night lifted, replaced by the fierceness of their bond. Elle settled deeper under the sheet, the heat of the August night still pressing against her skin, but comfort from Tansy's closeness chased away the chill of loneliness. Outside, the crickets continued their lullaby, and inside, traces of lavender reminded them both that Ruby's love had not disappeared with her passing.

They stayed like that until their breathing slowed, tears drying into the quiet acceptance that, closed doors or not, life in the old shotgun house had only begun a new chapter. Tansy turned her head to face Elle, eyes tender, and repeated her conviction.

"This legacy belongs to you. It may be scary, but you have more strength than you know. You're here to claim it."

Elle felt a tide of emotion welling up again. She sensed the shift in the air, a silent promise that she would walk the path her grandmother had left, no matter how daunting. She closed her eyes and drew on Tansy's unwavering presence. Weary relief coursed through her, and clasping her cousin's hand as the moonlight faded along the windowsill, she resolved to learn the magic that had begun to spark inside her.

CHAPTER

TEN

The morning sun filtered softly through the lace curtains in Ruby's cramped bedroom, illuminating drifting specks of dust in the sticky air. Elle pushed aside a shallow wooden box of half-burned candles, her fingers brushing the rough edges of a tattered grimoire tucked beneath them. She stood near the bed she and Tansy had shared the previous night, her thoughts drifting between the comforting scent of old lavender sachets and the persistent throb of uncertainty she had carried for days. No matter how many spells or half-scribbled notes she uncovered, she still felt as if the city's magic waited just around the corner, ready to test her again.

Tansy yawned dramatically from the doorway, her hair an untamed tumble around her shoulders. "You look busy," she said, voice thick with remnants of sleep. She crossed over to Elle and peered at the grimoire pages, eyes widening at the complexity of the runes curled along the margins. "Any chance that's the silver-bullet guide that will save us from the next magical surprise?"

Elle smiled, though it arrived tinged with self-consciousness. "I wish. Ruby's entries here are scattered. It's more like half a recipe for an herbal potion, then a big circle to represent a ward. I can't tell if it's a partial idea or if it's specifically about the necklace." She lifted the leather cover, noticing flecks scraping off at the corners. For all the volumes Ruby had collected, not one neatly combined answers in a single place.

Tansy sighed, plucking the old grimoire from Elle's grasp and placing it carefully atop a pile near the window. "Let's pack this one with the other essentials," she said, nodding to a stack of journals on the rickety side table. "I figure we can bring them back to your hotel room. That way you can keep studying without trekking back and forth all the time."

Elle's heartbeat fluttered. She remembered how the hotel's power went haywire the other day, flickering the moment she tried to relax. Still, she recognized the sense in Tansy's plan. If she intended to reach the bottom of her uncanny connection to Ruby's legacy and the stolen, now mysteriously returned necklace, she needed all the resources close at hand. "It is a good idea," she admitted, grabbing a battered notebook with a pink Post-it sticking out one side. The pages rustled, loose from repeated turning.

They spent the next twenty minutes scouring the shotgun house for anything else that might prove critical. Tansy darted around, rummaging through shallow cabinets and pulling out dusty boxes. Occasionally, she would pause to read off a snippet, love charms, simple warding chants, or cryptic runic formulas, but came away with no single breakthrough.

Eventually, a silence fell between them. The small living room carried echoes of Ruby's presence, crocheted blankets draped over sagging furniture, half-used jars of spices, and spiritual tokens perched near the window. Elle's mind continued to surge with half-formed questions. Despite the warmth of the morning sun, a faint chill curled at the back of her neck.

Tansy glanced at the old clock on the mantel. "We should load the books into the trunk of my car," she said, retrieving a large canvas tote from next to the couch. "We have to leave soon if we want to beat the midday heat. I can practically feel the humidity creeping up my spine already."

Elle gathered armfuls of journals and placed them gently into the tote. The weight of them settled in her arms, and she wondered if she was seriously prepared to master everything Ruby had left behind. With a heavy sigh, she followed Tansy to the front door and stepped over a loose floorboard that squeaked in protest.

The morning clamored around them the instant they opened the door. Thick, moisture laden air hit Elle's face like a wave, and the sunlight, brighter than she expected, made her squint. She juggled the books in her arms, blinking against the glare. Tansy propped the screen door open with her hip.

Before Elle could exit, a solid presence nearly collided

with her from the porch steps, forcing her to rock back on her heels. She steadied herself and looked at Detective Mateo Cruz standing at the threshold, arms partially raised as if to catch her if she stumbled. His eyes held that steady calm she had come to rely on, though a trace of concern flashed across his features.

"Sorry," he said, lowering his arms carefully. "I didn't mean to barge onto your porch."

Elle was too surprised to speak at first. She registered the faint scent of soap and the quiet rustle of the morning breeze in the thick curls at his forehead. Beneath it, she caught a flicker of tension in his jaw. He stood there in casual clothes, a simple short sleeved shirt that highlighted the lean strength beneath. It was a sharp contrast from his usual work attire.

Tansy slid out onto the porch, arms akimbo. "We almost smacked you with an entire library," she teased, tipping her chin at the books in Elle's arms. "What brings you here so early?"

Mateo shifted on his feet, glancing between them. "You texted me the address," he said softly, directing the comment at Tansy. "You mentioned weird graffiti in the neighborhood. I wanted to check it out."

Tansy's face brightened in sudden recollection. She snapped her fingers. "Right. I noticed some new symbols scrawled on the corner two streets over, red paint, not the usual random tagging. Looked out of place. I thought it might connect to the bizarre flickering lights we keep noticing."

Mateo nodded, his attention drifting to the journals

in Elle's arms. "I've been following up on my own time," he said, voice quiet. "The department isn't exactly thrilled about chasing 'supernatural' leads. Officially, a graffiti job gets filed in the 'vandalism' category. But with everything that happened," he added, meeting Elle's gaze, "I just can't ignore the possibility it ties into your case."

Elle felt her chest tighten. She still recalled the dizzy surge when the necklace had flared hot against her skin days ago, nearly knocking her off her feet. The memory floated in the back of her mind each time she encountered anything out of the ordinary. She deposited the stack of books into Tansy's waiting arms, then rubbed the faint ache at her collarbone.

"Thanks for looking into it," she said, meeting Mateo's gaze fully for the first time that morning. "I know it might not be easy going against your precinct's stance."

His expression softened. "I'd rather follow my instincts than let a good lead slip, especially given the things we've both seen." He gave a half-smile, glancing at Tansy.

Tansy cleared her throat, hugging the old spellbooks to her chest. "I'll put these in the car. Maybe the two of you can talk about those strange leads. I'll pop back in a minute." She pivoted, stepping off the porch, leaving Elle alone with Mateo with the whir of cicadas buzzing around the overgrown magnolia tree by the sidewalk.

Elle folded her arms, feeling a prickly warmth slide along her skin. She noticed how Mateo's gaze lingered on her face before drifting to the spines of the journals Tansy was carrying away. "You still have that necklace, right?" he asked, speaking gently.

She nodded. "I'm keeping it close, but I've wrapped it in a cloth for now." She paused, not sure how to encapsulate the swirl of conflicting emotions she felt every time she touched that heirloom. "It flares up sometimes. Heat or strange vibrations. I'm waiting for clues from Ruby's notes on how to handle it."

He exhaled, shifting his weight from one foot to the other. A distant car horn sounded from a nearby street, echoing across the quiet neighborhood. "If you want me to keep you updated on any developments tied to these symbols, like the ones Tansy mentioned, I would be happy to. I also have a couple of tips from locals about lights across the Quarter. Probably nothing, but in case it ties back to the stolen purse incident or whatever else has been happening, I thought you would want to know."

Elle was not sure if she should laugh or bury her face in her hands. The "whatever else" portion seemed endless, from unexpected magical surges to her own spiraling confusion about New Orleans' supernatural undercurrent. She pushed a stray hair from her forehead. "Yeah, that would be great. I want to piece together how all this ties in. It is starting to feel bigger than a stolen necklace."

Mateo glanced at the front door and then back at her. His features, usually composed, showed something close to sheepishness. "Let me take some of those," he offered, gesturing to the few smaller notebooks she still clutched.

She hesitated. "They are dusty. You will get your shirt all grimy."

A small smile curved at his lips. He stepped forward and closed his fingers around the edges of the notebooks. "I once chased a suspect through three blocks of muddy yards in a thunderstorm. A little dust will not bother me."

Their fingers brushed as she passed the journals to him, and a subtle spark seemed to zip up her arm. She swallowed, her mind returning to the memory of how his arms felt around her waist when she nearly fainted. The moment lingered, charged with an intensity that had little to do with the items they held.

He cleared his throat softly. "Elle," he trailed off, glancing at Tansy's car, where Tansy was busy rearranging the larger books in her trunk. Then he met Elle's eyes, a hint of uncertainty in his face. "I was wondering, when all this chaos settles, maybe you'd want to grab dinner?"

Elle's heartbeat thumped louder. She stared at him, momentarily forgetting how to respond. He was so careful, so calm under normal circumstances, that the idea of him feeling awkward while asking her out felt refreshing, even sweet.

He pressed on, cheeks darkening slightly. "I know it might sound out of left field, and there's a lot going on. But once you're safe, once we get some answers, I'd like to see you outside the backdrop of stolen purses and shattered streetlamps."

Her lips parted in a slight smile. "That sounds really nice." She let out a breathy laugh, nerves tied up with a quiet jolt of excitement. "I'd like that too."

ELEVEN

Elle pressed her palm against the wide glass doors of the old boutique hotel, inhaling air that felt thick enough to drink. The night was unbearably hot, as though the humidity had conspired with every porch light and vinyl awning in the French Quarter to trap the summer heat. She had decided on a quick walk down the hallway, seeking relief in the lobby's air conditioning. Instead, she found the entire building wrapped in uneasy stillness.

A single rumble of thunder cracked overhead. The lights blinked twice, an instant flutter that made her heart pound. Then the entire lobby plunged into darkness. She gasped and stepped backward. Her reflection vanished from the glass, replaced by dim shapes, silhouettes of furniture, the faint outline of the concierge desk, the dull gleam of brass light fixtures that had all gone dead.

The sudden loss of light chilled her more than the storm outside. No generator kicked in, and the overhead fans stopped spinning. The quiet it left behind magnified everything else, her breath, her own pulse, and the low rumble of a gathering storm. She heard rain begin to slap the building with increasing fervor.

"It's fine," she muttered under her breath, trying to stay calm. She tightened her grip on the small purse slung across her body. Though she wasn't brandishing any incantations, she silently repeated a reassurance that Tansy had once taught her, a gentle chant about peaceful breezes. It did little good.

She realized her filigree necklace was growing warm, a gentle heat that pressed into her collarbone. Whenever her anxiety spiked, the necklace answered. Right now, it felt poised between a subtle vibration and outright burning. Anxiety coiled in her chest, pulling her heartbeat into a fierce staccato. She shut her eyes a moment and inhaled a lungful of humid air.

Lightning flared out on the street, illuminating the large windows for half a second. The thunder that followed rattled the front door in its frame. Something about the entire situation, shock from the power failing plus storms overhead, made her uneasy. She recalled too many mishaps lately involving her magic spiking at unplanned moments. The building's power grid had been faltering all week, or so the desk attendant had insisted. But a quiet part of her wondered if she had somehow coaxed this darkness into being, as if her presence had shorted out every circuit.

She fished out her phone and turned it on. The battery icon glowed a solid half-charge. Good enough, she thought, even if the reception might be spotty in the storm. She swiped across her contacts. Her first impulse was to text Tansy, see if she was still out or had gone to bed for the night. But she hesitated. Another approach gripped her. If she truly needed backup, who else could anchor her sense of relief better than Detective Mateo Cruz?

Her teeth gritted at the admission that she might want him here. She had never relished asking for help, certainly not from the calm, steady detective who had become her lifeline in the short time since their paths first crossed. Yet the building felt claustrophobic, and each bolt of lightning made her think of uninvited illusions. She typed out a quick message:

Storm knocked out power. Lobby is dark. Feel like I can't breathe. Are you close by?

Her finger hovered over the send button for two heart-beats. Then she tapped it. A wave of embarrassment followed. There was no reason for her to bother him unless something truly dangerous lurked in the gloom. But the necklace still buzzed at her throat, and sweat beaded along her forehead. She forced herself to exhale, thinking maybe she could handle this on her own.

Except the darkness did not just lie across the lobby. It curled into the halls, the corridors, the corners of her mind where half-formed nightmares sometimes waited. She remembered the last time she had felt close to blacking out, all because her magic threatened to surge. Her breathing sped up again, and she massaged her collarbone as if trying to keep the necklace from going molten.

Almost immediately, her phone vibrated in her hand. She unlocked the phone.

On my way.

That was it. No hesitation, no excuses. She found herself whispering a relieved thank you into the empty darkness.

Rain hammered the roof in thick sheets, and she listened to its constant drumming as she searched around the front desk. The old clerk must have stepped out, or else he was checking the building's fuse box in the back. A single emergency bulb cast the faintest glow across the tile. It made the entire lobby look haunted, as if reality had slipped sideways.

She tried to remain near the windows, hoping the occasional lightning flash would let her see more than shifting silhouettes. Twice, she spotted distant headlights passing on the street, but no immediate sign of any standard city emergency lights. The Quarter was prone to losing power, though rarely in such a sudden sweep. She felt a chill gather below her ribs.

In the next flash of lightning, a figure swept toward the door. He was soaked to the skin, the edges of a lightweight jacket clinging to his frame. He gave a brief push and stepped inside with a panting exhale, blinking like he had to reorient himself in the gloom. The swirl of outside air followed him, a humid gust that smelled like asphalt and ozone.

"Mateo," she said, heart twisting. She made it halfway

across the lobby before she realized he had extended a hand, checking if she was all right. He looked half-drowned, rivulets of water running off his curls. She swallowed her nerves at the relief that flooded her.

"You're okay," he asked, voice low. He smelled of rain and fresh sweat, as though he had sprinted from wherever he was. A glance at his face revealed worry etched between his brows, and the tension in his shoulders suggested he was still prepared for trouble.

She nodded, though her voice trembled when she spoke. "I think so. The lights went off, and it's so dark in here, it felt, I don't know. I panicked."

The emergency bulb sputtered again, sending the shadows dancing. Thunder rattled the windows, temporarily drowning out anything else. She tried not to flinch. Mateo put a hand on her forearm and guided her to a plush corner couch behind the reception desk, away from the glass. The couch's old cushions sank beneath their combined weight, reminding her that this place had seen better days.

She closed her eyes and focused on the anchor his presence provided. Neither one said anything for a moment. His breathing evened out, but his clothes dripped onto the floor. She almost apologized, but he shook his head, as though reading her mind.

"It's fine," he whispered, his tone gentle. "Better I'm soaked than you alone in the dark."

A shaky laugh escaped her. "I feel silly," she confessed. She set her phone down, screen illuminating them faintly from below.

He quietly shifted, taking her hand in his. His palm felt warm and reassuring, despite being damp. "Don't. I've seen enough weird outages in the French Quarter to know it can be unsettling, especially after everything." A pause that seemed loaded with meaning lingered between them. He knew well the sorts of illusions that stalked her. He had helped her more than once when she felt moments from buckling under the unknown.

She attempted a small smile, but thunder cracked again, closer this time. The windows rattled, and the building groaned as if protesting the storm's fury. Her necklace flared hot against her chest. She resisted the urge to yank it off and reminded herself that Tansy had said these older structures never withstood storms quietly. Still, a spike of fear twitched in her throat. Did the storm sense her frantic energy, or did her frantic energy feed the storm?

Mateo slipped an arm behind her shoulders and drew her closer. His quiet steadiness seeped into her bones and eased the tension that knotted her spine. The faint glow of her phone vanished as its screen went black after a minute of inactivity and plunged them into near-darkness. Only that overhead bulb remained, and its feeble light sharpened every angle of his face.

She felt his breath warm against her temple. For a heartbeat, she remembered the first time he had stood this close, protecting her from a threat neither of them fully understood. Now, in the powerless lobby, he felt like a shield against her swirling doubts.

A sudden surge of emotion welled in her chest, part

gratitude, part something deeper she hadn't named. She tried to ignore the pounding of her heart, but it was impossible. She turned her head slightly and met his gaze. His eyes looked almost black in the half-light as they searched her face for something. In that half second, she sensed him leaning in. The gentle brush of his lips against her temple flooded her with warmth she hadn't known she needed. She closed her eyes and wished there were no storms, no illusions, only the quiet press of his mouth against her skin.

When he pulled away a fraction, her breath caught. She wanted to say something, but words welled up and refused to form. Instead, she swallowed. The lightning flared again, this time streaking the clouds with a brilliant white fork that illuminated the entire lobby in a ghostly sheen. The thunder rumbled in tandem, making the pendant at her neck throb. She tried to banish the notion that her magic had triggered the outage, but the thought dug in. This moment of comfort with Mateo was over-shadowed by the fear that she had coaxed the darkness in.

"Elle?" he asked, sensing her tension.

She forced a small laugh, though her heart hammered. "I'm sorry. I just worry I did this," she gestured vaguely to the dark. "Every time my emotions spike, something weird happens with the lights or with me. Maybe it's just silly."

He squeezed her fingers gently. "It's not silly. But trust me, the city's power grid really is that unreliable." He gave a half smile. "I can't count how many times I've had to file reports on blackouts. You might be strong, but you're not responsible for every spark in New Orleans."

She almost laughed, though tears threatened. "You make it sound so easy."

He brushed a thumb across her knuckles. "It's not. But maybe we shouldn't shoulder blame for what we can't control. Let's just wait for the lights to come back. I'll keep you company until then."

She felt a flush of relief. Her fear might not be rational, but having him here made the darkness less claustrophobic. As if underscoring the fragile peace, the bulb overhead steadied for a moment, then winked out. They both looked up. Total darkness coated the lobby. Rain pounded the roof, a steady roar that seemed to have no end.

Multiple footfalls sounded on the tile just then. The front entrance opened, letting a flow of thick, rain-scented air swirl in. Elle blinked until she noticed short, frantic steps. A familiar voice called, "Elle? Mateo? You here?"

"Tansy?" Elle asked, relieved and startled at once.

Lightning flashed, revealing Tansy's silhouette in the doorway, balancing two paper grocery bags and a large bundle of candles. She stumbled forward, nearly dropping everything on the old tile. Mateo rose and crossed to help her. He took one of the bags, flashlight from his jacket pocket illuminating their faces in abrupt clarity.

"I saw the entire block go dark," Tansy said, breathless. "I was heading back from that 24-hour market, searching for some late-night groceries, and poof, no street lamps, no traffic signals, nothing. Figured I should load up on candles. I got some extra bottled water too. The clerk said the Quarter's having random outages again."

She glanced around. "Wow, this is gloomier than I thought. Everyone okay?"

Elle stood, hugging herself nervously. "Yes. We're fine. It just startled me."

Tansy offered a reassuring smile and hefted the second bag. Thunder rolled, and she cast a quick look at the broad windows, sheets of rain shimmering outside. "I can't imagine the hotel staff is pleased. Guess they're trying to fix it." She knelt, rummaging in her bag. "I have half a dozen candles. Should work until the power's back."

Mateo pointed his flashlight across the edges of the furniture, nodding at the thick fluted candles Tansy pulled out. "Good call. Let's light them up near the front desk so the staff can see if they come back. If not, we'll handle it."

Elle realized how close she had been standing to Mateo mere moments before Tansy arrived. She stiffened, warmth lingering on her cheeks. She braced for a sly comment or an arched brow from Tansy, but it never came. Tansy seemed preoccupied with distributing the candles. If she noticed the tension, she pretended not to see it.

A minute later, Tansy handed out small tea lights and lit them with a lighter. Tiny flames sprang up, dancing in unpredictable drafts. The glow elongated their shadows, and for the first time that evening, Elle felt something like normalcy. The candlelight banished the worst corners of the lobby's gloom.

"It's downright cozy now," Tansy joked, her voice kept intentionally light. "Might as well have a little impromptu sleepover if the power doesn't come back soon."

Mateo sent her a grateful look. He propped a candle on the corner of the reception desk, then handed one to Elle, who held it carefully between her palms. The soft glow played over his drenched jacket and tall frame. She succeeded in meeting his eyes for one second before anxiety and a faint blush made her glance away.

The crash of thunder made the windows shiver once more. The outside sky was a sprawl of dark clouds, but the row of candles gave the interior a gentler cast. Elle felt her heartbeat slow, no longer galloping in her chest. She breathed easier, knowing Tansy's arrival chased away the sense of lonely dread.

Tansy cleared her throat. "I'll see if the clerk's in the back office. Maybe we can figure out how to get the generator running." She hoisted a candle and made her way into the hallway, leaving Elle and Mateo near the couch.

Elle finally exhaled, letting her shoulders relax. "Thank you," she murmured, focusing on Mateo's warmth, on the safety that clung to him like a second skin. "Really," she added, voice low as though she feared the dark might steal her confession if she spoke louder.

He gave a small nod. The candlelight moved across his features, highlighting a tenderness around his eyes. He reached out, brushing a wet strand of hair from her cheek. "Anytime," he said.

Her heart fluttered with a series of quick, unsteady beats. She thought of the subtle brush of his lips on her temple and the tension that curled in her belly. Awareness sparked between them, heightened by the moody storm.

Then Tansy's voice echoed from somewhere behind

the desk. "Found someone! Looks like the manager is working with a breaker box or something. Want me to see if they need a hand?"

Elle almost laughed at Tansy's breezy tone. She turned to Mateo with gratitude shining in her eyes. He squeezed her hand and nodded for her to answer Tansy. The sense of closeness pulsed between them, but Tansy's presence reminded them that they were not alone in this half-lit realm.

"We'll wait here," Elle called back, clearing her throat. "Just in case you need us."

"Got it!" Tansy shouted. She scurried away, footsteps retreating down the dark corridor. The faint glow of her candle bounced across the walls until it vanished into another room.

In the front lounge, rain continued its steady assault on the roof. Each clap of thunder was softer now, as though the storm's anger was fading. Elle placed her candle onto the marble coffee table. Her heart had slowed, and the burning at the necklace's pendant had cooled to a gentle warmth. The storm had not destroyed them, and the world felt solid again. She lifted her eyes to Mateo, searching for the right words.

Before she could speak, he settled on the couch beside her, letting the candlelight wash over both of them. "You seem calmer," he observed softly.

"I am," she admitted. "And I appreciate you showing up." She paused, glancing at his soaked jacket. "You're probably freezing."

He shrugged. "I've been through worse. More importantly, you're safe." He rested a hand at the nape of her neck, a quiet gesture that sent warmth lighting every nerve in her body.

A delicate tension wove between them once more, nearly as palpable as the candlelight. She allowed herself a small laugh, brimming with relief. "We might both laugh about this tomorrow," she said, cheeks flushing. "I was so convinced my magic was behind it."

Mateo's expression softened. He opened his mouth to answer, but Tansy's approaching footsteps signaled her return. They widened the distance between them, though the air still vibrated with unspoken awareness.

Tansy appeared, balancing one last candle. She placed it on the desk, then raised an eyebrow with an apologetic grin. "Manager's still poking around. They think we might have lights again soon. Meanwhile, I brought a bag of random snacks if you two are hungry. At least we can pretend it's a mini-adventure."

Elle smiled at that. She took a long, steadying breath. The anxiety that had threatened to unravel her now felt contained. Tansy's arrival had diffused some of the fierce closeness she shared with Mateo, but it had not erased the gratitude that flowed in Elle's chest. She couldn't quite meet Mateo's eyes now, her heart pounded too fast whenever she tried, but she found comfort in the fact that he was here, unyielding in the darkness. The chaotic swirl of fear had morphed into something calmer.

Gathering her composure, Elle nodded to Tansy. "Let's see those snacks, then." She caught the faintest smirk on Tansy's lips, as if Tansy knew exactly what she was inter-rupting but chose to remain tactful. The tension in the air lingered, but it felt safe rather than stifling. Outside, the thunder began to roll more gently. A mild quiet kissed the edges of the night, and the candles painted soft amber arcs across the lobby walls.

Elle's heart tingled with warmth each time she thought about how quickly Mateo had come. Maybe she was not foolish to call him. Despite the awkwardness of Tansy's arrival the storm lashed world outside, a sense of cautious comfort settled over her. This strange half shadowed moment in the hotel lobby would remain a reminder that some fears vanished when someone steady was near.

TWELVE

Her eyes flew open at the faint brush of sound against her window. At first, she thought it might be rain, but the night sky was clear and full of quiet stars. She lay motionless in the hotel bed, trying to recall if she had dreamed the noise. Her pulse thudded in her ears. Days had dragged by since she felt fully rested, and every muscle in her body fought her mind's urge to investigate. Yet there it was again, a soft whisper, barely louder than a sigh of wind.

She told herself it was only tree branches scraping the glass. But the voice, yes, it sounded like a voice, persisted, gentle and coaxing. She peered at the clock on the bedside table. It was past midnight, an hour when even the late-night revelers in the Quarter typically began winding down. She inhaled slowly, anticipating the overhead lamp or some odd shift in the air, but the room stayed dull and silent. Her breath trembled. She wasn't sure she wanted to acknowledge that voice at all.

Yet the whisper tugged at her. She caught the vague impression of words she couldn't understand, a melodic lull that tempted her to move, to get out of bed, to follow. The last thing she wanted after too many sleepless nights was more strangeness, but a prickle of magic skimmed her arms, urging her to leave. She swung her legs over the edge of the bed and her toes met the old carpet. A jolt of faint but definite energy shot from the soles of her feet. It felt like the city itself vibrating with expectancy.

When she reached for her phone, her fingers slipped against its surface. She accepted that she likely would not need it to text anyone because she had no clue what she would say. The compulsion pulling at her felt oddly personal, almost intimate. Even so, part of her bristled at the idea that something could guide her decisions without her explicit permission. She did not want to be a puppet. She pressed her phone into the pocket of her pajama shorts anyway. Just in case.

A shaky laugh escaped her lips. She was about to stroll out of a hotel in the middle of the night, lured by a disembodied whisper that tugged on her exhausted mind. Was she sleepwalking? Her pulse jumped as she walked to the door and slid her room key off the small dresser. The corridor lights flickered when she emerged, but she pressed on toward the stairwell with purposeful steps that matched the throb of curiosity beneath her skin. Each heartbeat seemed to echo with the summons.

In the lobby, the night clerk was nowhere to be seen. Only a single lamp glowed near the empty reception desk and cast tall shadows across the checkered tiles. Outside, the air felt heavier than it had all day. The moment she passed the threshold, a swirl of wind caressed her cheek. She wiped damp sweat from her brow and headed down the silent street. Something was guiding her, or at least encouraging her to follow, and she was too tired to resist.

She did not notice Tansy slipping out of the shadows behind her. Tansy had been restless, dozing on a chair near the half-lit hallway, ever since they started sharing a temporary arrangement in the same hotel. She had glimpsed Elle crossing the lobby, recognized the distant look on her face, and grabbed her phone. The only coherent thought in Tansy's mind was that Elle kept mentioning thick oak trunks and whispered voices. City Park's ancient trees were the logical destination for anything connected to that kind of midnight lure. Fearing that calling out would spook Elle, Tansy typed a frantic text to Mateo.

She's leaving. Think it's City Park!

The wide road ahead shimmered with faint lamplight, each pool of illumination broken by an expanse of darkness. The warm New Orleans nights typically carried music or distant chatter, but the city seemed to hold its breath. Elle felt the small hairs on her arms lift when she passed a corner store with its shutters closed and dusty windows. She caught a hint of something drifting through the air, moss or maybe damp earth. The voice pressed at her senses, weaving around her thoughts like a lullaby she had half-forgotten.

She turned onto a narrow side street, drawn forward as if an invisible thread linked her heart to an unknown place. With each step, her weariness gave way to a focused daze. She could not turn back. She could not even form a sentence to ask herself why. A persistent part of her realized how truly unwise it was to set out alone, yet the gentle urgent call in the wind drowned out caution.

At last, she reached an old wrought-iron arch crowning the entrance to City Park. Beyond lay rows of towering oaks, each trunk draped with Spanish moss that swayed in the faint breeze. The half-moon overhead bathed the branches in silver light, carving haunting patterns on the walkway. She hesitated, breath catching. The voice felt stronger here, fluttering in her chest. For an instant, she expected the necklace strung around her collarbone to flare hot, but it stayed cool, resting motionless against her skin. The relative quiet unnerved her more than if it had blazed with power.

She stepped off the pavement and followed a small dirt path. Damp moss coated the edges of the trail, glistening with dew or some watery residue left after the sprinklers. She barely registered the sensation of her shoes slipping slightly on wet grass as she pushed deeper into the park. Her heart pounded in a nervous rhythm. She glanced from trunk to trunk, searching for the origin of the whisper. It might be an illusion or a memory or perhaps some distant echo of her grandmother's presence.

Each oak rose like a sentinel, branches coiling overhead in shapes that resembled archways in a cathedral. She thought of Ruby's voice for a moment, then decided that what she heard now felt sharper, more like a summons than a message of love. She swallowed a knot of anxiety. The trees were not malevolent, but they exuded a dim expectancy that pressed against her temples. She tried to speak, but her words caught in her throat. She wanted to ask, Who is calling me? Why here?

Her gaze moved around the clearing. A lone streetlamp cast light through the thick canopy, adding a weak glow to the path. The voice moved in the wind, Elle. Or so she thought. It vanished the moment she tried to pinpoint the direction. She pressed a hand to her chest, realized her heart beat too loud, and forced herself to keep going. The path ended in a wide, grassy area overshadowed by an ancient cypress whose roots formed thick, twisting shapes above the ground. The trunk looked impossibly old, bark knotted with age. Everything felt suffocating.

Her grip on reality slipped as if she had awakened from a deep sleep and discovered she was no longer in her bed. She saw strange silhouettes out of the corner of her eye, perhaps illusions or the interplay of moonlight with moss. The cypress towered overhead, branches swaying to a breeze she could not feel, and she sensed the voice swirling around her again, a faint murmur of her name. Elle. Her head spun. The world seemed uncertain, as though she stood on half-formed ground. She needed something to tether her.

Out of nowhere, the sound of heavy breathing made her jump. She turned, heart racing in her chest, ready to bolt. Instead, she saw the lines of a familiar silhouette stepping over a low bush. Detective Mateo Cruz, panting from what must have been a sprint, paused near the edge of the clearing. Even in the dim moonlight, she recognized the anxious set of his jaw and the relief flooding his eyes when they locked onto her face.

She stared, too stunned to move. He hurried forward, a half-desperate whisper escaping his throat. "Elle. Are you all right?"

At once, her tension collapsed into a trembling wave. She nearly fell against his chest. He slipped an arm around her shoulders and surveyed the area, scanning the gnarled trunks and drifts of moss. His warmth cut through the eerie chill that had been cloaking her. She listened to the rasp of his breath as he tried to calm himself, likely from sprinting across the dark streets, weaving around deserted roads to find her.

"Did Tansy text you?" she managed through dry lips. She felt unsteady, as though any strong gust might sweep her away again.

He nodded, brushing back a droplet of sweat clinging to his forehead. "She said you walked out of the hotel in a trance, something about oak trees. I ran the last few blocks." His voice trembled with concern. "I was worried."

His hand on her shoulder steadied her, though her pulse still thundered. She whimpered softly, the day's exhaustion colliding with this midnight summons in a dizzying swirl. She wanted to tell him the truth that a whisper had led her here, promising some secret beyond the reach of normal senses. Yet explaining it seemed impossible.

He guided her to a slight clearing where the ground

was dryer. She clung to him, face pressed to the soft cotton of his T-shirt. The scent of him, rain, a trace of coffee, and a tinge of laundry soap, anchored her to something real. She stared at the cypress tree, half-expecting it to uproot and lunge forward. Instead, its branches merely creaked, a slow, mournful sound.

"What do you hear?" Mateo asked quietly while shifting to keep a protective stance at her side. She could feel the tension in his body, the coiled awareness of a man used to scanning every corner for threats.

"I'm not sure," she admitted. "A whisper that sounded like my name." Her throat tightened. "Nothing I can see, not physically. But it brought me here."

Mateo's jaw clenched. "The park is too quiet for this hour." He scanned the tree line, eyes narrowing at any movement. "You said you're hearing something call you. Is it from those illusions you mentioned?"

Her skin prickled at the memory of illusions she had encountered before, the ones that sometimes flared when the stolen necklace had first reappeared in her life. She shook her head, voice trembling. "It's not the exact same feeling. It's gentler. But it pulls," she whispered. "I couldn't stay in bed."

She noticed how his expression hardened, frustration mingling with fear. He exhaled a slow breath, calming himself. "All right. Let's step away from that tree." He moved them a few paces back from the cypress whose roots twisted like serpents across the ground. "You're shaking," he said. "Try to breathe."

She gave a shallow nod, inhaled, and choked out a

weighted sigh. No frogs croaked, no crickets chirped, as though the entire park had paused to watch them. The whisper lingered at the edges of her hearing, faint but persistent, like a half-forgotten dream. She wanted to close her eyes and push it out of her mind, to break the tenuous connection it had forged with her midnight thoughts.

Mateo kept his grip firm on her shoulders and glanced down at her face. "Elle, hey," he murmured, voice lower. "Look at me." He turned her gently so she could meet his gaze. She latched onto those dark eyes and found solace in his steady presence. The tingle of leftover fear pulsed along her spine as he asked, "Have you had anything like this happen lately, some new sign that someone or something wants you to come here?"

She swallowed. "Not exactly, though I'd been so tired. My dreams felt strange, but I never heard anything this real." Her heart lurched at the memory of a haze that tried to claim her just moments before. "It felt like it was waiting."

Waiting. She sensed the same tension in Mateo's posture.

"Come on. I'm getting you home," he said, voice tight with determination. "We can figure this out, but not in the dark with no backup." He wrapped his arm around her, the warmth of his body a stark contrast to the clammy air.

She almost answered that she was perfectly fine, but a single glance into the darkness told her a different story. She could still hear the wind brushing against the moss-laden branches, the faint syllables that might have been her name. She moved closer to him, forcing herself to break away from the invisible thread that had drawn her here. She felt its tug loosen and relief flooded her at having him beside her.

A sudden wave of dizziness made her grip his shirt for balance. She ignored the anxious flutter in her stomach and focused on the strong, steady beat of Mateo's pulse under her touch. Step by step, they inched away from the cypress tree and headed back along the path. Her legs felt stiff, but her breath gradually eased. Mateo mumbled quiet reassurances and scanned each shadow with unwavering vigilance.

They stepped beneath a patch of moonlight streaming through gaps in the oak canopy overhead. She took a moment to catch her breath with both hands pressed against Mateo's chest for stability. He looked down at her with a mixture of relief and lingering concern. Silence stretched as she tried to shake off the mental fog that had carried her here. Their closeness reminded her that she was not alone in this unsteady dance with powers she barely understood.

She tried to speak, but words refused to form. Instead, her gaze lifted to his. He gave a tiny nod and acknowledged the fear that still clung to her. The corners of his mouth twitched with an almost-smile.

"I've got you," he murmured, a final confirmation that she could rely on him. Slowly, she slid her hands from his chest to curl them around his arm. The rest of the park lay in silence with only faint starlight and sleeping foliage bearing witness to her midnight wandering.

She turned her attention back to the cypress tree. The branches loomed in the distance and swayed gently. Her heartbeat throbbed once more, uncertain if that elusive voice might break free of the darkness again. Even now, she sensed a faint stirring along her spine. Yet Mateo's presence steadied her. She realized she no longer had to stand here alone with that fracturing sense of reality. A breath she had not realized she was holding seeped out in a trembling exhale.

Without a word, he touched the back of her hand. They took a few more paces away from the clearing, the moisture in the grass clinging to the edges of their shoes. Elle watched moonbeams ripple through shifting leaves, a final reminder of how easily illusions might hide among natural shadows. She tasted anxiety on her tongue. But the detective's arm around her shoulders provided a warmth that broke the spell of that haunting whisper.

Somewhere along the edges of her mind, the voice still hovered, but its power had receded. The night air smelled of damp bark and distant river mud, showing the city's constant interplay between water and ground. She glanced over her shoulder at the twisted roots and let the moment settle. The panic in her chest began to loosen. She could feel her breath returning to a steady pace, guided by Mateo's calm energy.

When at last she forced herself to turn from the looming cypress trees, relief flooded her veins as she realized that despite the growing strangeness, she was no longer wandering it alone.

THIRTEEN

Elle woke to the reminder of last night's unsettling calm in City Park. Though the sheets on her bed felt cool and soft, her mind replayed the feeling beneath ancient oaks. She could still sense the faint echo of that whispered voice tugging at her thoughts, urging her forward in the dark. As she sat up, the midmorning light spilled through the bedroom curtains, illuminating her grandmother's well-loved quilt across her legs. Her heartbeat skittered when she remembered the pull of magic that almost swept her away again.

She forced herself to stand. The mirror on the dresser reflected the disquiet in her gaze, the faint tremor at the edge of her mouth. With a steadying breath, she reminded herself she was not alone. Tansy had watched her closely after Elle stumbled back from the park the night before, and the cousinly concern guaranteed a morning of well-meant lectures.

In the small living room, Tansy flipped through

Ruby's old journals, her brow furrowed. The aroma of fresh café au lait and sweet pastries filled the air, a comforting counterpoint to the tension that already pulsed between them. Tansy glanced up and set the journals aside, tapping her fingernail lightly on the worn cover.

"You're acting like you're fine," Tansy said, "but I know that's not true. I saw your face when you came home." She crossed her arms and studied Elle with an unwavering stare.

Elle gave a slight shrug. "I slept better than I expected. I'm trying not to let last night spin out in my head."

Tansy's eyes narrowed. "Last night rattled you more than you admit, and I don't want some random magical whisper turning you inside out again." She gestured at the small table bearing two steaming cups of milk-laced coffee and a small plate of sugared pastries. "Sit. Drink something. Let's figure out a plan."

Elle pulled out a creaky wooden chair. The seat squeaked in protest as she settled in. She reached for a warm pastry and flaked the top layer with her thumb. Fine sugar dusted her fingertips.

Tansy exhaled loudly. "Our problem is not just repeating nightmares. It is that your magic keeps surging whenever something unexpected happens. Sporadic flares will not protect you if whoever or whatever keeps calling you strengthens its hold."

Elle nibbled the corner of the pastry. "That is why I am reading Ruby's journals," she said softly. "She left pages of notes, spells, and a lifetime of experiences. She knew more than any teacher out there, so I feel like I can learn from her words."

"And that is amazing information," Tansy conceded, "but we both know you need real-time guidance. No offense to Ruby, but she is gone. She cannot stand next to you if your next spell backfires. She cannot show you how to channel your power so it does not blow up half the room."

The bitterness in Tansy's tone surprised Elle. They usually navigated arguments with half-joking jabs, not tense frustration. Elle set the pastry down as her appetite faded. "You think I cannot handle it on my own. Is that it?"

"I think you would do better if you had a structured approach," Tansy replied. Her voice stayed calm, though her eyes flashed with concern. "Earlier, you nearly fainted from exhaustion in the living room after that weird trance. And a few days before that, you panicked when the necklace flared hot. Did Ruby's journals help you stop it?"

Elle resisted the urge to fold her arms defensively. Instead, she drummed her fingertips on the table. "I need more time to study them. It is not as if I have had a chance to fully decode every scribble."

Tansy's posture softened as though she regretted pushing so hard. She leaned forward and wrapped her fingers around Elle's wrist. "I know you, Elle. You want to pretend you're in control because you're scared to rely on someone else. But this city's magic is so old and unpredictable. If the next wave of illusions hits you when you're alone, it might be worse than a dizzy spell."

Elle thought of the power that crackled in the French

Quarter, how she sometimes sensed wards failing or illusions prowling just out of sight. The inevitability of a larger threat weighed on her heart, and she stared at the swirl of her coffee in silence.

Tansy released her wrist and gave a weary sigh. "I already texted a teacher who practices a structured witchcraft system. She's known for helping witches refine their gifts. I told her we're interested in a consultation."

Elle almost choked on a sip of coffee. "You did what?" She coughed, then swallowed. "You arranged a meeting behind my back?"

"Behind your back is a stretch," Tansy said gently, raising both palms in a peace gesture. "I just asked if she'd have time this week. She said yes. If you decide you hate her approach, we'll leave. But you owe it to yourself to see if her instruction can keep you safe. You're my cousin, and I can't watch you struggle alone."

The thought of a stranger evaluating her magic made Elle's shoulders tense. She recalled how Madame Laveau examined her back in those early days, eyes unnervingly perceptive. The idea of another mystic drilling her in advanced witchcraft felt daunting, yet Tansy's earnestness struck a chord. "I understand why you want me to go," Elle admitted softly. "If the teacher can help, maybe that's a good thing."

Tansy raised her brow. "So you'll at least meet her?"

Elle nodded, though her stomach quivered at the idea. "Yes, I can do that," she said finally, then tried for a smile. "I still want to keep Ruby's journals. They're my connection to her. I can balance that with someone else's lessons."

Relief flooded Tansy's face. "That's all I ask," she said. "We can trust your grandmother's wisdom while also accepting extra guidance. It is not a betrayal of her legacy. She would want you to be safe."

Elle blinked away a sudden surge of emotion. The morning air felt less stifling at Tansy's reassurance, and the salty-sweet moment of acceptance gave her the strength to pick at her pastry again. "All right," she breathed, letting the sugar on her tongue soothe her nerves. "Will you come with me if I schedule that meeting?"

Tansy nodded emphatically. "Of course. We are in this together."

They ate the rest of their breakfast in more companionable silence, sipping coffee and exchanging small ideas on how to prepare. Elle leafed through Ruby's notebook as she chewed, scanning a half-faded incantation scrawled in the margins. She imagined how Ruby's voice might have guided her to channel the swirl of emotions coursing through her every time her necklace grew hot. The memory of last night's whispered summons still lingered near her collarbone. She vowed she would not be caught off guard again.

Later, as afternoon light slanted across the windowpanes, Elle found a text on her phone from Mateo. He invited her to the Garden District for what he called a "late dinner," if she was up for a quiet evening.

She swallowed hard at the flutter in her chest. Though

they had shared moments of closeness in the past days, the idea of a calm dinner felt like a major step toward letting him deeper into her life. She typed a quick yes, and hit send before nerves made her hesitate.

When dusk approached, Elle stood in front of her closet, rummaging for something that struck a balance between comfortable and presentable. Tansy peered in and teased her about overthinking. Elle swatted her away with a grin. "I am not overthinking," Elle said. "I just do not want to look like I rolled out of bed." In truth, the swirl of anticipation coiled in her gut. She selected a soft blouse in a dusky rose color and warmer-toned jeans, something that would fit the mild New Orleans night without feeling stiffly formal.

The ride to the Garden District gave her time to clear her head. She gazed at grand houses lined with trimmed hedges and ancient oaks. The neighborhood contrasted sharply with the vibrant noise of the French Quarter. Gas lanterns glowed a gentle gold on front porches, casting light across the sidewalk. It all felt surreal, like stepping into a painting of old New Orleans.

Mateo stepped out from beneath a sprawling live oak by the sidewalk. A low-hanging branch brushed the top of his jacket. His gaze locked on her the instant she approached. Warmth filled his eyes, and a slight smile curved at the corner of his lips. In that moment, Elle felt the tension of her day lift. She smiled back.

"You found the place," he said, voice low. "It's a quiet cafe a few blocks down. Not fancy, but definitely cozy."

"I'm glad," she replied, walking in step beside him.

They strolled beneath dim streetlamps that cast light against the old wrought-iron fences. Occasionally, the smell of jasmine drifted by on the breeze. When they reached a modest restaurant tucked between two large homes, Mateo opened the door for her. The interior was softly lit, with a handful of tables spaced for privacy. The ambiance suited the gentle undercurrent between them.

They settled at a corner table near a window that over-looked a small courtyard. Candlelight glimmered against the glass, reflecting the shape of Mateo's profile. The server took their orders, and Elle tried to keep the swirl of distraction in her mind from overshadowing the moment. She glanced at him, noticing how the low light softened the edges of his dark hair.

He ran his thumb along the edge of the menu. "I appreciate you coming out like this," he said. "I know your schedule's been unpredictable."

"Yours, too," she replied. She reached for her glass of ice water. "I'm just... glad you asked."

They spoke quietly about the day. Mateo mentioned some routine follow-ups at the station, though he alluded to tension with coworkers who dismissed strange case details. He shrugged, giving a small laugh. "A few think I'm chasing stories that can't be proven. But I've seen enough now to know there's more to the city than we put in the paperwork."

When the server returned with their plates, Mateo waited until they were alone before leaning forward. "I want to tell you something," he began. "I've always been drawn to the cures or leads that no one else will touch.

Cold-case disappearances, odd sightings... I used to think it was just a personal quirk, but then your case fell in my lap. It was the sign I'd been waiting for to follow my instincts and stop ignoring the city's more mysterious side."

He paused, letting his words settle. Elle's pulse skipped as she realized the significance of what he confessed. She and Tansy had speculated that his willingness to believe her unusual stories came from more than simple detective duties. Now, hearing him confirm it made the air between them feel electric.

She set her fork down with care. "So this is more to you than just finishing the job? You actually believe in magic, illusions, or the possibility of it?"

Mateo studied the candle flame. "I never had the evidence to fully embrace the idea," he said, "but I did notice patterns that made no sense through normal logic. When I met you and saw the stolen necklace and the power surges, it felt like the puzzle pieces might fit. I realized I was not imagining things."

Elle felt a subtle flush creep along her cheeks. "I was not sure if I had forced you into my whirlwind," she admitted. "I have been juggling the urge to run back to Chicago with the drive to stay. Sometimes I think it would be easier to walk away and leave the city's magic behind. But this is my grandmother's home, and a part of me cannot abandon it."

Mateo's gaze sharpened with gentle understanding. "I get that," he said softly. "It is complicated. But I have watched people run. They take the easiest path and never look back, even when the city's problems keep growing. You," he reached across the table and brushed his fingers lightly against hers, "you are facing it head on. That is brave."

His hand lingered, and she curled her own fingers around his. Emotions swelled in her chest, at once vulnerable and strong. The weight of that admission hung in the air, making her realize how rare it was for him to open up. The candle flame cast dancing shadows along the table, and the small restaurant allowed her to hear the soft hitch in his breathing.

"I don't feel brave," Elle said, voice catching. "I feel outmatched. The illusions, the surges. I'm never sure if I'll be strong enough." She swallowed. "But this city still smells like my childhood, barbecue smoke, sweet beignets, the damp air after a storm. Ruby wanted me to understand that magic isn't some separate thing you lock away. It's part of my heritage."

Mateo's fingers shifted to hold her hand more firmly. "You're not outmatched if you have allies," he said quietly. "Trust that some people won't run from what you're facing."

His words soothed a knot in her chest. She realized that for the first time she glimpsed how important it was for him to be heard and believed as well. The tension in her shoulders eased, and she let herself relax into the warmth of his presence. They spent the meal exchanging stories of odd experiences, laughing over old misunderstandings, and savoring the sense that they were forging something real in a swirl of uncertain magic.

When they finished, he walked her outside. The night air felt cooler than before, and a light breeze ruffled the leaves of the nearby magnolia trees. Stars flickered above, though many streetlamps claimed the sky's darkness. Elle looked up at him and suppressed a flutter of nerves. His calm expression, the quiet shape of his mouth as he searched her face, made her realize they were standing closer than ever.

"I appreciate your honesty," she said at last. "You could have dismissed my story like everyone else."

"I couldn't," he said. He brushed a strand of hair from her cheek, his fingertips warm against her skin. "Something about you made me want to believe."

Her heart flipped, and for a moment, she forgot to breathe. The city exhaled around them, crickets humming in the grass, the sounds of passing cars. She swayed closer, compelled by the magnetic current that drew them together in every shared glance.

He exhaled slowly, letting his hand drop but keeping his gaze on her. "I'm sorry if that was forward," he said.

She answered with a slight laugh, though she felt the intensity swirl in her chest. "It was the right amount of forward."

They lingered a little longer beneath the oaks lining the sidewalk. Finally, sensing the late hour, she glanced at her phone. "I should head back before Tansy starts texting me nonstop to check I haven't been abducted by illusions." She tried to keep her tone light, though her heart still pounded, and the idea of stepping away from his presence felt surprisingly difficult.

Mateo nodded, stepping back with reluctance. "I'll walk you to your car."

They walked side by side, shoulders nearly brushing. Before opening her door, she turned. "Thank you for tonight," she said. "It helped to talk about everything."

His dark eyes gleamed beneath the streetlamp. "I'm here," he said simply. "Let me know if you need backup. Anytime."

She got into her car, waving once before she drove off, pulse still racing from the warmth of his touch on her hand. The drive home passed in a blur, tinted by a sense of promise and mingled relief. He saw her struggle, and he still stayed.

When she arrived at the shotgun house, Tansy sat on the couch with a battered pillow on her lap. She watched Elle kick off her shoes. A slow grin spread across Tansy's face, as though she already sensed the shift in Elle's demeanor.

"That must have been some dinner," Tansy teased.

Elle felt her cheeks flush all over again. "It was nice," she admitted, trying not to gush too obviously.

Tansy's expression turned serious. "Did you think about the teacher I mentioned earlier?"

Elle slid onto the armchair across from her, hugging a throw pillow. "Yes," she said. "We can set up an appointment. I will at least do one lesson. I promise."

Tansy let out a soft, dramatic sigh, clearly relieved. "Good. That is all I needed to hear."

Relieved laughter bubbled from Elle as she sank deeper into the chair. The swirl of tension from the morning had blossomed into something steadier by day's end. Her thoughts lingered on Mateo's confession of curiosity and the gentle press of his palm against hers. She felt the city's old magic humming at the corners of her consciousness, but instead of dread, she sensed a small glimmer of possibility. She had Tansy at her side, Ruby's journals in her hands, and a detective who refused to dismiss what he could not explain.

For the first time in longer than she could remember, Elle felt a spark of genuine hope. She smiled at Tansy, imagining how she would navigate her next lesson in structured witchcraft and how she would explain her shifting dreams to a specialized teacher. Though fear lurked at the edges, her resolve felt stronger. Tomorrow might bring another challenge, but tonight, the lingering taste of sugar and the memory of Mateo's quiet devotion gave her a confidence that felt almost magical on its own.

FOURTEEN

Elle jolted awake in the dim glow of her bedroom lamp, the memory of that regal woman echoing through her rattled nerves. The nightmare clung to her consciousness, fragments pulsing behind her eyes. She had glimpsed obsidian eyes fixed upon her, along with a hallway that seemed to stretch into endless darkness. No matter how she tried to ground herself in the reassuring glow of the table lamp, the woman's silent call lingered, coiling inside her thoughts.

A sharp breath hissed through her teeth. She shifted upright and swung her legs over the side of the bed while pressing a hand to her pounding heart. The house walls exuded a faint warmth that sometimes comforted her but tonight provided little solace. She scanned the cluttered space for signs of movement, half expecting ghostly silhouettes on the walls although logic said she was alone. Her reflection in the small mirror caught her eye, and she almost thought she saw the shape of a crown in the background, an illusion surely. She bit down on her lower lip until the phantom image burned away.

She inhaled slowly, counting each breath. Nightmares were not new to her, but this dream felt different. The woman's presence had pressed down on her like a cloak of authority, and the swirling sense of a crown of thorns had pulsed with a life of its own. She recalled Tansy's whispered suspicions about a malevolent, regal figure lurking in the city's underbelly. A powerful witch, by all accounts. Elle was not sure how much of that chatter was rumor, but every fiber of her being told her that dream was no ordinary product of an overactive imagination.

She rubbed her arms and summoned enough firmness to stand. Cold air licked across her ankles as she moved. A small bedside table housed a partially open journal, the one with Ruby's simpler spells and the instructions for scrying. She had read that page a dozen times but never tried it in earnest. Fear of unleashing something beyond her experience had always held her back. Now, with images of that corridor looping through her mind, she decided she could not remain passive.

Her magic thrummed below her collarbone, that familiar tension she had learned to recognize after repeated brushes with forces she barely understood. She exhaled and walked to the living room, rummaging through the wooden trunk against the wall. Amid the leftover items from her grandmother's life, she found a small shard of polished obsidian, a canister of salt, and half a candle stub. Ruby's journal had said these items were essential for a rudimentary scrying spell, at least in the style her grandmother once practiced. The instructions emphasized that scrying was an active, deliberate ritual, unlike the involuntary dream visions that often blindsided Elle.

She lit the candle and placed it on a small plate in the center of the floor. After sprinkling a circle of salt, she set the glossy obsidian in front of her and knelt, forcing her heartbeat to settle. She ran her fingertips over the rough edges of the stone and noticed a faint flicker of candlelight reflecting on the polished face. Her grandmother's neat handwriting filled her mind.

Embrace the vision, but don't linger if the sight grows hostile. Find your footing before you can stand in another realm.

The living room's air thickened with tension as she began. She whispered the words she had memorized from Ruby's notes, voice low, nearly blending with the soft hiss of the candle's flame. Each syllable felt like a pebble dropped in water, sending invisible ripples through the space around her. Her breathing wavered, but she pressed on, calling upon her bloodline connection, acknowledging that she was Ruby's granddaughter who had every right to reach for clarity.

For a moment, nothing happened. She stared at the obsidian, the subtle shine reminding her of dark water on a moonless night. Then her vision grayed around the edges. She drifted forward, as though pulled into that tiny gleam of light in the stone. A chill swept across her shoulders, and she felt an otherworldly sense, like stepping into a silent auditorium.

Images slammed into her with no warning. At first, they were only fleeting shapes, a tall silhouette with regal poise, a swirl of dark cloth, and then an unmistakable glint of a thorny crown. She tried to focus, but the scene kept shifting, fracturing like shards of broken glass. One instant, she saw the silhouette stride through a crowded street. The next, she glimpsed that same figure turning, revealing eyes that glowed with vicious intelligence.

Elle's heart pounded. The flickers intensified, dragging her deeper. She sensed swirling magic that scalded her thoughts. The face in her vision was never completely illuminated, but there was an undeniable aura of command, of ambition. The swirling crown of thorns crackled with an energy that felt invasive, as if each thorn was meant to ensnare her. The woman beckoned her forward, silently demanding her obedience.

She tried to pull back but found it difficult. Her throat felt tight, and her pulse drummed in her ears. A strangled sound escaped her lips as she forced her gaze away from the obsidian. That silhouette refused to vanish, looming just behind her closed eyelids. She thought of Tansy's references to an ancient witch ruling from the shadows. Could this be the Queen everyone mentioned?

Even though she had expected some strain while scrying, Elle felt unbalanced by the intensity. Her arms trembled under the weight of the visions. She saw scraps of an unlit corridor, the same one from her nightmares. Slivers of candlelight lit the far edge, but the figure refused to let her see more. Then with a sudden surge, the vision poured into her mind again, each image sharp and overwhelming. She felt heat prick the back of her neck.

No. She could not risk letting the sight claim her entirely. Desperation rattled her focus, and she wrenched herself away from the circle, snapping the physical connection. She lunged for the candle, pinching the flame with her fingertips to extinguish it. The sudden darkness brought her spinning back into reality. She crashed onto her side, chest heaving, heart beating so hard she worried it might give out.

For several seconds, she stayed on the floor, struggling to slow her breathing. Her skin felt clammy, and sweat trickled down her spine. The taste of magic, sharp and bitter, coated her tongue. She pictured the flicker of that thorny crown and shuddered. Ruby's caution about powers too large for fledgling witches rang in her ears like an alarm bell.

She scrambled to her feet, every muscle tense. She needed support, someone to talk through this surge of confusion and fear. Tansy might still be out, likely visiting a late shift at her job or tracking some new tip about local witches.

Elle's phone sat on the coffee table, screen illuminating an incoming text from Tansy.

Checking in later. Sleep if you can.

Elle stared at it, then shook her head. She wanted

reassurance that she was not falling headlong into dangerous magic without a lifeline. She opened her contacts and found Mateo's number. Calling him felt almost impulsive, but she realized she needed his steadiness.

The line rang only once before he picked up. "Elle?" He sounded alert, even though it had to be late. The warmth in his tone cut through her anxiety.

She squeezed the bridge of her nose. "I'm sorry if you're busy, but I, something happened. I tried a scrying spell, and," She paused, breath hitching. She could not quite shape her words around the onslaught of images. "I just need you here."

His response was immediate. "Where are you?"

"Home," she whispered, voice unsteady.

"Stay there. I'm on my way."

The call ended. She stood in the center of the living room, arms wrapped around herself. She stared at the remains of the extinguished candle and the spilled salt ring. Her mind was still raw from the intensity of her attempt, but a small part of her was relieved. Mateo would come. She could almost imagine the comforting note in his voice, the smell of coffee that clung to him after a long day of work.

Perhaps fifteen minutes later, the front door clicked open. She had left it unlocked in her haze of panic. Mateo stepped inside, hair ruffled as if he had run his hands through it multiple times on the drive over. He wore a worn T-shirt and jeans, and the subtle aroma of coffee lingered in the air around him. His eyes searched the room until he found her in the hallway connecting the living space to the bedrooms.

She held up a trembling hand, embarrassed by her own state. "I—I'm sorry, I just—"

He did not wait for her to finish. He covered the distance in two strides and locked his arms around her. The moment his hands pressed against her back, the tension in her body began to recede. She inhaled, and the warmth of him replaced the chill that had seeped into her bones.

"What happened?" he murmured, voice low as though he sensed any loud tone might overwhelm her further. He guided her gently into her bedroom, flicking on the bedside lamp. The soft glow painted delicate shadows across the walls.

Elle closed her eyes. "I tried to scry," she managed. "I kept seeing that regal woman. She wore something like a thorny crown, and I felt her pull. It was so powerful. I don't even know if she's real, but every sign points to—" She swallowed the dryness coating her throat. "I triggered something bigger than me."

Mateo touched her cheek, concern in his gaze. "Sit," he said softly. He eased her onto the edge of the bed. He sat next to her, close enough that the heat of his body lulled her trembling nerves. "Tell me what you need right now."

She leaned into him, letting her forehead rest against his shoulder. "I just need to feel safe," she whispered. "I know that does not make sense. Nothing does lately. But it is like she is watching me, even in my sleep."

His hand came up to cradle the back of her head,

smoothing her tangled hair. "All right," he murmured. "You are not facing this alone."

Elle closed her eyes, heart pounding too fast to form coherent sentences. She detected the faint drip of a leaking faucet in the kitchen, the rustle of the curtains in the hallway. Each mundane detail reassured her that reality still existed, despite the illusions roiling in her mind.

He pressed a tender kiss to her temple, then to her cheek, guiding her closer until she breathed against his neck. She nestled into that warm pocket, half hidden by the collar of his shirt. The faint coffee scent and lingering city air seemed to wrap her. Normally, she might have worried about crossing boundaries, but exhaustion and confusion overrode caution. She sank against him, letting his presence shield her from the memories of that corridor.

A few deep breaths later, she managed to speak again. "I keep seeing her, even when I try to shut my eyes. I am afraid I am opening a door with these spells that I might not be skilled enough to close."

Mateo's voice rumbled against her ear. "You said it before. This city's old magic is unpredictable, and you're still new at handling it." He exhaled, adjusting his arm around her shoulders. "But I've watched you learn so much in the past weeks, more than most people might in a lifetime. You will figure this out, Elle."

She let out a shaky laugh. "You have more faith in me than I do."

He tightened his hold. "I've seen you handle illusions

and wards. That takes bravery and quick thinking, both of which you have. If you need to slow down, do it. You don't have to rush every spell."

Elle nodded against him, soaking in his words. A wave of fatigue tugged at her, the aftermath of channeling so much raw energy. She could still taste the scrying's residue, like metal on her tongue, but Mateo's closeness dampened the lingering pulse of fear.

She realized she could fall asleep right here, pressed to his chest. The notion made her cheeks flush, but he shifted slightly, as if giving her more room. When she glanced up, his expression carried no hint of impatience or discomfort. Instead, his brown eyes reflected a calm acceptance that disarmed her usual worries. She reached for his free hand and threaded her fingers through his.

The silence stretched between them, thick with unspoken understanding. Then he lifted her intertwined fingers and kissed her knuckles gently. She closed her eyes again, a faint sense of peace slowly taking hold. The swirling crown, the corridor, the obsidian eyes, those threats still loomed, but she found a reprieve.

She shifted her legs onto the mattress. Mateo guided her backward, leaning against the pillows so that her head rested near his shoulder. He let out a slow breath, and she felt the vibration of it in her own chest. Her limbs felt heavy, and she realized sleep was approaching her, eager to reclaim her senses.

"Stay," she whispered, voice barely audible. "Just a little."

He responded by pressing a light kiss to her forehead. "I'm not going anywhere."

The lamp's glow cast a fuzzy circle on the far wall, painting shadows that no longer seemed menacing. Elle inhaled Mateo's reassuring scent, and her eyelids fluttered. She felt him stroke her hair, simple and comforting, no urgency in his movement. The tension that had clung to her shoulders since she first woke up began to dissolve.

She let out a half sigh, half exhale, and whispered, "Thank you." It was all she had energy to say. He didn't reply, only moved his hand in slow circles along her back, steady as the pulse she felt under his shirt. In that quiet, her consciousness began to drift, lulled by the safety of his warmth and the softness of the room.

Her final thought before drifting off was that sharing this moment with him felt as intimate as any spell she might cast. No illusions shimmered at the edges of her vision this time, only the delicate hum of his heartbeat beside hers. The fear that had nearly shattered her only minutes before could not pierce the sanctuary of his presence. With each slow breath, she sank deeper into a hazy sleep, knowing that for tonight she did not have to face her nightmares alone.

As her mind teetered between wakefulness and slumber, her last conscious feeling was of the gentle weight of his hand on her spine, anchoring her in the here and now. Outside, the night pressed close, but inside her bedroom, quiet reassurance eclipsed the lingering shadows. So, with the taste of magic still tingling on her tongue and Mateo's calm breathing against her ear, Elle surrendered to sleep, content to let him keep watch as the final traces of the haunting dream slipped from her grasp.

FIFTEEN

Elle felt her pulse quicken when the radio fragment in the taxi buzzed through the static. The announcer's voice sounded strained, rattling off warnings about a tropical storm on the horizon. She leaned forward, tension knotting in her shoulders. The driver glanced into his rearview mirror, probably noticing the worry in her eyes. They were stuck at a red light, wind gusts rocking the car as if the storm had already found them. Dark clouds blotted out most of the afternoon sun, casting everything in a strange half-light. After what felt like an eternity, the signal turned green and the taxi lurched forward toward the Marigny neighborhood.

Spying the familiar shotgun house coming into view, Elle exhaled in relief. The wooden steps glistened with the thin sheen of moisture from damp wind, and one shutter clapped against the frame. She gave the driver a few bills and climbed out into the swirling gusts. The blast of wind whipped her hair against her cheeks. She clutched her small overnight bag close and hurried across the walk, mindful of the storm's building fury.

At the top of the porch, she wrestled with the old front door until the latch gave. Even before stepping fully inside, she smelled the comforting scent of pine cleaning solution and fresh candles. Tansy appeared from around the corner with a portable radio against her hip.

"You made it," Tansy said, voice laced with concern. Her eyes moved to the swirling sky beyond the door. "We've got a real one brewing, don't we?"

Elle kicked the door shut, fighting the wind that tried to wrest it open again. "I've never seen the clouds roll in this fast," she said, rubbing at the stiffness in her neck. Her gaze drifted across the living room. Dozens of tall, cylindrical candles lined the mantel, and a bag stuffed with lightly clinking bottles sat on the coffee table. Bottled water, she realized, plus an assortment of snack foods Tansy must have stockpiled.

"I wasn't kidding when I said I was prepping for the worst," Tansy said, setting her radio down. "Power outages are normal enough in storms, but everything on the radio suggests this might be worse than usual. I rearranged my work schedule so I can keep an eye on you here tonight. I figured you didn't want to get stranded in that hotel if the roads flood."

Elle gave a shaky nod and set her bag on a nearby chair. She had been planning to stay holed up in her hotel room, but Tansy's call that morning had changed her mind. A swirling knot in Elle's gut told her it was safer to be in a place that felt like home, around the leftover wardings her grandmother had placed. She unwound the thin scarf from her neck and folded it on top of her bag. The old house walls creaked as they were rattled by the wind. The entire city seemed to be holding its breath.

Tansy gestured for Elle to follow her into the kitchen. "I've got matches, flashlights, and more candles stashed here," she said, opening a cabinet where large jars of salt and extra batteries stood in neat rows. "We can block off the windows with towels if the rain gets any heavier. Did you eat at all before heading over?"

Elle hesitated. "Not since breakfast," she said, wincing. "There was too much to do today."

Tansy wrinkled her nose in disapproval. "We'll fix that soon. Mateo texted me an hour ago. He said he's bringing gumbo from his grandmother's recipe." She paused, a playful gleam breaking through her concern. "He was insistent you try it. Claims it's the best gumbo in the city."

Warmth fluttered in Elle's chest at the mention of Mateo. She recalled how dedicated he had been lately. He dropped everything whenever strange flickers of magic unsettled her. For the last few days, she had felt a lingering tension in the air, as if the city's wards were fraying at the edges. The radio's warnings about strong winds and possible flooding only intensified that feeling. She pushed a strand of hair behind her ear, trying not to look too transparent as relief mingled with anticipation.

"That's sweet of him," she said quietly. Then her voice gained a rueful edge. "But part of me wonders if I'm accidentally calling this storm. You know, fueling the weather somehow."

Tansy set down a box of water bottles and studied Elle's face. "I won't lie," she said, "I've never seen the city's sky go from calm to black in minutes. But storms happen often enough here. Don't blame every shift in the wind on your magic."

Elle forced a small smile, mindful of the weight at her collarbone. The filigree necklace, warm against her skin, pulsed subtly with her heartbeat. She sensed it was picking up on her anxiety. Whenever she got unnerved, the silver filigree heated as if responding to strong emotions.

An unexpected crash against the exterior shutters made them both jump. Tansy cursed under her breath, tossed a kitchen towel aside and rushed past Elle. They found the living room dimmer now that the clouds had thickened. Thunder boomed overhead so loud the wooden floor seemed to vibrate. Dust motes danced through the sudden gloom and swirled in the lamplight.

Elle swallowed hard and pushed away images of illusions that had haunted her dreams. She wanted to trust that tonight's terror was purely weather and nothing to do with lurking magic. Taking a deep breath, she found Tansy searching for something near the window. Her cousin finally wedged an old wooden wedge below the shutter to keep it from slamming.

"I don't want that banging all night," Tansy said with forced cheer. She shot a smile at Elle. "Better. Now we just need some actual food."

A buzz of the doorbell made them both jump yet again. Tansy shook her head with a soft laugh. "I swear if this is one more traveling salesman, they're about to get a face full of wind."

Elle eased to the door and peeked through the narrow glass pane. Mateo's tall shape stood on the porch, an umbrella tilted overhead and a plastic container balanced carefully in his other hand. Relief rushed through her, almost dizzying. She opened the door, letting in a swirl of damp wind and the spicy aroma of gumbo.

"You made it," she said, her voice mild but under-pinned with gratitude. She stepped aside so he could wrestle the umbrella shut. Rain pelted the porch steps in thick droplets. He gave her a warm, if slightly harried, smile.

"Thought I might get blown away," he said, pressing the container of gumbo into Elle's hands. "My grand-mother says this storm is a bad one. She claims the sky turned green before the clouds rolled in. You know how the older folks share these warnings."

Elle clutched the warm container against her torso. She noticed Tansy watching from the living room arch-way, an amused tilt to her head. "Thanks for this," Elle said to Mateo, carefully placing the container on a side table. She felt aware of every shift of her body near his, each brush of shoulders igniting a quick flutter in her chest. Tansy must have noticed too, given the way her eyebrows arched.

"Well, if you two are ready," Tansy announced in a teasing voice, "I'll set some bowls out. We can eat before the power flickers. You can confirm if this is indeed the best gumbo in the city, or if Mateo's grandmother needs to up her spice game."

Mateo laughed softly, offering Tansy a brief nod. He turned back to Elle, gaze gentle. "How are you holding up?" he asked.

She wanted to lie and say she was fine, but the tension in her neck refused to vanish. "A bit anxious," she admitted. "The wind is so intense, and my necklace has been reacting all day. I can't decide if I'm reading too much into a normal storm or if something more supernatural is at play."

Mateo's expression grew thoughtful. "Even if there's no direct magic behind it, your fear is real," he said. "I get it."

Before Elle could respond, thunder rumbled again, closer this time, rattling the windows. A lamp wavered, casting an unsteady glow across the living room. Tansy hurried over and started handing out bowls. She moved quickly, wanting them to eat while there was still a semblance of light. The gumbo's fragrance filled the small space, bringing an unexpected warmth that reminded Elle of neighborly potlucks from her childhood.

As they settled, Tansy made a point of lighting several wide candles on the coffee table for added illumination. Their soft glow turned the living room into a warm haven against the menacing gloom outside. Occasional gusts pushed at the windows, and every so often, the old house groaned in response.

The gumbo tasted rich with spices, and Elle found herself momentarily forgetting her worries. She noticed

Mateo observing her with a quiet intensity that made her heart flutter again. The chatter among them turned to easy remarks about comfort foods, how Tansy once tried to replicate a family recipe but ended up scorching the entire pot. Brief laughter followed, a small release of tension.

Then lightning flashed, brilliant and sudden, illuminating the front windows. A crack of thunder came so quickly after that Elle nearly spilled her bowl. The necklace flared hotter, a tangible sign of her frayed nerves. She drew a shaky breath, trying to steady her heart.

Mateo set his bowl aside. "You all right?" he murmured, leaning closer. His large hand came to rest on her arm, a simple touch that radiated reassurance. She caught Tansy stepping discreetly away, probably giving them space. The quiet hum of the portable radio on the table announced updates about heavy winds moving in with an alarm in the broadcaster's voice.

Elle tried to laugh off her jumpiness. "I'm all right, just keyed up," she said. "My grandmother used to talk about protective charms people used to hang in the windows. She said sometimes a single salt jar could keep a hurricane from claiming the heart of a household. I never knew how serious to take that."

"Maybe there's something to old wives' tales," Mateo said gently. "Some cultures leave bowls of water by the door or rose petals on the threshold. My grandmother told me about that once and said it helped friendlier spirits guard the house."

There was an awkward, tender silence. Elle realized

she wanted to trust in every scrap of old magic tonight. She could feel the house bracing against the storm, and in that moment, she felt her own power stirring. Was her anxiety feeding the clouds, or did the storm's raw energy latch onto her magic? That question made her skin prickle.

Tansy returned, tucking a strand of hair behind her ear. "I'm going to double check the windows down the hall," she said, glancing back. "Just in case. You two hold down the fort here."

Elle nodded, quietly appreciative that Tansy had an excuse to leave them alone. The necklace pressed against her skin felt like a small pulse of electricity, reminding her of the complicated swirl of longing and dread she carried everywhere. Mateo studied her face as if reading each flicker of emotion.

Outside, the wind roared, tossing branches against the roof. Rain battered the wooden walls in waves, and the lights flickered once more. Weak buzz gave way to the softer glow of the candles when every lamp abruptly shut off with a click. Complete darkness encased them for a moment, except for the candlelight dancing across the living room walls.

Elle heard her own heartbeat pounding. Her hand found Mateo's sleeve as thunder cracked again. The deep rumble vibrated through the floor, and the windows trembled in protest. She closed her eyes, steadying herself against him.

"Its just the power," he said quietly, voice warm enough to chase away a bit of her fear. "We've got candles. No need to panic."

She opened her eyes, face inches from his. The gentle candlelight grazed the strong lines of his jaw and cast a soft glow over his dark eyes. He offered a small, steady smile, and she found it hard to breathe for a moment. The closeness sparked the same flickers of interest she felt earlier, now magnified by the storm.

Over by the mantel, Tansy's portable radio sputtered, warning about possible flash floods in low lying areas. Elle forced herself to release Mateo's sleeve and move back slightly, clearing her throat with a nervous laugh. "Right," she managed. "We will be fine."

Mateo nodded, picking up one of the flashlights from the table and testing it. A bright beam cut through the gloom. "Good," he said. "Just in case we need to move around the house."

Elle sank onto the couch, swallowing a knot in her throat as another clap of thunder rattled the walls. She set her half eaten bowl of gumbo aside, losing all appetite. The tension in her chest felt almost electric, as if her own power fluttered against her ribs. A faint notion crossed her mind that if she closed her eyes, she might sense something intangible fueling the rain's unyielding fury. But she did not dare test it, not with the house already creaking beneath the storm's force.

Mateo settled next to her, close enough that his shoulder brushed hers, warming her side. The contact steadied her frayed nerves. Candles on the table wavered, their flames dancing in the cross breeze that snuck through the aging windows. She noticed the tight set in his jaw and realized he was likely worried too, though he tried not to show it. The old floor lamp in the corner flickered back to life for a moment, cast a weak glow, then died again with a defeated pop.

Outside, the wind howled. Tansy's footsteps pattered in the hallway, then she reappeared, shaking her head. "The whole street looks dark," she reported softly, turning off the flashlight in her grip. "No one has power. I saw neighbors fumbling with their own flashlights on their porches. We are in for a long night."

A brilliant flash of lightning lit the front window, and thunder slammed after it, making the glass rattle within the frame. Elle flinched so sharply that her necklace bounced against her collarbone. She caught her breath, acutely aware of the pulse beating in her ears. The swirling candlelight moved across Mateo's face as he leaned closer.

"It will pass," he said, voice low. "Let us just ride it out together." He tried to make light conversation, describing an old piece of folklore about leading storms away with copper bells. "My abuela swore by them," he said. "She hung them on her porch whenever the forecast turned bad."

Elle listened, half-lost in his voice. It was gentle yet unyielding. She clutched her necklace, feeling its warmth sync with the erratic rhythm of her heartbeat. The question lingered: was her fear feeding the storm, or was the storm amplifying her uncertain magic? She felt the edges blur in the humid, candlelit haze, knowing each heartbeat carried both apprehension and a longing for calm.

The next roll of thunder vibrated through the house,

and she inhaled sharply, letting Mateo's voice anchor her. His soft words about copper bells and protective charms washed over her, a shield against the howling wind outside. She closed her eyes and decided she would hold onto this fragile bubble of closeness. The candlelight painted patterns across their faces, and though the storm raged on, she found a small refuge in the space they shared.

SIXTEEN

Night settled around Ruby's shotgun house more quickly than Elle expected. The swirling storm clouds outside had deepened the gloom, pushing through the neighborhood. A stray gust rattled the front windows again, making her flinch as she lit another squat candle on the coffee table. A thick collection of them now dotted the living room, casting shadows against the walls in irregular patterns. The power had gone out entirely not long ago, and every lamp and overhead light had succumbed to the sudden darkness.

She and Tansy had carried spare candles from nearly every room, setting them in chipped saucers or dusty votive holders. Their soft glows staved off the eerie blackness that pressed against the house from all sides. Earlier, she had felt the sharp bite of her own anxiety, but the warmth of the candlelight provided a gentle buffer between that fear and her raw nerves.

From her perch on the couch, Elle took a shaky breath

and released it. She could still hear rain slamming against the windows in uneven sheets with distant thunder rumbling. Though her pulse hurried, she tried to focus on the welcome presence of her cousin and Mateo, both of whom had brought comfort in this tense atmosphere.

Tansy sat cross-legged on the armchair across from her, rummaging through a bag of snacks balanced on her knees. "I knew I had some leftover cookies in here somewhere," she muttered, voice determined. The candlelight gilded her face, creating bright patches against the worried pinch in her brow.

Mateo stood near the door, trying unsuccessfully to peer out through the front window. The darkness on the other side was complete. He turned and joined Elle on the couch, the faint aroma of coffee and damp cotton rising from his clothes. His closeness made the hairs on her arms stand at attention, as though her magic recognized him even before her mind fully did. Although she tried to quell the flutter low in her stomach, a thread of excitement wound its way through her despite the storm's roar. She found his presence deeply reassuring.

He exhaled as he settled beside her, the cushions dipping under his weight. "There's no sign of the power coming back," he said quietly. "The entire street looks out. Might be some blown transformer, or the lines could be down."

Elle nodded, watching the storm-lashed window for a moment. The house let out a subtle groan beneath another gust of wind, and she felt a touch of dread at how fierce the storm had become. "At least we have enough candles to last us a while," she said, trying to keep her voice light. She glanced around at the small points of flame dancing in glass jars and saucers. "And Tansy's cookie stash."

Tansy grinned triumphantly and retrieved a half-empty package of vanilla wafers from the bottom of her bag. "Never doubt me," she crowed, waving it as if it was a hard-won trophy. She eased back in the armchair and crossed one leg over the other. "We can't do much else but sit and wait for the storm to pass. Might as well share some stories, right? Something to distract from that howling wind."

Mateo adjusted one of the candle holders to ensure it was stable. "Stories sound good." His voice settled into that low timbre that made Elle's pulse accelerate. "What kind of stories did you have in mind?"

Tansy brushed a few stray cookie crumbs from her lap. "Oh, you know. Spooky, funny, random. Honestly, anything beats listening to the shutters bang. I was thinking about an old story from when I was in college." She paused, absently fiddling with the package. "I was crazy about a person who seemed perfect on paper, but I had these unexplainable chills in the back of my mind. Like something was trying to warn me. One night, a spirit popped into my dream, no joke, and flat out told me if I continued down that path, I would be miserable." She shrugged, lips curling in a rueful smile. "Even if you don't believe in dream spirits, it was enough for me. I broke things off. A friend told me later that person was already dating someone else the whole time. So maybe a little ghostly nudge saved me from heartbreak."

Elle raised her eyebrows. "That's weirdly comforting. Though I'd be shaken if a spirit actually came to me for relationship advice."

Tansy let out a short laugh. "I figured it was just a fluke, but I never forgot it. I learned to trust my intuition more, especially when everything seemed picture-perfect." She snatched a cookie and popped it into her mouth, speaking around the crunchy sound. "Nothing wrong with letting the universe throw a little red flag in your direction sometimes."

Mateo listened intently, his posture easy, but Elle could see the flicker of interest in his eyes. He rubbed his jaw thoughtfully. "I've had cases on the force that involved dreams or nightmares. People swore they saw figures in the shadows or heard voices that turned out to be real warnings." He paused and pulled over a cushion to rest his arm on the back of the couch. "The one that sticks with me most was never officially closed. We had a local man who claimed his wife vanished one night after describing a tall silhouette with eyes. None of it made sense, and we never found her. The husband described hearing footsteps on his porch, but there were no prints. The whole thing reeked of the supernatural. My captain told me to let it go, but I can't stop wondering what took her. It felt bigger than anything normal."

Silence fell across the room except for the steady drumming of rain outside. Elle squirmed slightly, unsettled by the notion of such a chilling case. She sensed the lingering weight behind Mateo's words. "It is frightening," she said softly, "how easy it is for people to disappear under strange circumstances. And in a city like this, well, it is no secret certain things lurk."

Mateo nodded, his gaze drifting to the nearest candle's flame. She understood that quiet resignation. Though he had tried to follow official channels in unexplained cases, he was often told not to push too hard. She reached for his hand on an impulse but remembered Tansy's presence a second too late. Her cheeks warmed as she withdrew, pressing her palms to her knees instead.

Tansy noticed, but she only offered a small smile. "We are safe right now," she announced, as if to soothe them all. "Thick walls, sturdy roof, enough wards left by Ruby to hopefully keep big nasty things from knocking at the door." She rose from the armchair and stretched. "But I am a big believer in double checking. Let me walk around the house. I can hear that window in the kitchen complaining about something. If I leave it alone, we will have water dripping everywhere."

She left them without much ceremony, clutching the package of vanilla wafers against her hip. Elle tracked her cousin's departure until Tansy disappeared into the corridor. The rustle of footsteps soon faded, leaving Elle alone with Mateo in the candlelit living room. The house creaked and thunder cracked overhead, making her jump. Her heart pounded in her ears.

Mateo leaned closer, keeping his voice low. "You all right?"

She nodded, though goose bumps prickled her arms.

"Just jumpy. Storms usually do not scare me, but this one, I cannot tell if the darkness is from the weather or something else." She glanced at the scattered candles that bathed them in gold. Shadows danced over the floor in long shapes that stretched toward his feet.

His eyes found hers, calm and watchful. "Want me to distract you more," he asked, half a smile tugging at his mouth.

A ripple of warmth cascaded through her, banishing some of the tension in her chest. "Yes," she admitted, clearing her throat. "I like hearing your voice."

He tilted his head, studying her face. "Well, this might not be the most uplifting story, but it is a strange one. A friend of mine used to work at the station. He once got a call from a woman claiming that her reflection in the bathroom mirror was not hers. He brushed it off, but the next day she went missing. When he and I went to search her place, the mirror was broken, as if someone had slammed something against it. We never found a body or her. It was not our case, so we could not investigate further, but it stayed with me." His voice lowered. "I know it sounds impossible, but I cannot help thinking maybe there was something in that reflection she saw."

Elle's skin prickled. She found it difficult to tear her eyes from him while a slight tremor of alarm worked its way through her spine. "Possession? Or maybe illusions?"

"Maybe," he said. "We see a lot more illusions than I want to admit."

She remembered the fleeting glimpses she herself witnessed in the city's streets, the rumors of illusions haunting those with open hearts. Instead of retreating from the conversation, she leaned a fraction closer, letting the warmth in his gaze anchor her. "Are you ever tempted to stop chasing these cases? To pass them off as some other detective's burden, so you can, well, return to normal police work?"

He paused, then shook his head. "I don't think I could pretend everything is normal. Not when I see the truth about what roams here." He matched her gaze, and she felt a quiet pulse in the space between them. "Though I can't say it's easy. Especially if it puts those I care about in danger."

Elle's breath caught. Her heart hammered, uncertain if he was talking about danger from illusions or referencing the precarious swirl of magic that seemed to follow her. Either way, the moment felt more intimate than anything else that night.

A flash of lightning illuminated the house's windows, lighting up his features for the span of a single heartbeat. She saw a flicker in his expression, a thought he couldn't quite voice. Thunder trailed behind it, rolling through the sky like a distant exclamation. She realized how close their knees were, not quite touching but nearer than before.

She swallowed hard. "I appreciate it," she whispered, her voice nearly lost under another gust of wind. "You being here. I feel safer."

He watched her for a moment, eyes dark and warm. Then his hand brushed her chin in a gentle motion, guiding her to face him fully. The simple contact sent a delightful shock across her skin. She caught a faint, earthy scent from his jacket, like fresh coffee beans laced with city air. The candles carved out the planes of his cheekbones, turning the living room into a private cocoon of light and shadow.

She parted her lips as if to say something else, but the words never formed. His hand moved from her chin to the side of her cheek, fingertips trailing a careful path, and Elle found herself leaning in. A spark filled the short space between them. Her heart thundered louder than the storm outside, and before she knew it, his lips met hers.

The kiss was soft but charged with an urgent current. Despite the faint drip of water and the groan of the wind, all she registered was the warmth of his mouth moving against hers. A wave of sensation rippled along her spine, leaving her half breathless. She parted her lips more, felt his exhale mingle with hers, and let the world beyond candlelight blur into nothing.

Thunder crashed again, sharper this time, rattling the windows in a scolding reminder of the storm. Yet she could not bring herself to pull away. Instead, she lifted a hand to rest on the back of his neck, marveling at the heat of his skin. The moment stretched, fragile and powerful at once, until a voice called from the kitchen doorway.

"All I can say is, the window is," Tansy halted, and Elle felt Mateo tense against her. "Uh, never mind." Tansy's tone carried a faintly amused lilt, but she made no move to interrupt further.

Elle reluctantly drew back, cheeks burning and breath unsteady. The loss of contact brought a slight ache, yet she could still feel the warmth of his lips buzzing on hers. She turned to see Tansy holding a dry towel and raising her eyebrows, though her face was mercifully free of judgment.

For a beat, no one said anything. Tansy finally cleared her throat. "I need a quick fix for that rattling frame in the kitchen, but I found a towel for the leak. Thought you'd want to know. I'll just," She gestured with the towel. "Give you guys a minute."

Elle opened her mouth to respond, but words remained stuck. Heat flooded her face, and her heart thumped wildly. Mateo's hand slipped away from her cheek, though he stayed close, his breathing uneven. The faint swirl of candle smoke made her head swim as she realized Tansy had no intention of scolding them, nor did she plan to linger.

Tansy vanished as she had arrived, footsteps padding into the hallway. A fresh gust droned through the living room, making the flames quiver. Elle turned back to Mateo, meeting his wide, steady gaze. Neither of them spoke, but she could see the same hunger in his eyes that pulsed in her chest. She pressed her lips together, still tasting the traces of that stolen kiss.

They pulled apart, hearts pounding, unspoken promises lighting up the thick, storm-torn air.

CHAPTER

SEVENTEEN

A faint lull settled over the living room, as though the storm had paused to catch its breath. The candles Tansy had lit on the side table still danced with trembling flames, casting shapes across the wallpaper. Elle stood near the open doorway, her pulse strong in her ears. Moments earlier, the rain had raged against the old shotgun house with the force of a waterfall while howling winds rattled the windows. Now the drums of thunder receded into the distance, and the downpour eased to a subdued patter.

She brushed damp hair from her forehead and inhaled the warm, saturated air. The house smelled of hot wax, pine cleaner, and the faint spice of gumbo that nobody had quite finished. She glanced at Mateo, who stood beside her, his tall frame outlined by the last glow of daylight. In the quiet, his gaze locked with hers, the corners of his mouth curving into an almost question. She read it back in her own heartbeat, a question about stepping outside, about trusting that the lull would hold.

In truth, a mixture of gratitude and tension tethered Elle's chest. It felt impossible to ignore the crackling expectancy that hovered between them, as if the energy of the storm had seeped indoors. He tilted his head in invitation and gave her a slight nod. Without speaking, he reached for the old brass doorknob. She swallowed and stepped closer. Her reflection glistened faintly in the window's glass, framed by the soft lines of candles behind her.

She pushed open the door. The screen creaked on its hinge. A humid gust washed over her as she followed Mateo onto the porch. Rainwater dripped from the eaves in a gentle curtain, and the battered rocking chair in the corner shuddered each time a stray breeze caught it. The porch's wooden planks felt slick under her sandals, forcing her to move carefully. She kept one hand braced on the doorframe until she could survey the scene.

Farther down the block, the street lamps glowed against the thick gloom. She expected to see torrents still flooding the gutters, but the rainfall had tapered to a soft haze on the pavement. She took in a careful breath and tasted the metallic edge of ozone in the air. She knew that the calm could be short lived, yet something about it drew her forward.

Mateo's presence warmed her side. She sensed the tension in his posture and the same undercurrent that tugged at each breath she took. The day had been intense, and the memory of thunder rattling the shutters still clung to every corner of her mind. Now the storm's heartbeat had slowed as though waiting for something else to take place.

She tilted her chin to look at him. A droplet clung to his dark hair, sliding along the strands before falling to his collar. The slight sheen on his skin told her he was as aware of the thickness in the air as she was. Their eyes met, and her pulse gave a fierce flutter as she searched his expression.

He lifted his hand, tentative yet sure. "You all right?" he asked quietly.

She nodded. "Still just keyed up," she answered, voice low. "I can't tell if this is a real lull or if the storm needed to breathe."

A small smile curved across his lips. "At least we can stand outside for a second," he said. "No more walls closing in on us."

Rainwater trickled over the porch's edge, beating soft patterns against the step. Elle breathed in the scent of wet wood. Wind ruffled the short hairs at the back of Matteo's neck. She had a sudden urge to run her fingers there, to feel the solidity of his skin and the warmth he radiated. She swallowed and tried to steady the swirl of emotion. The old porch lamp overhead gave off a weak glow and highlighted the lines of his face.

He shifted closer. She sensed him looking at her with a question again, as though gauging if she wanted to retreat back inside. Instead, she stayed.

They both watched the street and the glistening puddles on the asphalt. A distant rolling of thunder teased the horizon. Reflexively, Elle touched her collarbone, expecting the necklace to press hot against her skin. But she had taken it off earlier and longed for a moment free of its unpredictable pulses. Still, her power felt alive and tingled under her ribs each time she inhaled. Her breath felt thick, like she was breathing in magic more than air.

Mateo turned to her. His hand rose to gently tuck a damp lock of hair behind her ear. The touch sparked awareness along her cheek. She shivered, not from the cold but from the tension winding between them. The storm had been raging for hours and stranded them in candlelight with Tansy's anxious footsteps in the next room. Now they were almost alone. The moment spilled open, raw and unguarded.

He spoke her name softly. "Elle."

She leaned in, her body acting before her mind had time to second-guess. Her gaze fastened on his mouth. The worry, the thunder, the candles inside, it all faded. All that remained was the shape of him in the half-light, the promise in his eyes, and the warmth that coiled at the center of her chest.

His lips met hers in a firm, unwavering kiss. Her nerves seemed to catch fire, the sensation more electric than any arc of lightning could be. The world narrowed to the present, the place where her lips melded with his, broken by the uneven catch of her breath. Rain hissed off the porch roof, and her heart pounded so loudly she could not tell if it was her pulse or the distant thunder.

She pressed closer and her hands rose to clutch the front of his shirt. She felt the lines of his chest through the damp fabric, and her head spun at the heady mix of comfort and hunger that filled her. She had imagined kissing him before, but none of those fleeting daydreams matched the real thing. Every nerve in her body felt alive, as if the storm had settled in her bones, waiting for this moment to unleash.

The sky erupted in a blinding flash. She tore her mouth away from his, eyes darting upward. A jagged line of lightning speared the darkness, streaking down with eerie precision. It felt as though the city itself gave a thunderous roar in response.

A deafening crack snapped across the street, and both of them jumped. Elle gasped, heart lurching. She saw sparks dancing around the lamppost opposite the house, light strobing in wild arcs. The iron stand reverberated with the force of the strike. The smell of singed ozone rushed across the street and washed over the porch.

She and Mateo stumbled back together, adrenaline flaring as fierce as the lightning. She felt his grip on her arm, steadying her. Sparks flew from the lamppost's transformers, whirling through the rainy air like fireflies gone mad. Elle's heart pounded in her ears, and for one breathless instant she wondered if her power had sparked that bolt of electricity. Her mind flickered through the possibilities. Was it chance, a meteorological quirk, or had the storm answered the wild rush of magic simmering in her blood?

They pressed against the house's siding, the closeness of their bodies a counterweight to the sudden fear. Another rumble shook the sky. Adrenaline spiked, buzzing in her veins. She looked at him, gaze darting between him and the chaotic sparks.

He let out a short laugh, part relief, part giddiness. "Are you okay?" he asked, voice pitched high enough to carry over the ringing in her ears.

She nodded, swallowing. "Yeah," she managed. "You?"

He exhaled, a sound almost like a shaky chuckle. The corners of his eyes crinkled. She realized they were both flushed, hearts hammering in unison. Something about the sudden thunderclap and the electricity swirling in the air made them look at each other with renewed awe. It felt like the storm had answered them, acknowledging the spark they shared.

Elle's lungs seized a breath, and she let out a trembling laugh, giddy from the possibility that her magic might have fused with nature just then. "That was intense."

Mateo's eyes shone with the same realization. "Guess we should get inside," he teased, although his voice shook a bit. "Before we tempt another lightning bolt."

She nodded, adrenaline quivering through her limbs. They turned toward the door, stepping carefully around the large puddle that had formed on the porch near the steps. The lamppost crackled behind them, but the sparks were already fading, leaving a faint glow in the otherwise dark street. Rain started again in earnest, drumming a heavier tattoo against the roof. Wind cut across the porch, spattering droplets against their legs.

Mateo guided her inside, his hand hovering near the small of her back. They crossed the threshold, water trickling from their hair and clothes onto the floorboards as they fumbled to close the door. When they managed to shove it shut, they stood in the dim hallway and panted from the jolts of excitement.

Candlelight came from the living room, and the air felt thick inside as well, both from the humidity and the unexplained rush that crackled between them. Elle realized her arms were trembling, and she was unsure if it was from the kiss, the lightning, or the surging storm. Maybe all three.

Mateo drew in a breath, eyes bright with the remnants of adrenaline. His hair hung damp against his forehead, and droplets traced down one side of his jaw. She let out another shaky laugh and leaned briefly against the wall for balance. She felt the wet cling of her shirt, the sticky damp of her arms, and the thrumming heat in her cheeks.

"You saw that lamppost, right?" he asked, voice still tight with disbelief.

She nodded and let out a breath. "We could not have missed it," she said, her words a bit breathless. "I swear lightning never hit that close when I was a kid around here."

He rubbed his neck, as if trying to shake off the tension. "Looked like the sky singled us out."

They exchanged a long, wide-eyed look. Her heart hammered, still not over how impossibly bright the strike had been. She might have imagined it, but she thought she had felt a tug deep in her core at the same instant. As if her magic recognized the storm's ferocity. Or maybe the storm recognized her. The puzzling fascination in Mateo's eyes said he might wonder the same.

CHAPTER

EIGHTEEN

Elle sat on the edge of the couch in Ruby's dim living room, massaging the lingering ache in her shoulders. The storm that had ravaged the neighborhood last night had finally passed, leaving behind wet streets and dull skies. A humid warmth seeped through the open windows, carrying the distant hum of traffic. She was still reeling from the events of the previous evening, the thunder, the raw burst of energy on the porch, and the lightning that had nearly crashed into a lamppost across the street. Even hours later, she felt fragile, as though her skin was stretched too tight over her nerves.

Tansy appeared in the doorway carrying two mugs of coffee. She offered one with a small grin and set the other on a battered side table. A faint bruise colored Tansy's temple from where the shutters had rattled loose in the storm, but her expression sparkled with restless excitement.

"I know you are tired," Tansy said, "but I think we

should go to Algiers Point tonight. My friend Charisse says there is a séance circle gathering, and she is sure they can help with everything." She waved a hand about, indicating the swirl of tension still clinging to the house.

Elle exhaled slowly. She sipped her coffee, the chicory tang cutting through the heaviness in her chest. "Help with my rampaging magic, you mean," she said. "Or my inability to keep wind from howling indoors."

Tansy sank onto the couch beside her. "I know it is short notice, but you told me yesterday that you want answers. Maybe this circle can at least give us clues about your energy. Think of it like a small step forward." She placed a reassuring hand on Elle's knee. "I promise, it will not be too big or flashy."

A hollow laugh escaped Elle. "Flashy is exactly what scares me right now." She let her free hand drift to the filigree necklace lying cool against her collarbone. Even though the storm had passed, occasional pulses of magic still fluttered there, as if reminding her the danger was never gone. "What if I lose control in the middle of someone else's circle?"

Tansy paused, empathy softening her features. "We will be careful. They are used to dramatic things happening in séances. In fact, Charisse told me they welcome strong energy." She squeezed Elle's knee. "I am with you every step of the way."

Elle studied the steam rising from her mug. She thought about how the slightest tremor of her fear last night had seemed to feed the storm itself. She was desperate for clarity and even more desperate not to be alone in her confusion. If Tansy vouched for the group, maybe it was worth a shot.

"All right," Elle said softly. "I'll go."

Relief flooded Tansy's eyes. She bounced up, nearly sloshing coffee from her mug. "Good. I'll text Charisse and let her know. The gathering starts just after sundown. We can take the ferry across if the schedule cooperates."

"Before we go," Elle added, setting her mug aside, "I'm letting Mateo know. Just in case," she stopped, unsure how to phrase the knot of worry lodged in her throat.

Tansy nodded with a knowing smile. "He's your safety net."

Elle pulled out her phone.

> Heading to Algiers tonight for a séance circle. Tansy's idea. Thought you should have the address just in case. Be safe.

She hesitated, thumb hovering over the keys, then added a simple **Thank you for last night** before sending it. She tucked the phone away and tried not to dwell on the memory of Mateo's arms around her amid flickering candles. Her pulse still fluttered remembering that warmth.

An hour later, she and Tansy boarded the ferry to Algiers Point. The short ride across the river was peaceful enough, the dark water lapping against the hull. The skyline faded into dusky shapes, and the wet breeze off the water clung to Elle's skin, layering her in a fresh sense of anticipation. She kept one hand on the steel railing, scanning the horizon. Somewhere across the city, she imagined Mateo reading her text and frowning in concern.

Algiers Point greeted them with quiet streets and scattered lights in the windows of old Creole cottages. Tansy led the way through a narrow walkway, eventually stopping in front of a small house with colorful paper lanterns strung along the porch. The air smelled of jasmine and faint incense. Low chatter drifted from within, punctuated by the occasional clink of glass or shuffle of footsteps.

Charisse opened the door, a petite woman in a loose top and patterned pants, her short hair dyed a vibrant orange that glowed under the lantern light. She offered Tansy a warm hug, then turned to Elle. "You must be the one with the powerhouse aura," Charisse said, giving Elle an appraising look. "Sorry if that sounds forward, but Tansy warned me you're exceptional."

Elle inhaled, wondering how many more times she would hear whispers about her aura before she finally believed it. "I don't know about exceptional," she mumbled, stepping past the threshold into a narrow hallway. "But I do have a knack for attracting trouble."

Charisse's expression softened. "We'll see if tonight can help. The host of the séance is already getting things set up. We'll go to the back room."

Elle followed Charisse and Tansy through a corridor lined with flickering sconces. The house smelled of sandalwood, thick and heady. At the far end, an arched doorway opened on a wider space crammed with mismatched chairs. Twinkling lights ran along the walls, turning the dark corners into welcoming alcoves. A circular rug took up most of the floor, and several people had already settled into seats around it. Several glass bowls sat in the center atop a low wooden stool. Incense swirled overhead, curling into shapes that reminded Elle of storm clouds.

An older man with an air of authority stood as soon as they entered. He wore a draping shawl and had long, braided hair streaked with silver. "These must be our final arrivals," he said. His voice was deep, carrying a lulling quality that made Elle's skin prickle. "Welcome."

Tansy introduced Elle to the rest of the group, a handful of practitioners and curious attendees. All of them gazed at her in open curiosity. One younger witch, wearing a floral bandana, whispered audibly, "She's the one?"

Elle's stomach lurched at the attention. She forced a polite smile and gripped Tansy's arm for reassurance. When everyone had finished murmuring, the older man, whose name turned out to be Cornell, gestured to the open circle of chairs. "Please, sit wherever you feel comfortable."

Elle moved to slip into a seat beside Tansy, but Cornell lifted both hands, the corners of his mouth curving in a mysterious smile. "Actually," he began, "I sense your energy might be best in the center."

Elle's pulse thudded. "Why the center?" she asked, trying to keep her voice steady.

Cornell's dark eyes looked at a candle near the stool. Its flame trembled as if the air had shifted. "Because your aura has a bright intensity, and I suspect you can ground the rest of us better from the center." He paused, then added warmly, "We mean no harm. We only want to see if equilibrium can be achieved."

Tansy shot Elle a questioning glance. Elle swallowed, unsettled by how certain the man sounded of her place in this gathering. But something about his calm presence put her at a relative ease, so she nodded. "I'll do my best," she said.

She perched on the low wooden stool, feeling everyone's stares. The other witches and curious onlookers formed a wide ring around her, crossing their legs or clasping hands in their laps. Charisse offered an encouraging wink. Tansy stayed near enough for Elle to see her reassuring smile.

Cornell started them off with a soft chant, calling on guiding spirits to lend clarity. One by one, the others joined in, layering their voices in a lilting harmony. The candlelight wavered, and quiet settled around them. At first, Elle closed her eyes, feeling the churn of her own nerves. She tried to breathe slowly, inhaling the incense-laced air and exhaling anxiety. But as the chant grew louder, a strange sensation crawled over her skin, almost like an invisible hand brushing her arms.

When she opened her eyes again, the flames around the room seemed brighter. The circle's energy pulsed in time with her racing heart. She spotted Charisse from the corner of her vision, her mouth parted as if marveling at something. A few others pressed themselves back against their chairs and stared at Elle in open astonishment.

Cornell's chanting took on a purposeful rhythm. The

air thickened. Elle felt an urge to speak, to pray, or to call upon something more potent than her fear, but she stayed quiet and let the circle's energy wash over her. She thought back to Ruby's old lessons scrawled in half-finished diaries. The best strength sometimes lay in silent acceptance.

A fierce gust of wind tore through the room, rattling the windows. The candles burned wildly, and at least half of them went dark in an instant. Gasps rippled around the circle, and the droning chant faltered. The summer humid air turned icy, sending goose bumps down Elle's arms.

She tried to breathe but found herself choking on something impossible to name. Her throat felt squeezed, as though unseen fingers clutched it. She managed a brief, panicked cry. Chairs scraped against the floor as some participants scrambled away. Frantic voices rose on all sides, shadowy figures stepping back, uncertain how to help.

Tansy jumped to her feet, but a stray swirl of wind knocked her off balance. Elle coughed, eyes stinging. The candles that still remained lit cast strange, dancing lights that made the situation even more surreal. She tried to claw at her throat, forcing air into her lungs, but the pressure only grew.

The door slammed open, letting in a slice of streetlight from outside. A familiar voice cut through the chaos. "Elle!"

Mateo. Relief jolted her, mingling with desperation. She barely heard calls of alarm from the other witches as he crossed the threshold. His eyes darted to the center, found her struggling on the stool, and he sprang forward without hesitation.

"Move," he commanded whoever blocked his path. He shouldered past them, ignoring startled protests. In the dim glow, Elle could see tension carved into his features. She tried to speak, but the choking sensation pinned her voice. With decisive strength, he scooped her off the stool and anchored her against his chest. One of the overturned bowls clattered at his feet, but he did not stop.

Her vision blurred. She braced an arm around his shoulder, inhaling his familiar scent of soap and faint cologne. The suffocating pressure loosened a little, and she coughed again, tears burning her eyes.

The other practitioners pressed toward them in a halo of confusion. Charisse exclaimed, "We didn't do anything, something else hijacked it!"

Tansy's urgent voice rose above the fray. "Let her breathe!" Her frantic gaze locked with Elle's for a heartbeat, checking that she was conscious.

Mateo held Elle, looking ready to fight if anyone dared stop him. She could feel the frantic beat of his heart through his shirt, each thump a stark reminder she was safe in his arms. Her own pulse skittered as he pushed past those who had formed the circle, brushing aside curtains of tangled incense smoke. The wind still whipped around them, rattling shutters and causing the paper lanterns outside to flicker. Elle's chest heaved, partly with terror, partly with gratitude, as if her magic had recognized him before her mind caught up.

NINETEEN

Elle slowly blinked awake to a dull throb at the base of her skull. The world felt muffled, as though all the noise from last night's séance had drained away into dawn. With a shallow inhale, she took in Mateo's living room. Faint grayish light from the half-closed blinds fell across the worn sofa beneath her cheeks, illuminating the swirl of dust motes drifting in the air.

She flexed her fingers and found them stiff from tension rather than rest. Her bare feet were tucked under a thin quilt, the faded pattern evidence of how often it had been washed. Some quiet part of her realized this was the second time she had ended up on his couch. Only this time, Tansy was present too, curled up in a nearby armchair, her limbs splayed in exhaustion. Tansy's mouth hung open as she snored softly, her dark hair mussed.

Elle shut her eyes again, momentarily dreading what morning might bring. The séance had gone out of control, leaving her breathless and terrified. She was sure Tansy felt the same, a protective worry that had kept her from letting Elle out of her sight. At least in Mateo's apartment, they had found some measure of safety after the chaos. Yet that safety was fragile and new.

A subtle flutter under her collarbone made her open her eyes again. She pressed the palm of her hand to that spot. Something tingled there, a warmth that felt more alive than just the usual thud of her heartbeat. The ache that lingered from nearly being choked last night shifted and gave way to a faint spark in her skin.

Her curiosity pushed her to sit upright. She carefully lifted the collar of her T-shirt, the one she had borrowed from her cousin's spare bag. Where the short sleeves draped awkwardly on her shoulders, she could still see the top edge of her collarbone. In the bluish dawn light, she caught a faint glow.

She pressed two fingers to the spot. A mild heat pulsed against her touch, as though responding to her curiosity. Biting back an exclamation, she tilted her head to the side and pulled the collar away enough to see it fully, a whorl of lines, delicate as filigree and shaped almost like the edges of a spiral. Sharp angles connected the spirals, creating a symbol unlike the fleur-de-lis images that had occasionally haunted her dreams. This was new, a design that looked ancient yet intimate.

She swallowed, heart pounding. It glowed like a dim ember beneath her skin. When she removed her fingertips, the glyph brightened, then receded to a duller shimmer. She could almost feel it tapping in time with the push and pull of her pulse. It was mesmerizing in its strange beauty.

A soft sound in the kitchen made her glance over the back of the sofa. Mateo stood behind the narrow counter, rummaging in a cabinet for blankets or towels. He wore an old T-shirt, loose over well-worn jeans. At the sight of him, her chest fluttered with both gratitude and guilt. He had stepped in last night at the séance without hesitation, carrying her right out of that circle.

Last evening was a blur of swirling incense, chanting that had grown too strong, and then a suffocating force around her neck. The memory tightened her throat. She recalled Tansy's voice screaming somewhere behind the circle of startled witches. The moment she thought she might pass out, Mateo had charged into the room and scooped her up. His embrace had felt like the only real thing in a haze of panic.

She breathed deeply, forcing the tension back. She was safe. She just needed to figure out what was happening with this new mark. Her mind whirled with uninvited questions. Was last night's mishap truly the séance group's doing, or had something darker hijacked their attempts at summoning clarity? And why was she bearing the sign of it on her skin?

Soft footsteps pulled her attention. Mateo, arms laden with folded blankets, stepped closer. He paused when he saw her awake, and relief spilled across his face.

"You're up," he said quietly, dropping the blankets onto a nearby chair. His gaze skated across her expression as if checking for new bruises. "How do you feel?"

"A little sore," she answered, voice rasping. She cleared her throat. "And I found something." She lowered her voice to avoid waking Tansy, then beckoned him closer with a small hand gesture.

He set one knee on the edge of the sofa, leaning over her. In the muted morning light, concern etched every line of his brow. There was no dismissive skepticism as he bent to see what she wanted to reveal.

"I think I have a mark," she said. Carefully, she pulled the collar aside to expose the faintly glowing lines adorning her skin.

He inhaled sharply. In response, the glyph pulsed bright for a fraction of a second, as though reacting to the heightened energy in the room. Mateo's hand found her shoulder, fingers light but steady.

"Does it hurt?" he asked.

"Not exactly," she answered. "It's more like a slow burn under the surface. It's reminding me something is there, but it isn't painful. Just present."

Mateo touched the skin just below the mark with the tip of his forefinger, and she felt a jolt that wasn't unpleasant. The swirling lines flickered brighter for the span of a heartbeat, and she bit her lip to stifle a gasp.

"Sorry," he said, drawing his hand away. "Didn't mean to startle you."

Elle reached for him, pressing his palm back to that same spot. "No, it's okay. I just have to get used to everything changing so fast." She locked eyes with him. "You've been so calm about all this. I wouldn't blame you if you decided it was too much."

She expected him to keep a guarded expression or to offer a polite reassurance. Instead, the corners of his mouth tensed with an earnest determination. His fingers slipped to the side of her neck in a light stroke.

"You've seen me handle plenty of bizarre things," he said, voice tinged with gentle humor. "I've chosen to be here, no matter how strange it gets."

He was so close that she caught the faint scent of coffee clinging to his shirt. She felt a warmth blossoming in her chest that matched the new glyph's pulse.

A moment later, an unexpected snuffle drew both their gazes toward Tansy, who stirred in the armchair with a loud yawn. She opened her eyes and blinked. When her gaze landed on Elle and Mateo huddled at the sofa, Tansy exhaled in relief.

"Morning," Tansy murmured groggily. She sat taller, rolling her stiff shoulders. "I guess we all survived." Her eyes moved to the mark on Elle's collarbone. "Is that new?"

Elle nodded, letting her shirt drop back into place. "Yes. It started glowing when I woke up."

Tansy pressed her lips together, concern overshadowing the remnants of her drowsiness. "You have a knack for collecting weird magical brandings. But this time, it looks..."

"Different," Elle finished, glancing at the now-covered glyph. She felt it throb lightly beneath the fabric. "It's more complicated. Not like the simpler motifs we've been seeing around the Quarter."

Mateo rose and guided Tansy to the small table by the kitchen so she could have more space. Then he returned to Elle's side, offering a supportive arm for her to stand as well. The three of them hovered near the table. Outside, a car engine rumbled by, and the faint smell of fresh bread from the bakery down the block drifted through a partially open window.

Tansy raked her fingers through her hair. "I hate to say it," she muttered, "but last night felt hijacked. I've known many witches who host séance circles, this was not normal. Whatever we tried to do, something else cut in and singled you out, Elle."

Elle nodded grimly, remembering the sensation of invisible hands clamping around her throat. "It felt personal," she admitted. "Like it was waiting for me."

Mateo pressed a palm flat on the table. "Any idea who or what it could be?"

Tansy rubbed her eyes, thinking. "No name leaps out right now, but a group of us suspected that the city's older influences were stirring. And you, Elle, might be the biggest magnet for it. The necklace, your grandmother's journals, everything has been building, right?"

Elle caught the slight edge in Tansy's voice, equal parts dread and protectiveness. She swallowed and glanced at Mateo, who listened fiercely. "I used to think I was in over my head," she said quietly, "and that staying out of those circles was safer. But maybe it's worse to pretend it's not happening. Now I can't deny it's happening on its own, anyway."

The new glyph tingled, as if it agreed with her. The sensation sent awareness through her entire body, reminding her it was no ordinary mark. Fear flickered in her chest, weaving with curiosity. She looked at Mateo, half afraid to voice her next thought.

He tilted his head. "What is it?"

She stepped closer. "I am worried it is permanent like a tether or a beacon, something that might attract more trouble." She hesitated, then forced the words out. "I do not want you or Tansy getting hurt because I am walking around with a literal target on my skin."

"You told me once," Mateo said, his tone gentle, "that you felt alone in this. But you are not alone now, are you?" He looked at Tansy, who nodded firmly.

"Damn right you are not," Tansy grumbled, though her expression was warm. "I am not going anywhere. And neither is Detective Cruz, from the look of things."

Mateo's lips curved in a half smile. "You will never drag me away," he teased, though the determination in his eyes was serious. "We will figure out if it is a beacon or a shield. Maybe it is marking you, but that can mean different things. It might even be a protective side effect."

"You are oddly optimistic," Elle said, relieved but cautious. "Chalk it up to a detective's hunch?"

"Call it a personal vow," he answered. He turned toward the counter to rummage for cups. "Let me at least get you some coffee," he said, "and then we can talk about a plan."

Elle sank into one of the wooden chairs and exhaled in a surge of gratitude. With Tansy by her side and Mateo rummaging for coffee grounds, she had the strange impression of a new normal. It was not the quiet life she once envisioned, but in this worn apartment, she felt safe enough to examine her anxieties without being swallowed by them.

Within minutes, the aroma of fresh coffee filled the apartment, dark, reassuring, tinted by the slight bitterness of chicory. Tansy accepted her steaming mug gratefully and blew on it. Elle leaned her elbows on the table, sipping carefully, the warmth of the cup soothing her trembling fingers. Mateo leaned his hip against the counter and sipped from his own mug as his gaze often moved to Elle's collarbone. She could tell he was recording every detail for some private mental log.

The adrenaline haze from last night had left behind a weariness that hollowed Elle's limbs. But she refused to wallow. "After coffee," she said, "maybe we can see if any of Ruby's notebooks mention glyph changes or references to newly etched symbols."

Tansy shrugged, exchanging a glance with Mateo. "Might be helpful to check if you're not the only one who's ever had a mark appear after a failed ceremony."

Elle nodded. "Agreed. I'll call a couple folks, well, maybe not the same folks from last night," she said, shivering at the memory. "But there are a few others who sometimes handle lost or forbidden spells. They might have some insight."

Mateo nodded. "Do you want me to reach out to any of my contacts? I still have a friend or two in the precinct who don't mind chasing unusual leads." He offered a small, wry grin. "They might keep an ear out if any weird incidents show up in the next day or two."

Her lips curved into a smile before she realized it.

"That'd be good. Thank you." An unspoken tension passed between them, the recognition that he might risk professional scrutiny for her sake. Yet she couldn't find the words to dissuade him, not when she needed him so badly.

They fell silent for a moment, each sip of coffee noticable. Tansy's shoulders slumped in exhaustion, but she seemed calmer, the panic of last night fading with every breath. Elle noticed how the new mark on her own skin pulsed with an almost lullaby rhythm, as though it sensed her acceptance of help.

At last, Mateo set his mug aside and crossed the short distance to Elle's chair. He crouched next to her, resting a steady hand on the back of her arm. "You're sure you're okay?" he asked gently. "No dizziness or leftover pain from last night?"

Her throat tightened at his quiet concern. "I'm okay now," she said, her earlier fear loosening. "No more choking sensation. Just this." She tapped the collar of her T-shirt.

He nodded, expression thoughtful. She felt herself leaning into him, drawn by the surety in his presence. He placed his free hand lightly over hers. His fingertips skimmed her skin in an unspoken promise. She closed her eyes, letting herself breathe in the warmth of his closeness, the faint residue of soap on his collar.

Tansy made a small, sheepish cough that might have been to give them privacy or to break tension. Elle shot her cousin a grateful, teasing look. Yes, Tansy had teased in the past about them being "cozy," but in the aftermath of danger, that closeness felt more essential than romantic fluff.

"By the way, thanks for letting us crash here," Tansy murmured. "I know we just sort of jumped into your space."

Mateo straightened and shook his head. "I insisted. You both needed rest, especially after that fiasco." He combed a hand through his hair, then settled it on the back of his neck, a gesture Elle recognized as a sign of mild self-consciousness. "I could not let you go back to that séance house or anywhere else that might leave you vulnerable."

A pang of affection tugged at Elle. "We appreciate it," she said softly. "I am sorry to drag you into more weirdness, but I cannot seem to avoid it these days."

His warm gaze locked onto hers. "You are not dragging me." There was a moment of weight in those words as though he wanted to say more but left it at that.

Even Tansy, usually quick to fill lulls, let it stand. Dawn streamed brighter through the blinds, coloring the walls in pale gold. The city outside roused with the shuffle of footsteps on the sidewalk and the rhythmic call of a distant street vendor peddling pastries.

Elle set her mug down and tugged aside her collar one more time, letting the two of them see the mark clearly in the fresh daylight. The glyph glimmered, a complex design with lines that seemed both precise and fluid. It was linked to a power she still had not harnessed. She wanted to be ready for whatever that meant.

In the stillness, she felt every trace of the city's magic

hum under her breastbone, as if she were more attuned to the undercurrents than ever before. The corner of her mind whispered that something big was in motion. The presence that had hijacked last night's séance was one whisper away from trying again.

She set her jaw, letting determination push aside fear. "I need to learn what this means," she said. "Because ignoring it will not make it go away. If it's a sign or a claim or whatever else, I will not stand by and let it control me."

Tansy smiled, admiration sparking in the tired lines under her eyes. Mateo placed a gentle hand at Elle's shoulder again, a silent vow that they had her back. Her heart thrummed in response, matching the glow beneath her collarbone.

As the sun rose higher, she found herself drifting into fragile hope. Perhaps this was not a curse etched on her skin. Perhaps it could be the start of something that gave her power she could finally wield, with Tansy and Mateo at her side. They had navigated everything so far. Maybe they were not unstoppable, but they were united.

She brushed her fingertips over the swirling glyph, then slid her hand over Mateo's. The lines within her skin kept pulsing, reminding her that the city's story was carving itself into her bones. Despite the tension fluttering in her stomach, she let her lips tilt into a small, determined smile. She might be marked, but she was not alone.

Gazing at Mateo's steady brown eyes, she felt the faint ache recede. A softness spread through her chest, a kind of warmth that replaced mere survival with something stronger, resolve. Whatever force prowled the city's edges had no chance against a heart that refused to face this alone.

She squeezed his hand and allowed herself to imagine a future that extended beyond fear and doubt. The city might be brimming with unknown dangers, but it also offered a chance to anchor herself in real connections. She knew in that delicate glow of sunrise that if Mateo continued standing beside her, she could push back against any lurking shadow. The glyph beneath her skin pulsed one final time, a silent beat of acceptance.

She allowed her eyes to close and leaned into the promise that together they could outlast the watchful presence creeping through New Orleans. In that fragile dawn moment, hope felt like magic all its own.

TWENTY

Elle stepped from the car onto the cracked pavement, nerves pressing at her from all sides. The early light of morning did little to diminish the lingering apprehension that clung to her chest. Barely twelve hours ago, she had been lying on Mateo's couch, breath trembling from the aftermath of the séance gone wrong. Now she found herself back at the very house where it happened, her pulse already racing. Tansy hovered at her left, and Mateo stood closer at her right than usual, as though preparing to catch her if something unnatural happened again. She gripped the handle of the car door for one extra moment before letting go with a sharp exhale.

The small house in Algiers Point looked eerily normal from the outside, at least at first glance. In the weak daylight, its colorful paper lanterns still hung drooping across the narrow porch, though several had winked out, their lightbulbs shattered by last night's gusts of unexplained wind. Her mind reeled back to the swirl of frightened people in that back room, the chanting that faltered, and the equally sudden breath as if invisible hands were gripping her throat.

Tansy stepped forward. "Looks quiet," she said. She clutched a canvas tote bag over her shoulder that presumably held a few warding supplies or crystals. Elle half expected her cousin's eyes to betray some sense of dread, but Tansy's face remained keen, refusing to show fear. Still, the small hitch in her breath gave her away.

"We can skip this," Mateo offered gently, his gaze moving from the house to Elle. "We haven't even been gone an entire day. If it feels too soon, we don't have to go in."

Elle wanted to accept that offer, to tell them that her need for answers wasn't worth stepping back into a space that had threatened her life the night before. But the memory of suffocating terror, of an unseen force shutting off her airway, crawled under her skin. She couldn't endure another night wondering what power had hijacked the circle and singled her out. She was done letting fear make her decisions, especially now that she bore a strange glyph on her collarbone, proof that something had marked her.

She shook her head and forced a calm tone. "I need to see it," she murmured, stepping forward. "I need to know the energy here. Maybe we'll find a clue, something to tell us if it was a random presence or someone with an actual plan."

Mateo's expression hardened in quiet support. He nodded and led the way up the creaking steps of the porch. The front door was unlocked and slightly ajar. Elle's heart hammered as he pushed it open. The hinges groaned in protest, revealing the narrow hallway where last night's incense still haunted the air. Only now it smelled stale, like perfumed smoke trapped in a sealed chamber.

The boards under her feet creaked. She took a slow step, her eyes drifting to the sconces that had flickered during the group's chanting. Dust and faint streaks of light revealed the house was empty, at least physically. Tansy reached for Elle's elbow and squeezed.

They walked toward the back, passing a half-open door that led to a small kitchen. Abandoned cups and half-melted candles lined the counters. It reminded Elle of a hastily deserted gathering, as if the circle's members had cleared out the moment the séance broke. She pictured the frantic shouts, the confusion when strong winds rattled every window. The host had apologized, if she remembered correctly, but none of that changed the fact that Elle had nearly collapsed from that terrifying grip around her throat.

The final doorway in the corridor opened into the parlor where the makeshift circle had once been. The overhead lights had burned out, so only a dull beam of outside light streamed in through a curtained window. Empty chairs jutted in disarray around the edges of the room, their cushions dented from the people who had sat there. Scattered salt gleamed in patches along the floor, and someone's half-finished chalk scrawl flaked near the center of the wood planks. The space reeked of leftover incense mixed with anxiety, if such a scent could exist.

Elle's chest constricted at the memory of herself perched in the middle. Chanting voices swirled around her. That had been the moment the house shattered into chaos.

Tansy ventured forward, one step at a time, scanning the scene. "They really cleared out," she noted softly. "Even the host is gone. Not a single sign of their usual after-ritual cleanup." She sneezed at a small swirl of dust that rose from the floor.

Elle's gaze snapped to a shape on the far wall, near the corner where a single candle still drooped in its holder. The shape was a smear of chalk lines that hadn't been there last night, she was certain. She edged closer. Curiosity drew her too powerfully to remain at the threshold.

"Is that some kind of writing?" Tansy asked, stepping behind her. "Because it might just be leftover patches of old sigils."

Elle tilted her head, trying to decipher it. From her angle, it was an uneven circle, or maybe a spiral. She moved two paces to the right and froze. There scrawled across the cracked plaster rose a faint message in ghostly lavender: "*The Queen is listening.*" The words glowed with an unnatural luminescence, as if lit from behind by moonlight that did not belong in this daylit room.

Her husbanded composure cracked. A memory of Madame Laveau's warnings about an old power in the Quarter rushed through her mind. The Queen. The rumored witch, the presence that seemed connected to everything swirling around Elle's life. She reached up on reflex and touched the spot beneath her collar of her shirt where that new glyph had appeared after the dangerously botched séance. Immediately, the skin under her palm prickled with heat, like an echo of the night's fear.

A cold breath on the back of her neck made her jolt. She turned, half expecting to see someone there. She saw nothing, just dust motes drifting in a kaleidoscope of sunlight. But the sensation of being watched tightened the base of her spine. Her pulse sped up.

Mateo must have noticed her terror because he stepped forward, sliding a steadying hand against her elbow. "Elle?" His gaze scanned the air near her shoulder. "What's wrong?"

"I felt something," she whispered. The new glyph pulsed again, radiating a faint warmth she could not ignore. "Like a breath. Right here." She pressed her fingertips to the back of her neck, goose bumps rippling across her skin.

Tansy peered around the room, her brow furrowed. "Is it the same feeling from last night?" she asked. "Or something else?"

Elle's throat constricted. "Similar, but not as strong." She paused, her eyes moving back to the faint writing on the wall. *The Queen is listening*. The words pulsed like a silent warning. "Last night felt more physical, more violent. This is more like someone's simply watching, testing me."

She swallowed hard, the dryness in her mouth scraping. Tansy approached the glowing message, though she maintained a cautious distance. Behind them, Mateo stepped to the nearest window and inched aside the curtain, letting a little more daylight spill into the dim space. The sudden brightness only accentuated the glowing text, making it seem more unnatural in the morning sun.

Elle forced herself to center her attention on the presence. She tried to recall a protective phrase from Ruby's journals, some half-finished lines that could ward against malignant watchers. Her grandmother's handwriting had been scrawled in all directions across the pages, but a phrase about *barrier and breath* came to mind. It was not something she had fully memorized.

She parted her lips and spoke the words she could remember. Her voice quavered. *"Let the watchers find no door. Let these walls shield every core."* Then she closed her eyes and added fragments of another verse. *"Bound by faith, hidden from sight..."*

Her memory faltered. A flush of warmth spread across her collarbone, and she felt a stuttering thrum in the air, as though her own heartbeat had spilled outward. She exhaled, praying it was enough to dampen the room's oppressive energy. Her entire torso prickled with tension, and she squeezed her fists tight to keep them from trembling.

A sudden whistle of cold air blew across the parlor. Salt scattered, swirling as if caught in a miniature vortex. The incensed odor vanished, replaced by a sharp chill that stung Elle's nose. Tansy yelped, stepping back. Mateo readied himself, his posture tense, scanning for a visible threat.

The temperature drop hurt, a gnawing iciness that pressed in from all sides. Elle found she could scarcely breathe. She gripped the fabric of Mateo's jacket and half crouched as a wave of dizziness battered her. And then, as quickly as it came, the chill receded, leaving the air stale and normal once more.

Elle's legs threatened to buckle, and Mateo caught her, sliding an arm around her waist. She pressed her forehead against his shoulder, letting out a shaky breath. That swirling wind had done no harm, but it felt like a test, some intangible presence seeing how she would respond to a fleeting intrusion.

Tansy's eyes went wide. "Are you okay," she rasped, voice trembling with unspent adrenaline. Salt crystals still twinkled on the floor, scattered like broken glass.

Elle nodded weakly, although her pulse still thundered. "Yes," she managed between shallow gasps. She forced herself upright, leaning into Mateo's solidity. His heart pounded beneath his shirt, a reminder that he felt every shred of tension with her. She lowered her voice. "We should leave. I don't think we'll learn anything more here." Her gaze moved to the chalk scrawls that had lost some of their glow.

"My question," Tansy said, pressing her palm to her chest, "is why that phrase is here. None of the circle members would have scrawled it if they were just a normal group seeking answers. It sounds like a threat."

Mateo nodded in agreement, though worry clouded

his expression. "It might be a clue about who we're dealing with. Or it might be a promise." He looked at Elle, arms still firm around her. "Let's not risk another demonstration. Come on."

She felt an odd mixture of relief and shame. Relief because she wanted nothing more than to walk out that front door. Shame because a part of her had wanted to prove she could face down anything brewing inside these walls. But that swirl of cold air, that ghostly breath on her neck, both made her realize she was still new to handling magic, especially if it was an extension of whatever the Queen wanted. She needed to be cautious.

They drifted back into the corridor, Tansy leading the way with brisk steps. Elle glanced over her shoulder one final time, eyes lingering on the chalk text. She imagined it pulsing again, whispering over her shoulder: *The Queen is listening.*

The unearthly sound in the parlor pressed on her eardrums.

She tore her gaze away and let Mateo guide her down the hallway. They stepped outside into the mild daylight as though surfacing from a tunnel. The morning sun warmed her face, but it felt jarring after that icy wind. She blinked rapidly, her lungs expanding as she sucked in fresh air. A slight tremble made her knees uncertain.

Tansy bade them onward, down the porch steps and onto the cracked sidewalk. "I can't believe how awful the energy felt in there," she murmured. She wrapped her arms around her midsection, as if trying to stifle a chill that clung to her from within.

"So it wasn't just me." Elle's voice came out frail. She tucked her hair behind her ears, arms tight against her sides. "It's not the same as last night, but that presence felt wrong. Like it was measuring me for something."

Mateo slid a comforting hand along her arm. "You're not imagining things," he said softly and gave Tansy a small, grim nod. "We'd be foolish to ignore it or to chalk it up to leftover séance energy."

A flash of fear crossed Tansy's features, quickly replaced by concern. "Now we have more questions than answers."

Elle swallowed, drawing in the humid morning air. Mateo's hand lingered on her elbow, offering unspoken support. She could sense him fighting the urge to ask if she was truly all right. The trembling in her limbs was real, but so was her resolve not to let fear rule. Madame Laveau's warnings echoed in the back of her mind. The city harbored old powers, and some might cling to any surge in a new witch's aura.

"Come on," Tansy murmured, stepping toward the car. "I'll drive, if that's okay. I just want us out of here." Her voice cracked on the last word. She set a determined pace, indicating no time should be wasted lingering outside the house.

Elle threw one last glance at the drooping lanterns on the porch. They swayed slightly in a faint breeze, as though some invisible presence took one final jab at her nerves. She felt the new glyph on her collarbone hum faintly again, not painful but insistent. It was as if it recognized a threat or recognized a claim. She deliberately turned her back on it, stepping forward with Mateo at her side.

They reached the car without incident, though her skin still tingled with the memory of that cold breath on her neck. She drew in a purposeful inhale, summoning whatever composure remained. Her heart still pounded with each step.

Mateo opened the passenger door for her, his eyes never leaving her face. She sensed the quiet question he hadn't voiced. Are you sure you're not hurt? She offered a small nod, hoping to reassure him. She was frightened but uninjured.

Tansy slid into the driver's seat, letting out a shaky sigh as she gripped the steering wheel. Matteo helped Elle into the backseat, then slipped in beside her. The car's engine rumbled to life, a soothing sound of normalcy in a morning otherwise drenched in tension. The wheels squeaked away from the curb, leaving that battered porch behind.

Elle couldn't help glancing at the side mirror, half expecting movement at the front door. There was none. Still, the fear refused to fade. That message on the wall, *The Queen is listening*, possessed a weight that didn't vanish just because they'd driven away. The uninvited swirl of air, the biting chill, the words scrawled in chalk, each sign pointed to a greater puzzle. Who or what had singled her out, and why?

Mateo sat close. The warmth of his presence steadied her. A memory flashed of him holding her in that same house only hours ago, protecting her from the choking darkness. The earnest concern that etched across his face told her he sensed the same creeping dread. Tansy peered back at them through the rearview mirror, frowning.

"I think," Tansy whispered, "that we should talk to Madame Laveau again. Maybe she's heard something about this scribbled phrase. If it's a direct threat, we need more wards." She paused, her breath shallow. "Unless you two think we can handle it alone, but after what happened in there, I'm not sure we should."

Elle's mouth felt dry. She swallowed, leaning into the seat. She didn't want to rely on others for every supernatural hiccup she faced, yet seeing those words, *The Queen is listening,* made her realize how outmatched she might be. The events of the last day had proven her raw power could be dangerous if she didn't know how to direct it, and the Queen's watchers might sink claws into any gap in her knowledge.

Mateo brushed a knuckle along Elle's arm, drawing her attention to him. "I think we talk to anyone who can help," he said firmly. "If this is the Queen's doing, we would be unwise to go it alone. We have seen that she or her followers are not shy about scaring us away."

Elle's lips parted in a shallow sigh. She hated feeling helpless but hated ignorance even more. She forced a nod and turned to watch the passing streets, where the growing sunlight bathed the sidewalks in gentle warmth. Inside, her pulse refused to settle. She thought about how that swirling wind had coiled around her, how it had pulled her breath toward a freezing emptiness. She had never felt so sure that an invisible presence monitored her, hungry for the magic she possessed.

As Tansy navigated toward the ferry that would bring them across to the main part of the city, Elle began to replay the warding phrase she had attempted. She had only half its lines in her memory. Next time, she resolved to carry a direct reference from Ruby's journal, not a guess. Because if the Queen's watchers had found her once, they could find her again.

Mateo's hand slipped into hers. "We will figure this out," he said, his voice quiet. "You're not alone."

She squeezed back, though her mind lingered on the intangible eyes that seemed to track her. She felt that same pinprick pressure deep in her collarbone where the glyph's lines still burned with a quiet glow. Her gut twisted with the thought that the Queen might not be rumor or scattering illusions. If the phrase was right, the Queen was actively listening, actively searching.

They arrived at the ferry landing, the breeze from the water smelling faintly brackish. No one spoke as Tansy pulled to a stop. None of them moved to exit the car right away. Everything felt heavy, and Elle could see tension in Tansy's jaw, in the line of Mateo's shoulders. The sense of being watched lingered in the corners of her vision, pressing like a half-seen silhouette beyond the innocent morning.

She closed her eyes, inhaling the humid air. "We're dealing with something older than we realized," she whispered, mostly to herself.

Mateo caught her eye. "Then we will fight with everything we have," he said, sliding a gentle hand up to her shoulder. He leaned closer and kissed her temple with a sweetness that made her cheeks flush. Tansy noticed, her gaze flicking back, and though her expression was tense, she didn't object. She was worried enough to let them have this small comfort.

But even that tenderness could not drive away the image of glowing chalk scrawl. *The Queen is listening.* A tremor coursed through Elle, though she pushed it down. They were in this together, she told herself. She was not alone. Tansy would not let her drift from reality, and Mateo, with his unyielding sense of protection, would guard her from the worst. Yet somewhere in the pit of her stomach, she felt that small coil of dread refusing to loosen.

"Let's get home," Tansy murmured, eyes forward again. "We can figure out the next steps from there." She pulled onto the exit lane, and the car rolled onto the ferry that would head across the river.

Though the sun had climbed higher, giving the day a clearer warmth, Elle shivered against the seat. Madame Laveau's warnings echoed in her mind. The Queen's watchers might be anywhere. The city breathed with old magic, and some corners thrived on secrets. Her own glyph seared softly under her clothes, reminding her that it had flared in that house not by coincidence. She felt certain the Queen's presence was more than a distant rumor. It was near, entangled in every swirl of leftover power.

They arrived on the other side, passing quiet streets

where a few pedestrians strolled, oblivious to the chilling events that had unfolded just across the water. Mateo rested his hand on Ella's, nodded once, then helped her out when the car came to a stop near a cafe block. Tansy climbed out too, stepping onto the pavement and eyeing the brightening sky. None of them spoke for several long seconds. Their silence was a shared realization. None of them knew how to outrun an ancient watcher or break a centuries-old hold.

Elle straightened her spine and took a slow step down the sidewalk, letting the heat of the day warm her skin. A tingling dread trailed behind her like a shadow, persistent and unyielding. "We'll go for help," she said quietly, glancing at her cousin and Mateo. "We'll talk to whoever can give us a real defense." She hesitated, breath hitching as she recalled the quiet malice in that scribbled message. Her eyes found Mateo's. "But if the Queen is listening, then we better learn how to stay silent or shield ourselves."

Mateo's jaw tightened. "We'll craft stronger wards," he promised. "Every lead we can find, we'll follow." Then he looked to Tansy, who nodded in silent agreement.

They turned up the block, heading toward a place that promised coffee or at least a reprieve from the tension. Elle could not expel the heavy sensation thrumming in her chest. Every glint of morning sun across the pavement made her think of luminous chalk scrawls, staring back from a cracked wall. Even here, her glyph still held a faint glow, as if it too recognized that the city's hidden magic was paying attention.

As they walked in the gathering daylight, the question pounded in her mind, echoing Madame Laveau's caution. How do you escape a watcher that is rooted in the oldest magic of the Quarter? Her heart gave no answer. But she felt the slow creep of that presence behind her, as though it followed each step and waited for the moment she let her guard fall.

TWENTY-ONE

Elle inhaled the thick evening air on Frenchmen Street, trying to banish the memory of her latest brush with dark magic. The night market spread out in a tumble of tables and patterned tarps. Colored lanterns glimmered overhead, and every breeze carried the scent of hot peppers, frying dough, and spilled beer. Street musicians played a rhythmic beat nearby, weaving a lively soundtrack that felt both comforting and jarring.

She had wanted to greet this evening with fresh confidence, but her heart still thudded with leftover tension from the séance days earlier. Tansy lingered by her side, a steady presence though visibly cautious. They had come here hoping the music and bargains might help them breathe again. Neither said the word séance, but the memory of it lingered like a chill that would not quite leave Elle's skin.

"I'm starving," Tansy announced, though her tone remained subdued. She scanned the line of food vendors along the sidewalk where a small crowd waited for fried alligator bites and loaded fries. "We could grab some dinner first, then stroll around," she added. She fiddled with the strap of her canvas bag, something Elle recognized as a nervous tic.

Elle nodded, but her attention drifted across the stalls. She felt restless, aware of the gentle pulse of the newly reclaimed necklace tucked under her neckline. The chain pressed lightly on her collarbone, its familiar weight ensuring she never forgot its presence. The faint heat against her skin reminded her how power surfaced in times of stress.

They passed an array of candlelit tables packed with handmade jewelry, luscious soaps, and intricate paintings of New Orleans street scenes. Vendors called out greetings: "Candles half price." "Local honey and beeswax, come try." The swirl of color should have lifted Elle's spirits, but tension glued itself to the back of her neck. It felt as though dozens of unseen eyes tracked her every move.

She pretended interest in a table filled with crocheted stuffed animals shaped like miniature jazz musicians. Tansy stopped beside her, poking at a plush saxophone figure and chuckling softly when the crocheted sax started to unravel.

"Watch out," the artisan teased, stepping forward. "That one's a bit of a troublemaker." She spoke with a grin, eyes warm. "You ladies need anything else tonight?"

"Just browsing, thank you," Elle answered. She tried not to fidget. Her mental alarm bells kept ringing, telling her that they stood in the open, ripe for another unexpected intrusion. But she swallowed those nerves, returning a polite nod. Tansy offered a quick thanks, and they moved on.

They soon found a stall advertising handmade scented candles. Square tins sat in rows, each labeled in swirling script: Magnolia Dream, Spiced Lavender, Voodoo Blooms, and Rainy Jasmine. Tansy reached for one labeled River's Edge, lifting the lid to sniff its contents. Elle fumbled for a moment with her own tin, her mind flicking through random thoughts: Was it safe to hold items imbued with a stranger's energy? She realized she was being oversuspicious in a place that was meant to be fun. This was exactly why they had come, to shed the fear.

Yet the hair on her arms pricked upright. The back of her neck tingled in that too familiar way, as though a current of magic flitted through the crowd. She forced a breath and resolved to keep her composure.

"Which one do you like?" Tansy asked, her voice gentle. She sensed Elle's hesitation but tried to keep things normal. She offered a half smile. "I'm torn between Rainy Jasmine and that spicy clove one."

Elle picked up the spicy clove, took a tentative sniff, and found comfort in its warmth. Behind them, laughter flared as a group of tourists jostled past with large plastic cups of lemonade. A guitarist perched on a stool near the corner and strummed a soft melody.

The crowd shifted, and someone bumped Elle's shoulder hard enough to make her stagger. "Sorry," she muttered as she pivoted to catch her balance. She glimpsed a wide brimmed hat, a fleeting shadow of a face, but no apology came in return.

Her pulse quickened. She tried to remind herself it was a busy night market and collisions happened. She replaced the tin on the table with unsteady fingers. Tansy continued to examine a candle, oblivious, until she noted the worry on Elle's face.

"Everything okay?" Tansy asked as she stepped closer.

Elle forced a small smile. "Yes, just startled." But her inner sense warned her otherwise. The necklace heated more intensely, a faint warmth that spread across her collarbone. She placed a hand there as if to quell a growing ache, then let her palm drop.

They moved on to the next stall, which displayed homemade soaps molded into baroque shapes. Tansy grew animated in conversation with the soap vendor, who chatted about coconut oil and exfoliating scrubs. Elle found it hard to focus. The crowd felt heavier, the street narrower, as though the press of bodies tightened around her. She looked at her shoulder more than once and searched for the wide brimmed hat in the sea of faces.

A few minutes later, they passed a station where a local band was setting up. The drummer tested a beat and the bassist plucked a few warmups. Elle forced her shoulders to relax and decided she was overreacting. She needed to trust that not every bump in a crowd was malicious. People lived here, unafraid. Why couldn't she slip back into that sense of normal?

Tansy caught her arm gently. "Maybe we can circle to the food trucks first, then see if there's any spice vendor.

I'm running low on that smoked paprika I love." She pointed toward the far side of the street where string lights hung above an assortment of trucks.

Elle nodded and let Tansy steer them forward. A flicker of laughter brushed her ears from a nearby couple sharing a plate of beignets. The crisp edges of dough sparkled with powdered sugar. She tried to let that simpler joy seep into her thoughts. The tang of fresh fried treats tugged at her memory and reminded her of nights in the Quarter that had once been carefree.

Before she could revel in that moment, something large and fast closed in from behind. She sensed it more than she saw it. Her hand instinctively flew to her collar just as a sharp tug jerked her sideways. A violent yank tore at the necklace chain, wrenched her neckline askew, and sent a stab of adrenaline surging through her limbs.

Yet the hair on her arms pricked upright. The back of her neck tingled in that too familiar way, as though a current of magic flitted through the crowd. She forced a breath and resolved to keep her composure.

"Which one do you like?" Tansy asked, her voice gentle. She sensed Elle's hesitation but tried to keep things normal. She offered a half smile. "I'm torn between Rainy Jasmine and that spicy clove one."

Elle picked up the spicy clove, took a tentative sniff, and found comfort in its warmth. Behind them, laughter flared as a group of tourists jostled past with large plastic cups of lemonade. A guitarist perched on a stool near the corner and strummed a soft melody.

The crowd shifted, and someone bumped Elle's

shoulder hard enough to make her stagger. "Sorry," she muttered as she pivoted to catch her balance. She glimpsed a wide brimmed hat, a fleeting shadow of a face, but no apology came in return.

Her pulse quickened. She tried to remind herself it was a busy night market and collisions happened. She replaced the tin on the table with unsteady fingers. Tansy continued to examine a candle, oblivious, until she noted the worry on Elle's face.

"Everything okay?" Tansy asked as she stepped closer.

Elle forced a small smile. "Yes, just startled." But her inner sense warned her otherwise. The necklace heated more intensely, a faint warmth that spread across her collarbone. She placed a hand there as if to quell a growing ache, then let her palm drop.

They moved on to the next stall, which displayed homemade soaps molded into baroque shapes. Tansy grew animated in conversation with the soap vendor, who chatted about coconut oil and exfoliating scrubs. Elle found it hard to focus. The crowd felt heavier, the street narrower, as though the press of bodies tightened around her. She looked at her shoulder more than once and searched for the wide brimmed hat in the sea of faces.

A few minutes later, they passed a station where a local band was setting up. The drummer tested a beat and the bassist plucked a few warmups. Elle forced her shoulders to relax and decided she was overreacting. She needed to trust that not every bump in a crowd was malicious. People lived here, unafraid. Why couldn't she slip back into that sense of normal?

Tansy caught her arm gently. "Maybe we can circle to the food trucks first, then see if there's any spice vendor. I'm running low on that smoked paprika I love." She pointed toward the far side of the street where string lights hung above an assortment of trucks.

Elle nodded and let Tansy steer them forward. A flicker of laughter brushed her ears from a nearby couple sharing a plate of beignets. The crisp edges of dough sparkled with powdered sugar. She tried to let that simpler joy seep into her thoughts. The tang of fresh fried treats tugged at her memory and reminded her of nights in the Quarter that had once been carefree.

Before she could revel in that moment, something large and fast closed in from behind. She sensed it more than she saw it. Her hand instinctively flew to her collar just as a sharp tug jerked her sideways. A violent yank tore at the necklace chain, wrenched her neckline askew, and sent a stab of adrenaline surging through her limbs.er's sleeve, but he jerked away and stumbled back.

The moment was chaos. Some bystanders formed a loose circle, exclaiming and pointing. Others rushed toward the fallen merchandise, hoping to salvage their goods. Elle pressed a hand to her collarbone, feeling how her magic still quivered beneath her skin. She noticed a faint scorch mark on her T-shirt near the necklace's chain, as if her power had burned through the fabric in her panic.

The security officer barked for him to stay where he was, but an older man stepped into the path, blocking her line of sight. That gave the attacker an opening. He darted sideways, weaving between the tables and gawkers. In seconds, he vanished into the throng, his hood regained, leaving a panicked feeling in his wake.

Tansy made a noise of alarm, as if she wanted to chase him. Her eyes moved back toward Elle. Elle was too shocked to urge her forward, the pounding of her own heartbeat muffling any coherent thought. A taller bystander called out, "He's gone that way," but no one seemed prepared to give chase in the crush of people.

Exhaling shakily, Elle realized the security officer was now standing beside them again. A uniformed officer who must have heard the commotion strode up. He had the bored expression of a man used to festival scuffles. He glanced between the scattered candles, the small scorch mark on Elle's shirt, and the crowd that still murmured in alarm.

"What happened here?" he asked, pulling out a small notepad.

Tansy jumped in. "The man tried to grab her necklace. He ran off that direction." She gestured to a gap in the milling crowd. "We're not hurt, officer. It was just shocking."

Elle found the courage to speak. "Yes, I, he, I'm fine." She swallowed, trying to mask how badly her hands shook. "He's gone now."

The officer's brows drew together. "You sure you don't want to make a formal statement, miss? We have patrols posted, we can file a complete report." He studied the tension in her stance. "If you were attacked, we can get more details. We have cameras on some corners."

Tansy took a small step forward, her voice quiet. "We

appreciate that, but she's all right. It happened so fast. We didn't see much of his face."

Elle looked at Tansy, aware that the entire scene was too public for discussing the magical explosion that had just thrown a man across the pavement. She mustered a polite nod. "Please, officer, I'm okay. I don't want to press charges or anything. He only grabbed my necklace, and now he's gone."

The policeman hesitated. He looked around as if debating whether to urge further investigation, then scratched his chin and closed his notepad. "All right, ma'am. Just be careful out there. If you happen to recall anything else, find any detail about him, you can call this number." He handed Tansy a business card. "Night markets can get tricky with the crowds," he added in an almost dismissive tone.

"Thank you," Tansy said, taking the card. She managed a polite smile, though it didn't reach her eyes.

With that, the officer stepped off, presumably radioing a brief mention of the disturbance. The tension left behind weighed on Elle's shoulders, and the group of onlookers drifted back to their stalls or resumed their shopping, though many kept glancing sidelong at the place where the attacker had fallen. A vendor knelt to gather her spilled items, throwing Elle an uncertain look. She mouthed a reluctant, "All good," but her gaze held a flicker of unease. Elle could only nod.

At last, the circle dispersed, leaving Tansy and Elle standing together under the lantern glow. A faint reek of something burning still lingered. Elle peered down and realized it was coming from the edges of her T-shirt, where a dark pattern of singed cotton fanned outward from the necklace's chain. She touched it gingerly, feeling the hot metal of the pendant. She clenched her teeth at the realization that her magic had fully manifested again, right in a crowded public space.

Tansy placed a hand on Elle's arm. "Take a breath," she said softly. "You're safe. That guy's gone. It's okay."

Elle sucked in air and tried to calm the trembling in her ribs. People were still watching them from corners of the market, though at a distance. Somewhere, a jazz tune started anew, upbeat and bouncing, in stark contrast to the tension in Elle's chest. She forced herself to release the necklace. Her hand stung from gripping it so hard.

"I never wanted to do that," she admitted, voice low and tight. "To fling someone away like that. And in front of everyone."

Tansy glanced around carefully, ensuring no one else was eavesdropping. "He attacked you first," she murmured. "If you hadn't reacted, he might have ripped the chain right off or worse. You did what you had to do."

Elle's eyes flicked to the spot where the attacker had collapsed. "But that jolt of power, I'm terrified I could have hurt him badly." She remembered the blowback at the séance and the swirl of panic that followed. Even if he had been a stranger possibly working for darker intentions, she could not push aside the guilt twisting in her stomach.

Tansy squeezed her arm gently. "You didn't kill him, and we don't even know if he was just a thief or something else. But you and I both know that necklace is a beacon for trouble these days." Her gaze hardened as she glanced at the chain. "Wish we could go half a day without it attracting turmoil."

Elle let out a shaky laugh, though no humor touched her eyes. "Same," she said. Her voice quavered, and she closed her eyes to steady herself. "I guess we know now that whoever wants it, they're not shy anymore." The faint quiver in her voice betrayed the fear she struggled to bury.

Tansy scanned the small lantern-lit stalls once more. Passersby kept shooting them curious or pitying glances, then looking away quickly.

"Elle, your shirt is slightly burned. You smell it, right?" Tansy asked, wincing at the acrid scent. "We can't stay out here much longer. You need to get changed, calm down. Maybe call Mateo—"

"No," Elle said softly, though her free hand curled into a fist at her side. She longed for his steady presence, but she also despised the idea of always depending on him to mop up her battles. "We can handle things for now. Let's just..." She exhaled. "Let's go somewhere quieter. I could use a break from all these eyes."

Tansy nodded. "Yes, let's get out of this crowd."

They turned, picking a path through the bustle with Tansy gently guiding Elle by the elbow. The marketplace felt like it was returning to normal, or at least attempting to. A few vendors cast them worried glances but seemed reluctant to ask questions. The music resumed its steady pulse, and overhead, the city sky glimmered faintly with stars struggling to be seen through the light pollution.

"Are you actually okay," Tansy repeated when they

reached a slightly emptier patch of pavement. She rested a hand on Elle's shoulder, her face marked with concern.

Elle closed her eyes for one heartbeat, then two. Her trembling had partially subsided, enough for her to realize they had just witnessed how quickly her power could surface in public. The memory of that man's desperate eyes lingered. She wondered if he had known exactly what he was grabbing or if he was just after any valuable chain. But the directed purposeful yank on the necklace made doubt shrivel. He had zeroed in on the filigree pendant without hesitation.

"I will be," she whispered, forcing a measure of control into her voice. She glanced around at the swirl of market lights, the hum of conversation, the bright glow of neon signs behind them. The feeling in her gut told her that the city's undercurrent was rising, and it was no longer content to stalk her from a distance. It had stepped into the open, claws bared. Her necklace seemed to radiate that same dread, its metal still warm. "This isn't me overthinking," she added, turning back to Tansy. "Whatever hunts me, it's coming out of the shadows now."

Tansy's lips thinned, but she nodded, her hand squeezing Elle's in silent agreement. The night pressed in with the smell of warm concrete and leftover fryer grease. Music rippled across the street. In the midst of that lively tapestry, Elle could think only of how the mood had shifted, how joy had turned to shock.

Unsteady, they started walking again, weaving around chatty groups. The burn mark on Elle's shirt stung each time it brushed her skin. She wanted more than anything to vanish into the crowd, but her presence felt magnified by her own magical aftershock. With Tansy's support, she paced herself, ignoring the leftover stares.

"As soon as we get home, I'll make tea," Tansy said. Her voice trembled, but she forced a resolute edge. "And tomorrow, maybe we figure out a way to shield you more so that these attacks don't happen again."

Elle nodded, though answers felt far off. She clasped the necklace carefully, guiding it under the collar of her singed shirt, out of sight but not out of mind. A warning flickered in her thoughts: the Queen isn't the only threat. The city thrives on secrets, and any fragment of magic might tempt those hungry for power.

A swirl of anxiety tightened in her chest, matching the rhythmic pulse of the music drifting on the breeze. As they reached the edge of the market, the street opened enough to breathe, but the sense of being watched remained. Tansy pressed a reassuring hand against Elle's back, urging her forward with gentle steadiness.

Biting her lip, Elle exhaled a shaky breath. She glanced once more at her shoulder, scanning the crowd for any sign of the hooded figure or other uneasy watchers. Nothing stood out except the normal swirl of tourists and locals. Yet her gut told her that the city's hidden currents had shifted. Tonight, under the lanterns and lively tunes, something had proved it would not remain in the dim corners. If it had to reveal itself in public, it would.

Fighting an urge to run, Elle clenched her jaw and moved on with Tansy, the two of them retreating from the thrumming heart of Frenchmen Street. The memories of the attacker's grip remained, fueling a knot of fear. She tried to calm the spark she still felt under her skin. It refused to disappear entirely, reminding her that no matter how much she wanted normalcy, her connection to deeper powers would not let her be.

The market lights receded behind them, and the acrid smell of singed fabric followed like a ghost. Each step away felt like walking into a new and more dangerous reality. Tansy's worried sideways glance confirmed Elle wasn't alone in that thought. She pressed the necklace flat against her collarbone, bracing herself for whatever new confrontation lurked. The city's energy buzzed with a too-familiar intensity as she and Tansy disappeared into the quieter streets, well aware that the line between hidden threats and everyday life had cracked wide open.

TWENTY-TWO

Mateo parked his car on a small side street lit by a single flickering lamp. Elle sat beside him in the passenger seat, her breath still unsteady from everything that had happened at the market. Her slender fingers remained curled around the edge of the seat, and she couldn't fully steady them no matter how hard she tried.

Tansy's call had been frantic. She had told Mateo how one moment Elle had been sampling candles, and the next, someone had lunged for her necklace. Tansy had explained the force of Elle's magic pushing the attacker away. Then came the scrambling crowd, the questions from bystanders, and Tansy's decision to call Mateo for help.

Now, at his insistence, Elle was here, parked outside his apartment. The building was modest and had weathered plaster walls. It stood only a few blocks away from the market, but the short distance felt like a world removed. Nighttime humidity pressed down on the street, carrying the faint odor of stale beer and sweet flowers.

She felt the reassuring warmth of his palm on her arm. His voice was calm, yet concern shaped each syllable. "We should head inside. You don't owe anyone anything else tonight. Let's get you settled." He glanced at her trembling hands before adding gently, "Please. You're safe with me."

She drew in a breath and nodded. Her gaze flicked to the side mirror as if expecting their assailant to reappear, but the street was quiet except for a cat slinking into an alley. A single overhead bulb hummed above Mateo's door, highlighting a set of chipped steps that led to the second-floor landing. The building wore its age in chipped paint, but it offered comfort in its familiarity—this was his home.

He led her up those rickety stairs, one hand at the small of her back. The wooden railing creaked under their combined weight. Wind rustled the leaves of a potted plant by the door. The night air felt thick, as though it carried the echoes of her magic that had exploded in the marketplace. Her heart still drummed an uneven rhythm inside her chest.

Mateo keyed in, flipping a light switch in the narrow hallway. The overhead bulb gave off a soft glow that revealed framed photographs and a few scuff marks on the walls. They stepped into his apartment, and immediately, a wave of comfortable warmth surrounded Elle. Soft lamplight glowed from a table lamp with a brass body. She noticed a handmade quilt folded over the back of a small couch. Across from it, a low coffee table held a few old case files, their manila folders splayed open to reveal typed pages and detective's notes. A single silver medal rested on one side, presumably a trooper award. It reflected the lamplight in a subdued gleam.

She inhaled shakily, aware of her necklace's persistent buzz under her collarbone. The filigree felt almost hot to the touch. Mateo closed the door behind them and locked it, then turned to study her face.

"You're still shaking." His voice was so gentle that her eyes stung with unshed tears. He pushed a blanket into her arms, letting her hold it against her chest while he angled himself to meet her gaze. "I'll grab you a glass of water, okay?"

Elle wanted to say something, anything, but no words came except a hoarse "Yes, thanks." She managed a nod. That small motion made her temple ache. She had clenched her teeth and tensed every muscle during the ride over, and the fatigue set in now like a lead weight.

He disappeared around the corner. She looked around for somewhere to set her purse, realized all she had was a secondhand tote Tansy had handed her after the market fiasco, and placed it on a side chair. Curiosity tugged her attention to the pictures on the wall. Fading photographs showed a family gathering that must have included half a dozen aunts, uncles, and cousins. Mateo appeared younger in one image, baseball cap askew while leaning beside two older women who resembled him around the eyes. The edges of the frame had turned slightly yellow with age, making the moment look suspended in time.

Another photograph showed him in uniform, stoic in front of a police cruiser. The date scrawled on the edge suggested it was from his first year on the force. A gentle pang softened her chest. She thought about how he must have carried the confidence of a new recruit, determined to protect people. Now he was here, caring for her after yet another brush with supernatural incidents that defied logic.

"Here." Mateo's soft tone broke into her thoughts. He held out a tall glass of water. He must have slipped ice cubes inside, the outside of the glass beaded with condensation. She took it with trembling fingers, gulping a few grateful sips.

A heartbeat passed. Her knees felt weak, and she sank down onto his couch, leaning her head back. The overhead light made her squint, so he clicked on a lamp instead, adjusting the overhead fixture off. The new dimmer glow reminded her of being safe in some quiet sanctuary.

He cleared his throat and ran a hand through his hair. "I am going to check the local precinct's notes on any disturbances at the market tonight. I promise I will talk to my colleagues about the possibility of camera footage near Frenchmen Street. Someone must have caught that attacker on film."

She nodded slowly. "Thank you," she managed. "I keep replaying it in my mind. It is like everything was normal, then he was yanking on my necklace. And I was so scared."

She set the water aside on the coffee table, noticing the way its condensation dripped onto the scattered case files. She half expected Mateo to fuss about secret documents, but he did not seem to mind. He crouched beside the coffee table, rummaged in one folder's pocket until he found a notepad, and scribbled a few lines. Most likely recording the details Tansy had given him.

As he stood, he placed a reassuring hand on her thigh. "I am sorry this happened. The city can be unpredictable, but that was more than a random mugging, was it not?"

"It felt targeted," she answered, voice shaky. "He grabbed only the chain. Everything else was right there. My phone, wallet. He did not bother with any of that." She swallowed, remembering the attacker's expression, a hunger that did not look entirely human.

Mateo's jaw flexed, and he pressed his lips into a thin line. "I will figure out who he is." He exhaled and glanced at her hands, which twisted the blanket's corners. "Or at least who sent him."

Exhaustion dragged her forward, so she let the blanket fall onto her lap. Her eyes welled with tears that she could not hold back. Frustration mingled with terror. She tried to speak, but only a harsh sob tumbled out. It sounded louder than she wanted, echoing in the quiet apartment.

He eased down on the couch beside her, warm hand stroking her back. "Hey, it is okay," he whispered. "Let it out. You have been through too much."

She did not want to cry. She wanted to hold onto some semblance of composure. But the tension suffocating her chest finally demanded release. She choked out a curse under her breath. "I hate this," she said brokenly, wiping her cheeks. "I hate feeling like it keeps finding me. No matter what we do, there is always this chaos."

Every inch of her felt brittle. The constant threats, the surging magic, the sense that someone lurked in every shadow made her mind reel. She felt Mateo's arm slide around her shoulders, gently guiding her against him. His T-shirt smelled faintly of soap and coffee. She felt the steady rise and fall of his chest as he let her cry into him.

She had never realized how badly she needed a moment to shatter. Tansy had tried to keep everything afloat, and Elle had tried to stay brave for them both. But now, in Mateo's apartment, it all spilled out. She cried until the tension behind her eyes dulled, her breath hitching in irregular intervals.

Mateo silently passed her some tissues, never inter-rupting, letting her emotions run their course. She drew in a ragged breath and noticed fresh tears dampening his shirtfront. Heat pricked her cheeks in embarrassment, but he gave a small, kind shake of his head as if to say she owed him no apology.

The phone on the coffee table buzzed. She glimpsed the screen, noticing Tansy's name. Mateo, still cradling Elle with one arm, reached out to pick it up. "Yeah," he murmured softly. Then he nodded, eyes flicking to Elle. "Everything's fine here."

Elle heard Tansy's voice faintly through the speaker, the tone anxious but calmer than before. Mateo ended the call with a soft "Thank you," setting the phone back down. He turned to Elle, clearing his throat in relief. "She's heading home in a rideshare, said she texted you a screen-shot. She's okay."

The knowledge that Tansy was safe freed a small weight from Elle's shoulders. She released a trembling sigh. Her tears were mostly spent. Now only weariness drummed against her skull.

Mateo's hand brushed gently across her brow, measuring the exhaustion in her expression. "Try to rest," he urged in a quiet tone. "You're shaking, and you're worn out. We can talk about everything tomorrow."

She nodded, letting her shoulder slump against the couch. She felt no inclination to argue. The day had fractured her composure, and the only strength she had left was the knowledge that no immediate threat existed inside these walls.

Eventually, she moved to stand, but her legs faltered under the lingering adrenaline crash. Mateo rose with her, his grip steadying her. "I've got you," he said simply. A faint flush of comfort bloomed in her chest at those words.

When her knees nearly buckled again, he scooped her up. The sensation of weightlessness startled a gasp from her throat, but he held her close, cradling her thighs and hooking an arm around her back. She pressed her face to the crook of his neck, breathing his warmth. A swirl of gratitude and vulnerability twisted inside her.

He carried her into a small bedroom illuminated by the gentle glow of a single lamp on the nightstand. The bed in the center was neatly made, an earthy green comforter folded down at the top. She spotted the corner of a framed photo resting atop a chest of drawers, another family portrait, she guessed, though she couldn't see it clearly. The air smelled faintly of detergent and something woodsy, maybe an old cologne that lingered in the space.

Very gently, he let her feet touch the floor. She felt him unbutton the top of her shirt with careful fingers, eyes searching her face for permission. She gave a shaky nod. The earlier tension in her chest was now replaced with something else, an undercurrent that made her exhale in shallow, unsteady pulses.

She tried to speak, to tell him yes, she wanted the closeness, the reassurance, but her voice came out as a barely audible whisper. He guided her shirt off her shoulders, folded it on a nearby chair, then brushed his lips across her temple. Every nerve in her body trembled, half from the remnants of fear, half from the spiraling warmth that only he seemed able to conjure.

His movements were slow, not rushed, as though giving her time to stop him if she changed her mind. She didn't want to stop. She wanted to feel something other than terror, to let the dark swirl of the night transform into safety. Her necklace hummed again, and she automatically reached up to unclasp it so that its chain wouldn't glow unexpectedly. She set it carefully on the nightstand. It gave off a muted warmth that reminded her of the power she couldn't entirely control.

Mateo eased her pants down, then lifted the quilt from the bed. She turned to him, cheeks flushed. He quietly tugged his own shirt over his head, revealing lean definition in his torso. He wasn't a showy man, but his every movement reflected a coiled strength that grounded her.

She touched his chest lightly, palm skimming over the faint scar near his collarbone. She wondered if it was from an old scuffle or an accident, but she didn't ask. Tonight wasn't the time for more painful backstories. Tonight was for solace.

He kicked off his shoes, unfastened his pants, and slid them aside. The lamp's glow caressed the outlines of his frame, accentuating the tension in his shoulders and the gentleness in his gaze. She watched him fold clothes methodically, revealing a neat streak that matched her own. Then he turned back to her, stepping closer to place a kiss against the stray tear track on her cheek.

She closed her eyes. The world spun with the day's fear and adrenaline, but here, in this bedroom, she found calm in the slope of his arms. They moved onto the bed, skin meeting skin under that warm quilt. She felt the sweep of his fingers up her spine, his breath grazing her ear. Her pulse pounded, though not with panic this time. Desire and comfort interlaced, creating a moment she never realized she so needed.

He pressed his lips to her shoulder, and she let out a soft exhale that turned into a longing sigh. He whispered her name, and she clung to him, letting the tears from earlier shift into a different release, a surge of closeness and trust. She had feared that her power might spiral out of control again, but with him, she felt only an expansion of warmth.

They moved together as though finding a fragile harmony amid the day's chaos. Each touch soothed the ragged edges of her fear. The sound was filled by the muted hum of the ceiling fan overhead and the soft, shared breaths that coated the air with renewed intimacy. Her cheeks heated, and her limbs relaxed. The gentleness in his kisses sent flutters of reassurance through her chest.

Their bodies merged with careful tenderness. His forehead came to rest against hers in unspoken gratitude. She lost track of time, giving herself over to the sensation of safety he provided. Every anguished thought from the market, every stifling second of panic, receded. She was aware only of his nearness and the rhythmic current of their heartbeat together.

When at last their breathing slowed, she felt exhaustion returning in a wave so massive that she could barely keep her eyes open. The day's strain, the tears, and the final rush of emotion had burned all her energy. Sweet relief filled her chest.

He stayed close, one arm draped around her waist, the other curling under the pillow so he could cradle her head. She tucked herself into the curve of his body. Embers of warmth still glowed through her limbs, but now a strange sense of security anchored her. Outside, she faintly registered a siren wailing in the distance, or maybe just the wind against the building. It no longer frightened her. She drifted in the softness of his breath.

The last thing she remembered was the gentle brush of his lips on her temple and the steady beat of his heart against her back. For the first time since coming back to New Orleans, real sleep claimed her. Not fitful, not haunted by illusions, but deep and unbroken, guided by the presence of someone who made her feel safe.

She let herself sink into that darkness without fear, trusting that come morning, she would have the strength to face the aftermath. The city might still hide its shadows and the quest for answers would continue. But for tonight, in the protective circle of Mateo's arms, she finally let her guard down completely, surrendering to rest and letting the distant hum of her necklace fade into dreamless quiet.

TWENTY-THREE

Elle woke to the soft glow of morning light drifting through the curtains. For a groggy half second, she wondered if she was back at her grandmother's house, but the unfamiliar scent of coffee and the faint hum of a nearby fan reminded her that she was in Mateo's apartment. She stretched beneath the light sheets, realizing the other side of the bed was empty. Her heart squeezed with a tinge of disappointment, though she reminded herself that he had promised to head into work first thing.

Slipping out of bed, she glanced down at the rumpled clothes folded on a nearby chair. Her cheeks warmed at the memory of falling into an exhausted doze after the intensity of the previous night. She caught her reflection in a small mirror on the wall. Tired eyes, hair mussed around her face, and the faint outline of a spiral-born glyph near her collarbone that never seemed to fully fade. It was the same glyph that had flared when her emotions ran high, one that reminded her of the Queen's twisted symbol.

She spotted a handwritten note on the small round table. She padded over in bare feet and picked it up.

Elle, had to step out for a few hours. Make yourself at home. I left some pastries on the counter. If you want to pass the time, feel free to look through the unclassified files on my desk. I'll be back soon.
– M

The simple courtesy of his message made her smile. It was a sweet contrast, a stoic detective who left pastries and an invitation to look into his cases. She wandered into the kitchen, discovering a little plate covered in cling wrap. Beneath were two flaky croissants and a small container of jam. Hunger teased at her stomach, so she took a few bites, then poured a glass of water from the sink to chase away her lingering sleepiness.

Her legs felt slightly sore, a reminder of how fiercely they had clung to each other when everything had finally quieted last night. She also felt a gentle hum of contentment in her chest, as if the city's usual anxiety had relaxed its grip for a brief moment. Finishing the croissant, she decided a shower would help clear her mind. As she headed to the bathroom, she let her fingers drift along the edges of the doorframe. She liked this space of his, small but full of quiet warmth.

The shower ran hot, steam billowing around her until

the mirror fogged. She tried not to worry about potential illusions in the steam. Instead, she leaned into the water, letting it run over her shoulders until the tension eased. Flashes of memories stirred, the shock of someone grabbing at her necklace in a crowd, the way her magic had sparked in defense, the sound of Mateo's voice when he reassured her. She exhaled, thankful that for once she had woken without immediate chaos pressing in.

She finished and wrapped herself in a soft towel, rummaging through the clothes at hand. On a whim, she chose one of Mateo's shirts from a dresser drawer. The worn cotton felt large on her, falling to mid-thigh, but she liked how it smelled faintly of him, clean aftershave and a hint of laundry detergent. Her pulse fluttered at the simple intimacy of wearing his shirt.

A restless spark in her chest spurred her out of the bedroom. She still held the note from him, the invitation to sift through some unclassified case files. Part of her hesitated, these were personal documents linked to the work he rarely shared with others, but she trusted that he truly wanted her to understand the bigger picture.

His makeshift desk took up one corner of the living room. It bore a neatly stacked array of file folders, a half-empty coffee mug, and a small lamp. She sank down on the edge of the couch, pulling the first folder onto her lap. The label read "Unexplained Apparitions: French Quarter." Her pulse kicked a little harder. Apparitions. She gingerly opened the folder, spotting typed police statements with handwritten notes along the margins.

Strange lights reported in an abandoned townhouse.

Ghostly chanting in the courtyard behind an old place that had since collapsed. And again and again, references to odd markings, incomplete graffiti shaped like hearts or spirals. Elle's eyes flicked to the faint glyph on her collarbone through the gap in the shirt. The swirling pattern on these forms might have been a simpler variant of hers, but the resemblance was unmistakable.

Swallowing hard, she reached for the next folder. It held black-and-white photos of what looked like chalk scrawls across alley walls. The lines curled in an elongated heart shape with a spiral core. Each accompanying report included an address, a date, and the times the illusions were observed. In more than one statement, a witness claimed hearing whispers that urged them to wander deeper into the city at night.

A heaviness settled in her stomach. She had braced herself to find a few vague parallels, not direct matches. The third folder was older, the papers a little yellow. This one focused on missing persons cases, many of which had been abruptly dismissed or deemed unsolvable by other officers.

Small lines in Mateo's own writing scrawled across.

Possible arcane link? Victims claimed visions, complained of nightmares.

Her eyes stung with sympathy. She could not imagine how many times he had tried to bring these connections forward, only to be undermined by superiors who scoffed at the idea of magic.

The final folder made her breath catch. She saw a scrawled note pointing to the symbol that combined a spiral with a twisted fleur-de-lis shape. It resembled a warped heart, or maybe a flower with a swirling center. Her grandmother's journal had a reference to that shape, scribbled in the margins near recipes for protective charms. At the time, Elle had not understood the significance, simply assuming it was another magical filigree. Now, seeing it framed as evidence in a missing-persons file chilled her blood.

She carefully opened her grandmother's journal to one of the last pages and scanned until she found the note she remembered.

Beware the spiral heart. Old illusions feed on innocent hopes.

She pressed her fingertips to the text and read the line three times before her stomach twisted in dread. This was not a mild scrawling. It was a warning. If the Queen's symbol was manifesting across random alley walls or scaring tourists, it meant the threat ran deeper than a personal vendetta.

The apartment's front door clicked. Elle looked up, startled. Her pulse leapt before she reminded herself that she was safe here. She rose from the couch with the folder still in her hands to see Mateo stepping inside. His gaze landed on her, relief easing the tension in his shoulders.

He held a small bag from a nearby coffee shop but set it down immediately.

"You're still here," he said, smiling the softest smile. It was enough to make the corners of her eyes prickle with unexpected warmth.

"Of course," she replied, placing the folder on the coffee table so she could close the distance between them. He cupped her face with one hand, pressed a welcoming kiss to her forehead, then drew back slightly to look into her eyes. She inhaled, feeling the faint rasp of his stubble against her cheek. After a moment, he leaned in and kissed her properly, the gentle pressure sending a bright surge of comfort through her chest.

When they parted, she nodded at the papers. "I've been looking at your files," she tried to keep her voice steady. "These sightings and illusions. The repeated motif... it's the same as the glyph near my collarbone, or at least suspiciously close."

Mateo exhaled. "I know. I've seen that design turn up for years. I couldn't prove it was connected to anything supernatural, but I recognized the pattern." He reached out, carefully sliding one finger over the edge of her shirt collar, revealing just a glimpse of the swirling mark. "That's how I realized there was something bigger happening than we had on record."

She gestured to the stack of folders on the table. "All those missing people? The illusions? How long have you been tracking it?"

His gaze moved aside, as though collecting himself. "A while," he acknowledged quietly. "Before I met you, there were multiple unexplained cases, people mentioning nightmares, booms of red light, the same spiral shape repeated in strange places. Whenever I brought it up officially, my superiors brushed me off. I kept investigating on my own time." He swallowed, turning back to meet her eyes. "After everything you've shown me, I'm certain it leads to a single source, something or someone manipulating the city for a deeper purpose."

She closed her eyes for a moment, recalling her grandmother's repeated scribbles about illusions that feed on fear. The weight of that truth settled between them. Elle felt exposed, simultaneously grateful for Mateo's unwavering dedication and alarmed by how far-reaching this threat seemed. Pressing her lips together, she drew a shaky breath. "So the Queen's symbol has been haunting people for years," she murmured. "No wonder I kept sensing I wasn't the only one."

He nodded, stepping closer to her. The intensity in his eyes made her heart pound. "When I saw that same pattern near your collarbone, it felt like a puzzle piece clicking into place," he said. "It scared me too because if it's tied to these missing-persons cases, I didn't want you getting dragged into something you couldn't escape."

Warmth and tension coiled in her chest. The sincerity in his face, his need to protect her, stirred a fierce gratitude in her. She glanced at the file in her hands one more time, noticing a typed account of "ghostly chanting" in a condemned warehouse. The details were specific, flickering lights, singing in an old language, footprints disappearing right in front of onlookers. She placed the file aside, feeling the prick of fear up her spine. Then she looked into Mateo's eyes.

"You've been dealing with this alone," she said, voice low. "Trying to show people the truth. It must have been..." She trailed off, words failing her. She reached out and gripped his free hand. "Thank you for keeping the evidence safe, and for trusting me enough to share it."

He covered her fingers with his other hand, gaze unwavering. "I'm done hiding it. The city deserves better than blind denial, and you deserve better than me dancing around the facts."

Before she could speak, he leaned down and caught her lips in a kiss that stole her breath. He kissed her as if the words they had just spoken weighed too heavily, as if only touch would soothe the reality swirling around them. She responded, letting the folders slip from her lap onto the couch, pressing trembling palms against his chest. Every nerve in her body sparked with heightened awareness of how this man had quietly fought on her side before they ever met.

He guided her backward a half step, sinking with her onto the edge of the couch. She felt his warmth through the thin fabric of the shirt she wore. A rush of longing swept away her remaining caution. This was more than comfort. She wanted to show him that she saw him fully, every steady, selfless part of him. Her hands slid up his shoulders, forming a magnetic pull that no logic could break.

Their kisses deepened, slow and hungry, interspersed with the soft rasp of shared breaths echoing in the small apartment. She curled her fingers in his hair, letting out a low sound of need that he echoed in a rumble from his chest. When his mouth trailed to the side of her neck, she gasped softly, the stimulating edge of desire rolling through her limbs.

He shifted and urged her to lie back against the cushions. Heat rose in her cheeks as she helped him tug his own shirt off. She traced the contours of his shoulders, marveling at the taut lines of muscle and the faint dusting of old scars she had never properly seen before. Each kiss left her heart thundering louder, the empty apartment amplified every rustle of clothing, every soft thud as a shoe or garment hit the floor.

Time lost its shape. A swirl of limbs and whispered praises filled the small space. She felt his pulse racing beneath her palms. He murmured her name when she bit gently at the base of his throat, breathless with want. She responded in a voice that sounded unlike her own, low, charged, and unconcerned with the logic of the files scattered around them.

They moved from the couch to the floor, then back onto the couch in a graceful tangle of shared urgency. She arched beneath him, her body flush with desire and trust. The fleeting thought of the Queen's symbol threatened to intrude, but it vanished behind her need to celebrate this connection that left no room for fear. When he drew her closer, all illusions or threats from outside melted away.

At some point, they made their way to the hallway, bumping gently into a wall as they laughed quietly, pushing each other's hair out of flushed faces. Then they stumbled into the bedroom again, the sheets rustling as they tumbled onto the mattress. Full sunlight spilled through the curtains, illuminating every curve, every earnest expression. She pressed her lips to his, marveling at how the day had begun with anxious curiosity but morphed into this intimate sanctuary. Over and over, their mouths sought each other, feeding both reassurance and raw passion.

A hazy, blissful eternity later, Elle lay panting on rumpled sheets, half atop Mateo, her ear over his beating heart. His arms were locked around her like a promise he couldn't break. Their laughter drifted across the small bedroom, quiet and breathless. She heard the steady hum of the fan, the distant city outside, but none of it seemed as compelling as the warmth of his skin against hers.

She shifted, feeling a renewed pulse of desire spark in the lingering lull. Mateo's dark eyes caught hers, and a slow smile curved over his lips. There was no need for words. They both sensed there was still space, still time, to lose themselves in the heat that thrummed just below the surface. Her legs slid against his, and the whisper of cotton sheets against bare skin reignited the electricity dancing between them.

They made love again with an unhurried tenderness that left her trembling. Daylight spilled across the bed, casting the shape of his silhouette over her body. She breathed in the subtle salt of his sweat, and he kissed damp trails along her shoulder. Their moans intermingled with the gentle creaks of the bed, echoing like a soft refrain.

Later, they paused long enough for him to brush aside a stray lock of her hair, and he pressed his lips to her temple. She smiled, her eyes half-closed as the afterglow worked its way through her system. Something about the day's revelations and the intensity of their connection made it feel like time had paused, allowing them a moment to step outside the city's threats and illusions.

When she rose to sip some water, he followed, capturing her against the wall in a fresh wave of need. They laughed at their impatience, but neither refused the magnetic draw. Clothing lay abandoned across the apartment, discarded in the heat of passion. The half-eaten pastries on the counter waited unnoticed. Afternoon sunlight replaced morning's golden hue, and they lost track of hour or meal, aware only of the tangible closeness that pulsed between them. She held on to him, each breath full of quiet wonder and undeniable longing. Tension unraveled in her chest, replaced by a sweet ache that went beyond lust, something uniquely theirs.

They let the world outside slip away, giving themselves completely to the moment. The couch saw them next, then the narrow rug near the desk, then the bedroom again, each encounter building a new level of intimacy. She surrendered to the rhythm of his heartbeat and trusted the rightness of it, knowing that whatever awaited them, they would face it together. For now, neither illusions nor glyphs nor daily worries existed. Only this unspoken promise in the quiet corners of his apartment, where they spent the afternoon making love all over his home.

TWENTY-FOUR

The beaten skiff bumped against the island's muddy bank with a muted thud, jostling Elle in her seat. She looked at the small patch of land, no bigger than a few cramped living rooms. Towering cypress trees overshadowed the island's center, and a dense growth of reeds formed a rustling perimeter along the waterline. The twilight sunlight trickled through drooping moss, painting everything in shades of pale gold and muted green. Humidity pressed in on her, but the quiet of the bayou gave the air an almost sacred quality.

Mateo cut the outboard motor, his forearms flexing against the warm metal of the controls. He glanced back at her, concern etched on his face despite the calm around them. "Are you all right?" he asked quietly.

Elle nodded, though she felt her pulse jumping. She clutched Ruby's journal to her chest, its worn edges a reminder of everything she had yet to master. "Just nervous, I guess," she confessed.

He steered the skiff a little closer until the hull scraped sand. With careful movements, he pulled a rope from under the narrow seat and hopped into the shallow water. Mud swirled around his ankles as he guided the boat to a more secure spot and tied it off. When he lifted his gaze, it moved across the reeds and the quiet waves licking the shore.

"Let me give you a hand," he said, extending his arm. She took it, feeling a steady warmth as he helped her out of the boat. The water was cooler than she expected, a welcome shock against her skin as she stepped down.

The fisherman who had rented them the skiff had only muttered halfhearted warnings to watch for gators, so the idea of wading in bayou water had made Elle's stomach tense. But the sun's waning glow offered enough visibility to reassure her that no reptiles lay in wait. She and Mateo made their way onto slightly drier ground.

Elle exhaled in one shaky breath as she surveyed the thick web of flora inland. It was quiet apart from the occasional frog's croak and the soft lap of the current. Standing on the island felt unreal, as if stepping into one of her grandmother's old stories. She tightened her grip on the journal. She could still picture Ruby, messy handwriting scrawled on every line, describing how water might cleanse or further awaken any deep-seated magic. Those notes had brought them here. The bayou was older than any paved street in the Quarter, a place that held an ancient, powerful energy.

Mateo offered to carry the small pack of supplies they had brought a clay dish, a coil of herbs from Tansy's stash, a slim candle, and a single matchbook sealed in a plastic pouch. Elle followed him across the bank until they found a patch of firm ground near a natural rise of roots. The space formed a shallow clearing, enough for them to set their items without risk of everything toppling into the marshy water.

"I think this is good," she said, scanning the uneven terrain. It was far from the perfect circle she might have liked, but Ruby's notes emphasized the necessity of finding a spot where the water's energy could quietly feed the ritual. She heard the gentle drip of moisture running down the cypress bark, a dampness made the air feel electric. A bead of sweat trailed down the back of her neck.

Mateo dropped the pack and removed the clay dish and placed it on a flat rock. Then came the candle and the spiral of potent-smelling herbs, still wrapped in a slender piece of twine. Elle knelt in front of the dish, the soggy ground staining her pants. She set Ruby's journal carefully on a small dry edge of the rock. The battered leather cover looked strangely at home here in the wilderness, as if it remembered a dozen older ceremonies.

She traced a finger over the scribbled lines she had marked earlier. Her grandmother's voice came through in the text.

An invocation of the bayou's spirit. Used for clarity and awakening the next stage of power without letting illusions slip in. Water for transformation, herbs for bridging realms, and fire to shape intention.

The memory of Ruby's laughter tightened Elle's chest. Her grandmother had always believed water to be the purest conduit for magic. Now, it was Elle's chance to follow that teaching.

She scooted closer and turned to Mateo. "Can you fill the dish?" she asked, pointing at the bayou swirling beyond the bank. "I know it's muddy, but the spell calls specifically for local water. I think it needs that energy."

Mateo picked up the dish with care. He stepped down to the water and dipped it in slowly. The surface reflected thin stripes of the setting sun, turning the bayou into a mosaic of purples and oranges. The dish emerged brimming with murky liquid. Distracted by the swirling silt, he looked at her, brow knitted with concern. "It's not exactly crystal clear," he said.

"It's fine," Elle answered, summoning a confident edge to her voice. "We want the bayou as it is. The silt is part of the magic."

Mateo brought the dish back and set it on the rock. The water sloshed gently, swirling with pale flecks of reflection from the sky. Elle placed the candle next to it, then coiled the herbs on the opposite side. She stood and rummaged in the pack for the matchbook.

The frogs had gone silent, and even the gentle trickle of water between reeds turned subdued. Over her shoulder, she noticed Mateo scanning the perimeter, the detective in him refusing to drop his guard. A flicker of relief spread through her chest. She always felt safer when he was near. He might not fully share her grandmother's brand of belief, but he never belittled it. His presence was a calm axis around which her fears could revolve. She took a deep breath, trying to settle her racing heart.

"Should I light the candle now?" he asked, voice quiet so as not to disturb the moment.

Elle nodded. "Light it and place it next to the bowl." She consulted Ruby's notes again and read the quick lines about timing: Wait until the evening air settles, then speak the words.

The evening air had certainly settled in an almost unnerving stillness.

Mateo struck a match with a swift motion. The tiny flame was bright in the dim environment. He lit the candle, shielding it from any stray breeze until the wick flared orange. Then he placed it carefully beside the dish. A soft glow outlined the edges of the clay container, reflecting on the water's surface.

Elle cleared her throat, voice trembling with a combination of excitement and dread. She pressed both palms together, centering herself. "I'll recite the lines, and you hand me the pieces when I ask for them," she said to Mateo. "At least that's what Ruby's note suggests."

He gave a curt nod. "I'm right here. Take your time."

She inhaled deeply, feeling the thickness of bayou air

cling to her. This was the first formal invocation she had attempted that wasn't purely protective or reactionary. Her grandmother's instructions described it as an invitation to the water's spirit, a call that could heighten magical senses and reveal deeper truths. But with heightened senses came the risk of illusions. A flutter of apprehension danced in her stomach.

She began in a low voice, reading from the journal's open page.

Cypress and silence, water and flame. I call forth the spirit of these roots. May your clarity flow through this vessel...

Her words came halting at first. Then she found a rhythm, letting the shapes of the incantation roll off her tongue in a mixture of old phrases Ruby had scrawled in the margins. The candle sent dancing shadows across her hands and the dish. When the incantation prompted her to cleanse the water with the herbs, she paused.

"Pass me the coil," she whispered.

Mateo did so, placing the spiral of herbs gently in her palm. She dipped the coil into the water, stirring until the muddy swirl changed texture. Thin ribbons of greenish tint spread out. Then she continued the chant, her voice rising slightly, though the words remained almost a whisper in the stillness.

For a moment, nothing happened except the sound of her own breath. Then the surface of the water began to glimmer. Sparks, faint as tiny lights, appeared under the water's surface.

Mateo leaned in, his eyes widening. "I see it," he murmured.

Her chest constricted in awe. Soft pulses of luminescence radiated from the center of the bowl, as if a hidden moonlit current rippled through the murk. The herbs bobbed gently, leaving watery trails of color. Encouraged, Elle closed her eyes and recited the next set of lines from memory, feeling Ruby's presence in every syllable. She envisioned the bayou's ancient depths swirling outward, responding to her call.

Then, in a single breath, she felt a shift resonate up her arms. The hair at the nape of her neck prickled. Her eyes fluttered open. The dish now glowed in earnest, shimmering with translucent tendrils of power that curled like phantom ribbons. They reached the rim, and the candlelight seemed to intensify. Every nerve in Elle's body was suddenly alert, as if she had touched a live wire. She heard a faint humming that might have been the water's spirit or her own heart pounding.

She glanced at Mateo, who had shifted closer. His mouth hung open slightly, a protective reflex capturing his features.

"Easy," he warned her softly. He placed a supportive hand beneath her elbow.

The chanting was done. The magic was reaching a peak, waiting to be guided or released. She swallowed hard, remembering the final line of the invocation.

Accept what the water shows, do not turn away.
Let the transformation begin.

Elle blinked. The intensities in the water made her vision wobble. Heart hammering, she tried to maintain her focus, but her mind drowned in a sudden onslaught of images. Lights flashed, not just from the dish but from the corners of her eyes, as though illusions were pressing forward to be seen. A roaring sound built in her ears, or maybe it was just her pulse echoing.

Mateo must have sensed her distress because he whispered her name, pressing his palm more firmly to her arm in an effort to anchor her. She parted her lips, about to reassure him, when a wave of dizziness slammed into her. The ground seemed to tilt, and her eyes rolled back. Over the roaring in her head, she heard Mateo shout her name, the word elongated in the quiet night.

She barely registered his arms catching her before she hit the ground. The journal tumbled off the rock, but she could not even spare a thought for it. Her entire awareness had narrowed to the unbearable spinning and the sudden darkness that swallowed her vision. Her breath hitched. In that eclipse, faint outlines of a female figure appeared: tall, regal, draped in black like a living shadow. A chill seized Elle's heart. She recognized that presence from whispers in her dreams.

The vision sharpened until she made out the woman's eyes, cold, luminous with hidden triumph. She radiated a power that coiled at her feet. It was the Queen, she was sure of it. The swirl of illusions around the figure suggested something more solid than before, as if the Queen no longer lingered on the far edges of reality but stood only a few steps away.

Elle heard her own gasp echo in some distant corridor of her mind. She wanted to tear her gaze away, but her limbs felt pliant, no strength left. It was only the fierce warmth of Mateo's hands that pinned her to the present. She sensed him cradling her, kneeling in the mud with frantic pleas for her to wake up.

When warmth seeped back into her body, she opened her eyes slowly. The sky overhead churned with a swirl of pink and gray clouds, but her entire focus landed on Mateo's face. His jaw was clenched, fear etched in every line of his expression. She distantly felt the wet ground soaking into the back of her legs, though the worst of the dizziness had subsided.

"Elle," he said, voice raw. "Stay with me. You fainted or, I don't know. You were gone for a moment."

She released a shuddering breath, pulses of pain throbbing at her temples. She tried to lift a hand to cling to him and realized he had already pulled her into his lap. She clutched the front of his shirt. The world still felt two steps from normal, but she managed to speak in a scratched whisper.

"I saw her," she rasped. "The Queen, she was so close."

TWENTY-FIVE

Elle first sensed the shift in the air when the breeze lost its gentle warmth and became a sharp, cool gust across her cheeks. She glanced up, catching a glimpse of the sky through the tall pines on the bayou's edge. Ominous clouds slid across pale sunlight at an unnatural speed, and her stomach fluttered with dread. Only moments ago, she had been listening to the drip of water along the bank and the faint hum of insects in the marshy undergrowth, but now everything seemed suspended. Even the cicadas paused their metallic rasp.

Mateo looked at her, eyebrows raising in a silent question. His steady presence gave her a flicker of calm, but she could see the tension in the line of his shoulders. He too noticed how the light had vanished behind thick clouds. In the distance, a rumble of thunder cracked the humid air.

"We should head back to the skiff," he said. He spoke softly, as if to avoid disturbing whatever power lurked beyond the cypress trunks. They had journeyed out here at Elle's insistence, driven by cryptic pages in Ruby's journal that mentioned cleansing magic in the water. Now, dark thunderheads loomed overhead, and the bayou felt too heavy with foreboding.

Elle nodded and hurried after him, nearly slipping on damp leaves when the first droplets began thrumming against the canopy. A moment later, the deluge struck, catching them off guard with sheets of cold rain. Each fat drop battered her exposed arms and soaked through her thin shirt in seconds. She gasped at the chill. The bayou floor turned slick as the water rose around fallen roots.

"There," Mateo called, tilting his head toward what looked like a small structure near the muddy bank. Through blurred vision and the haze of rain, Elle caught sight of a battered fishing shack. Its planks looked warped and stained by years of swampy humidity. The roof jutted out at an angle that threatened collapse, but it was their only hope for shelter.

Together, they trudged through mud and shallow water until they reached the shack door. It hung crooked on rusted hinges. The wood gave a protesting shriek when Mateo pushed it open. Long rays of watery light slipped through gaps in the siding, illuminating a cramped space where an old cot rested against one wall. A battered shelf leaned precariously on the other side, holding dusty jars and broken lantern pieces.

Mateo gestured for Elle to go inside first. She stepped over the threshold, letting out a shaky breath at the relative dryness of the interior. The floor was still damp and the air stagnant, but at least the torrent of rain no longer pounded directly on them.

He peeked around, careful not to disturb any rotted boards. Then he closed the door, latching it with a bent strip of metal. Raindrops pelleted the roof, forming a steady roar overhead.

Elle took another step in and recoiled slightly when her boot squelched on a patch of wet moss that had invaded the shack's corner. She pressed her lips together, trying to find composure. The earlier ritual had shaken her, and the sky's sudden fury felt like a cosmic warning. She could not tell if the Queen's shadow still hovered just beyond her awareness, but the memory of that presence was enough to make her tremble.

Mateo paused near the center of the shack, scanning for anything salvageable. "There's wood here," he said, pointing to a small stack piled beneath a corner shelf. The boards looked worn but appeared mostly dry. An old wood stove occupied one corner, rusted on the exterior but intact. He gave Elle a reassuring nod. "We can get a fire going. It might help dry our clothes."

She eyed the stove and let a small thread of relief ease through her. "I'll see if there's something we can use for kindling," she replied. In truth, she needed to keep moving so her limbs would not seize from the cold. Her shirt clung to her torso, and her hair dripped water onto her shoulders.

She opened a crooked cabinet near the shelf, rummaging past spiderwebs until she found a roll of old newspaper. The pages disintegrated at the edges, but the center was dry enough. She handed them to Mateo. He worked methodically, feeding a few crumpled scraps and small splinters of wood into the stove, then striking a match from the emergency pack he always carried. His willingness to come prepared for nearly any situation stood in stark contrast to her own impulsiveness. He whispered soft encouragement at the pile. Soon, flames leapt up in the dark interior of the stove, throwing warmth into the cramped space.

Elle shivered, hugging her arms over her chest. She could feel the chill in her soaked shirt. The hood of her jacket was full of water, dripping steadily onto the shack's floor. Each drip made her skin crawl, reminding her that the heavy downpour might last for hours.

Mateo looked her over. "You're freezing," he said, concern threading his voice. He rummaged in a dusty corner and produced an old cotton quilt with crumpled folds. It smelled faintly musty, but it was warm and appeared mostly free of discolorations or mold. With careful steps, he moved closer and draped it around her shoulders. His fingertips grazed her arms through the damp cloth of her shirt, sending a bolt of warmth down her spine. She exhaled slowly, momentarily forgetting the uneasy flickers of magic that had haunted them all day.

She glanced around the shack. Rays of pale afternoon light glimmered through the cracks, catching floating motes of dust. "Do you think this place will hold up?" she asked. The wind rattled the thin walls, and she imagined them pitching forward any second.

He nodded, eyes calm. "It is better than being stuck

out there in open water." The hiss of rain pounding the shack's roof confirmed his point. With a sigh, he reached for his pack. "We can wait out the storm, and maybe it won't last too long."

Elle sat on the makeshift cot, relieved to be off her feet. The day had drained her, between the earlier tension in the bayou and the ever-present worry over the illusions that might lurk behind each cypress. She watched Mateo search inside his pack with single-minded focus. Finally, he pulled out a bottle of red wine, along with a small cloth-wrapped bundle. He unwrapped it, revealing a chunk of bread and a wedge of cheese.

A tiny laugh escaped her. "You packed provisions for a swamp outing?" The idea sounded oddly comforting. So typical of him to ensure no one went hungry or unprepared.

"I guess I was hoping we'd have a calmer afternoon," he said, a rueful smile tugging at his mouth. His gaze moved to her, warm and watchful, as if checking that she found the notion acceptable. "But since we're stuck, we might as well share what we have."

Her chest tightened with affection. "Thank you," she said, softer than intended. The next rumble of thunder echoed outside, but for the moment, they could pretend the storm was a distant thing.

He set the bread and cheese on a bit of folded fabric to keep them off the damp floorboards. Then he retrieved two dented tin cups from the shack's lone shelf. They clinked quietly when he set them up next to each other. The stove's blossoming heat enveloped them, lending the rustic shack a glow that almost felt cozy. Dismal, rain-soaked boards surrounded them, but they had light, warmth, and the closeness of shared space.

Elle shrugged off her jacket and replaced it with the warm quilt. She slid one foot out of her boot and then the other, letting them rest by the stove's open mouth so they could dry. She nodded for Mateo to do the same. He eased his shoes off and propped them carefully where the heat could chase away the mud and dampness. Outside, the storm hammered away, rattling branches and stirring the bayou waters with furious intensity.

Sitting close to the small stove, he poured a modest serving of wine into each tin cup. The aroma of ripe grapes mingled with the scent of wet earth clinging to their clothes. Elle accepted the cup and noticed how his fingers lingered at the rim before letting go. His eyes held a question she could not quite name, a hesitation that only strengthened the tension in her chest.

They sipped in silence at first. Each mouthful chased away a bit of the chill, and the cheese tasted sharper than usual, perhaps because her senses were attuned to every detail. The shack, though humble, felt quiet enough to bring her frayed nerves a measure of solace.

Mateo spread a piece of cheese onto a torn hunk of bread. He offered it to Elle. She inhaled the savory scent and realized her hunger outweighed her fatigue. She ate it slowly, her cheeks glowing in the warmth of the stove.

Between the sounds of rain and the flickering of firelight, she sensed something shift between them. They had shared many tense moments before, but this moment was different. The world outside felt wild, unreachable. Here, in this battered place, they were an island of two. She had not realized how much she had longed for a moment when neither illusions nor old grudges overshadowed them.

"You're quiet," he remarked gently. He pressed his back to the wall near her, the boards creaking beneath his weight.

"I'm thinking about..." She trailed off because she had no simple way to describe the knot of emotions in her chest. The day's events hovered on the edge of her thoughts: the ritual's uncertain outcome, the glimpse of darkness in the water, the possibility that something beyond the thunder was trying to claim her. Instead of finishing the sentence, she met his gaze. "I'm relieved you're here."

He studied her, the muscles in his jaw relaxing. "I'm not going anywhere," he whispered, as if to emphasize that he was indeed part of her anchor.

Lightning flashed outside, throwing a brief white glare through the gaps in the walls. The thunder followed, roaring overhead. Elle did not flinch. Instead, she looked at Mateo the same instant he looked at her, and the air in the shack seemed to surge with an awareness that surprised them both. Her pulse sped up.

She set down her cup. He did the same. The stove's warmth felt like an echo of the heat rising between them. Leaning closer, she reached up and tangled her fingers in the collar of his damp shirt. Her breath caught in her throat. She felt his heartbeat throb under her fingertips, and she could not deny the pull of longing that mingled with a hungry need for reassurance.

"Elle," he murmured, voice low. He was so close that she could see tiny droplets of water still clinging to his eyelashes. She tasted the wine on her lips and imagined that same taste lingering in his kiss.

She tugged him down, and their mouths met in a rush of sensation. Any lingering chill from the rain evaporated the moment they touched. His lips were firm, his breath urgent, and she felt the hot exhalation against her cheeks. It was both reckless and tender, an outpouring of the fear they had held at bay all day.

She sank deeper into the kiss and slid her hands around his shoulders. The quilt slipped from her shoulders to his arms. Her mind churned with too many unknowns, too many threats, yet none of those thoughts stood a chance against the immediate, vital presence of him. A soft groan escaped her when he carefully lifted her onto the cot. Its frame creaked but held. Rain crashed on the roof, and the narrow walls failed to mute the storm's crash, but that only intensified the glow they shared.

Mateo broke the kiss for a moment, looking into her eyes as if confirming this was real. With a shaky laugh, he brushed a few damp strands of hair from her face, and she pressed her forehead against his. "You're sure?" he asked softly. A hint of uncertainty crossed his face. She recognized it as the same protective streak he always wore when her vulnerability arose.

"I'm sure," she breathed and guided him back to her with gentle insistence. There was an urgency simmering under her skin, born of everything they had lived through. She wanted to forget illusions and ancient powers for one night, to reclaim some part of her life that was still hers.

He kissed her again, deeper this time. The lines of his body pressed close, and she reveled in the warmth radiating through his damp clothes. She let her hands travel over his shoulders and felt the tension that coiled there from stress and worry. Her own heart thundered as she soaked in the realness of him, his solid form, his ragged breathing, the subtle scratch of stubble. She felt alive in that moment, unburdened by the fear that normally clung to her.

A gust of wind rattled the shack's door, but it held. The stove's flame crackled, sending light dancing over their tangled silhouettes. Her pulse pounded in her ears as she cupped his face. He leaned into her palm. Instinct conquered caution, and she guided him down, losing track of the rest of the world in the press of their bodies. The faint aroma of musty wood mingled with the spicy scent of his skin, creating a heady mix that clouded her thoughts in the best way possible.

She closed her eyes and let the moment sweep her away. Each lifted edge of clothing felt like another step into territory she had wanted but never dared assume was safe. Yet here they were, the shack echoing with the breath and the occasional sigh as they explored the closeness they had skirted for so long.

They slipped into a seamless union, forging a quiet piece of solace in a world that had given them little peace. She surrendered to the rising heat, letting it meld her fears and hopes into the present. Somewhere halfway through, Mateo murmured her name, almost like a promise, and she answered with a trembling hand against his cheek.

Their whispers turned to murmurs that faded against the battered walls. The overhead storm raged on, thunder rolling in waves, but they hardly heard it anymore. The small shack, with its leaking corners and crooked door, became the safest place she had known in ages. She clung to that refuge, pressing closer to him as though afraid the storm might steal him away if she let go.

Eventually, the tension softened into a calmer quiet, and they lay entwined on the creaking cot. The makeshift pillows were just folded sections of the quilt, and the dryness in the air came mostly from the wood stove's persistent heat. Still, she felt content, the kind of deep contentment that only arises after facing the worst and finding a pocket of warmth in the aftermath.

He tucked her head under his chin. Her hair fanned across his shoulder. Their legs were still tangled, and she did not want to move. Everything felt almost unreal, a perfect stillness interrupted only by the patter of rain and the trembling rise of her breaths.

"We'll leave when the storm calms," he murmured. His voice was thick with drowsiness and relief. She nodded and stroked her fingertips over his collarbone. A part of her did not want the storm to ever let up.

She closed her eyes and exhaled in a gentle sigh. The swirling fears at the corners of her mind threatened to resurface, but for once, she had a bulwark in the warmth of his arms. If illusions lingered in the dark outside, they had not found a way into this battered shack. Her heart finally slowed to a steady rhythm, and the rain outside blurred into soft white noise.

They spent the night like that, huddled together in quiet intimacy, warmed by the stove and content to let the rest of the world remain distant for a little while longer.

TWENTY-SIX

Elle woke to the sound of a distant boat horn echoing through the humid morning air. Dawn light bathed the small fishing shack in a gentle glow, illuminating the curls of her hair sprawled across the thin pillow. She felt more rested than she had in weeks. A single wooden window shutter hung crookedly beside her. The breeze slipping through the gaps carried the scents of damp earth and mossy cypress. Memories stirred, and she smiled.

She turned her head. Mateo was already up, crouching by the small stove to check if any embers remained in last night's fire. He glanced at her. Their gazes met, and a soft warmth appeared in his eyes. They did not exchange many words, not yet. The feeling of sharing the first few minutes of morning was enough.

Her body hummed with a lingering contentment. Even though the shack's old cot had creaked through most of the night, she felt a tender reassurance in every breath.

She stood, stretched, and slipped into the denim shorts she had bundled at the foot of the cot. When she looked up, Mateo was readying the battered skiff outside. He tied off the rope with practiced skill. Their plan was to head back to the city soon. The morning pressed in gently, promising new routines and errands, but Elle still felt the glow of the previous evening's closeness. She inhaled the bayou's raw scent as if imprinting it in her memory.

She gathered her belongings and stepped outside. A faint mist lingered over the still water, and clumps of moss dripped from leaning cypress limbs. She saw how her footprints from the day before had partially washed away. If not for Mateo's watchful presence beside her, the swamp might have felt eerie. Instead, she felt invigorated.

Mateo gave the shack one last cursory scan to ensure they left nothing behind. They walked side by side to the skiff, and she climbed aboard while he steadied her. The small outboard motor spluttered before roaring awake. The morning air carried a hint of coolness, though she knew the day's heat would return soon. She leaned back and let the gentle breeze caress her face as the boat glided away from the muddy bank. Each bump across the water felt like an exclamation of something she could not name. Happiness, maybe, or relief.

They did not speak much on the short trip back to the marina where they had rented the boat, but every time she glanced up, Mateo's slight smile told her enough. They reached the rickety dock, and he helped tie them off. He exchanged a brief nod with the gruff fisherman who accepted the skiff's keys. A short while later, they were on the road, the city's skyline peeking around bends in the highway. Mossy wetlands gave way to aging storefronts and the gradual bustle of morning traffic.

"I can't wait to shower in my own bathroom," she murmured, leaning her head against the passenger window. She kept her voice light, though part of her already missed the unhurried bayou.

"All the hot water you want," Mateo said, looking at her. He tapped the steering wheel in time with faint music drifting from the radio. "I unfortunately have to head to the station soon. If I'm late, Reyes will never let me forget it."

She nodded, feeling a gentle tug in her chest at the thought of parting ways, even if just for the day. They arrived at her grandmother's shotgun house in the Marigny neighborhood, where slender iron fences and flowering shrubs stood guard. Mateo pulled up along the curb, and she hopped out, balancing her bag over one shoulder. He followed and placed a hand lightly on her back. "Let me walk you to the door."

She smiled at the courtesy, unlocking the front door to let them both step inside. The house was warm. Golden light fell across the floorboards, and the faint traces of old herbal smells reminded her of Ruby's presence that always lingered. She turned, and Mateo stood close, his expression tender.

"I'll give you space to unwind," he said, brushing a thumb across her cheek. "I'll call you when my shift ends."

Her heart gave a small flutter at the simple promise. "I'll be here," she said. "Thank you for everything."

He kissed her forehead, then his mouth curved into that quiet smile she was starting to love. Without another word, he walked back outside. The sound of his car heading toward downtown faded, leaving the house in a comfortable stillness.

Elle set her bag down and exhaled slowly. After a quick shower, she changed into a fresh sundress and ran her fingers through her damp hair. A sense of peace clung to her, but it was tinted with the knowledge of what day it was: All Saints' Day. Residents across the city would be honoring their loved ones in the cemeteries, and she felt the pull to do the same for Ruby. Even though it stung to think of her grandmother's final resting place, Elle knew this was one tradition she did not want to set aside.

She walked into the kitchen, where half-unpacked boxes lined the counters. Ruby's cookie tins, mismatched mugs, and chipped plates overflowed every nook. She spotted a jar of lemon extract that Tansy had brought over weeks ago. Her heart clenched with bittersweet memory. Ruby had loved lemon cake more than anything, claiming the tangy sweetness kept her mind sharp. Elle sent Tansy a quick text, then decided a homemade cake might take too much time. She remembered a bakery down the street that sold slices of fresh lemon cake. It would do for a graveside offering.

Before she hurried out, her phone buzzed. Tansy's name lit the screen, and she picked up with a brisk, "Hey, you up for a quick trip to the bakery?"

"I was about to ask you the same," Tansy answered, her voice weaving cheer and a hint of sadness. Most New Orleanians approached this day with a reflective cheer, but Tansy's tone revealed how close Ruby had been to both of them. "I'm already in the neighborhood. Meet you at the corner?"

Elle agreed. Buttoning the last of her sundress, she grabbed her keys and stepped into the balmy sunlight. Tansy was easy to spot, waving from under a blossoming magnolia tree. She wore a bright floral skirt that matched the rebellious pink streak in her hair. They exchanged a quick hug, and Tansy arched an eyebrow with a teasing grin.

"You look well rested," Tansy said, drawing out the words. "Better than you have in ages."

Heat rushed to Elle's cheeks. She shrugged, letting the comment pass without explaining too many details. "It was nice, being out there," she replied simply. A hint of Tansy's grin suggested she already suspected more.

They grabbed slices of lemon cake from a local bakery with cheerful yellow awnings. The woman at the counter recognized Tansy and asked about the holiday. Tansy explained their plan to visit a cemetery and pay respects. The cashier smiled in sympathy, offering them a small discount for the cakes. They left with a takeaway box and a sense of gratitude for the city's quiet kindness.

A short drive brought them to the cemetery where Ruby's grave lay. The wrought-iron gates stood open, welcoming a steady flow of people carrying flowers, fresh paint, or small plates of homemade food. Children darted around the narrow walkways, chasing each other between the bright tombs. Every year on this day, families gathered to celebrate the memory of the departed instead of sinking into gloom.

Elle and Tansy found a free parking space along a tree-lined avenue. They walked in together, arms linked. The morning sun was climbing, and already the day felt warm on Elle's shoulders. She heard a distant saxophone melody drifting from somewhere deeper in the neighborhood, mingling with the murmur of families sharing stories.

Near Ruby's tomb, she saw several neighbors and acquaintances from the quarter. They offered gentle nods of greeting but gave Elle and Tansy space. The tomb itself had been painted white in prior years, though now it showed signs of scuffs and weathering. A pot of vibrant flowers rested at its base, likely from another relative who had visited at dawn. The sight made Elle's heart squeeze. She set her slice of lemon cake on a small stone ledge, along with a modest bouquet of magenta carnations.

Tansy knelt and touched the sun-warmed surface of the tomb. "Ruby was never shy, was she?" she said with a laugh. "I can still hear her standing in the kitchen, scolding us for not stirring the roux properly, or telling me my shoes were too loud for church. Then she'd wink like it was all part of a bigger secret."

A lump formed in Elle's throat. She nodded, remembering how Ruby loved to collect vivid Mardi Gras beads that she strung across the living room, claiming sparkle was essential to daily life. She recalled how her grandmother's hair smelled of lavender whenever she braided it. Memories rose like a wave, and she had to blink fast.

"She believed in everything unseen," Elle said, her voice trembling. "It never felt silly or impossible to her. It was like she had this unwavering faith that good magic lived in every corner."

Tansy's eyes shone with unshed tears. "She knew you'd find your place in the city," she whispered. Then she shot Elle a playful smile. "You know how she teased that one day you'd stop running and trust yourself?"

Elle let out a shaky laugh. "She was right. It took me long enough." She gently pressed her palm to the warm stone, imagining Ruby's voice telling her to breathe and believe in the next sunrise. In that moment, she wished she could share these recent revelations with Ruby: the cautious acceptance of her powers, the nights spent unraveling spells, and the promise she felt forming with Mateo.

The air carried the scent of candle wax from the altars other families had set up. A mass of white lilies, freshly polished tomb stones, and trays of homemade pastries dotted the rows. Voices merged in a soft tapestry of stories, jokes, and affectionate scolding. Mothers dusted old photos, while children giggled over melted ice cream. Somewhere, a small group of musicians plucked chords on a guitar and sang quietly in French. The overall effect was a celebration that held sorrow like a gentle undercurrent, proving love could outshine mortality.

Elle felt Tansy's arms link through hers. They stood a moment in comfortable silence, watching each family's own version of remembering. Then Tansy placed a slender candle next to the bouquet. "We'll light it," Tansy said. "A tribute to Ruby's unstoppable spark."

They fumbled a moment, trying to shield the small flame from the breeze, but it finally caught on the wick. The candlelight burned in the bright day, oddly steadfast in the face of the lively atmosphere. Elle let her tears slip free, a few. She felt no shame. Grief and gratitude wound together inside her. She ran a finger across the tomb's surface, as though her grandmother might sense that gentle goodbye.

A burst of laughter sounded behind them, where an older man was explaining a family recipe to his wife while she touched up paint on the tomb's lettering. The man gestured wildly with a spatula, and the bright clang of a tin pot knocked against a marble step, drawing more smiles from passersby. Elle could almost hear Ruby's echo in the comedic chaos: This city is never without color, child.

Taking a slow breath, Elle turned to Tansy. "I think I'm ready," she said gently. "We can stay longer if you want, but I need a moment alone with her. Then we can go."

Tansy kissed Elle's cheek, whispered she would wait near the cemetery entrance, and left her alone with the tomb. Silence wrapped around Elle as the other families drifted a respectful distance. After a few heartbeats, she placed her palm on the marble again, letting that final wave of sorrow pass through her. Then she whispered, "Thank you for everything, Gran."

In that second, the breeze ruffled her sundress, as

though an unseen hand offered comfort. She closed her eyes, inhaling the lemony sweetness from the cake. When she opened them again, the candle's flame danced gently. She took that as a sign of acceptance.

Elle wiped the tears from her cheeks and slowly made her way toward Tansy, who stood watching from the archway. They walked back to the car, arms linked, the memory following them until they reached the gates.

"In the mood for beignets?" Tansy asked as they stepped onto the sidewalk. The suggestion held a note of optimism.

Elle chuckled. "Sure, we can do that."

She paused when her phone chirped. A text from Mateo blinked on the screen. He had a knack for timing, it seemed. She opened it quickly, heart lifting at his familiar name.

> Guess what? My family is gathering for dinner tonight. Aunt Jenny cooking. Everyone wants to meet you (or re-meet you, for some). You up for it?

Her cheeks warmed, and Tansy peeked over her shoulder with a grin. "He's invited you over? On All Saints' Day? That's serious business, girl."

Elle typed back with a smile.

> Sure. Would love to see you and your family. Let me know what time.

Her chest felt lighter than it had all morning. The thought of stepping into Mateo's circle, especially after the intimacy they had shared, soothed the ache she carried from the cemetery. There was still so much to face in this city, old illusions and new challenges. Yet at that moment, she felt certain she could handle whatever came next, because love, like the lemon cake by Ruby's tomb, was a small but powerful offering that transformed sorrow into something bright.

TWENTY-SEVEN

Elle stepped through Aunt Jenny's front door and found herself in a swirl of color, laughter, and tantalizing aromas. The small foyer opened into a living room crammed full of family, cousins, aunts, uncles, and a few neighbors were chatting in overlapping voices. Someone in the corner boomed instructions to a pair of children playing with plastic cars, and across the room, a teenage cousin hollered at the TV whenever the Saints quarterback made a good pass. The entire house felt alive with warmth that the outside humidity only seemed to amplify.

"Elle, right?" A woman with a sleek ponytail, one of Mateo's cousins, rushed forward to greet her. "I'm Beatriz. Aunt Jenny's busy in the kitchen, but she told me to make sure you're not left stranded in the entryway."

Before Elle could reply, a stocky uncle in a faded sports jersey clapped her on the shoulder. "Mateo told us to expect you. We were starting to wonder if you got lost on the block." He shot Mateo a playful glare, as if accusing him of not driving fast enough.

Elle felt a self-conscious flush creep up her neck. She realized she had been gripping the strap of her purse and discreetly lifted her hand away. "I'm happy to be here. Traffic took a bit, but I'm glad we made it," she said, smiling at Mateo with a small grin. He gave her an encouraging nod and squeezed her fingers lightly before letting her go, clearly picking up on the nerves that crackled beneath her calm exterior.

Through an open doorway to the left, the smell of jambalaya spices drifted in waves. Someone in the kitchen was stirring a large pot that steamed so heavily the windows were fogged. Aunt Jenny's voice carried over the noise: "Yes, yes, a little more paprika. I promise, it's the secret to a good pot." Pots clattered, and the loud rumble of a stand mixer added to the happy clamor.

Mateo leaned closer and whispered, "She'll want to corner you and tell a hundred stories about me. Promise me you won't believe all of them."

Elle nearly laughed. "No promises," she teased. She hoped her voice sounded at ease. In truth, gratitude and anxiety both built inside her. Her phone buzzed with a text from Tansy.

> Leave some leftovers for me. Good luck, girl.

She quickly typed a short thanks and slipped the phone into her pocket.

They maneuvered down the hall, greeted at each step by a new relative. One asked how she liked the city, another complimented her sundress, yet another offered a cup of sweet tea. She answered as calmly as she could while a toddler barreled past wearing a glittery superhero cape. The child almost threw himself at her legs, and she laughed as she crouched to pat his head.

When the toddler ran off again, Mateo guided her into the living room. She noticed how he wore an easy familiarity here, speaking Spanish to one older aunt perched on a recliner, then switching seamlessly to help another cousin who was fiddling with the TV remote. The Saints roared onto the screen, the crowd noise pouring into the room, and half the family groaned at a missed field goal. Elle caught Mateo glancing across at her, a hint of softness in his eyes that made her heart flutter.

Aunt Jenny finally emerged from the kitchen. She was a stout woman with a floral apron wrapped snug around her waist. "Welcome, honey," she said, pushing up her sleeves and taking both of Elle's hands in a warm grip. "Mateo told us you might be nervous, so I have a plan. We'll put you to work. Pass out plates, get comfortable, and you'll forget you were ever anxious."

Elle breathed out a genuine laugh. "That sounds fair. Thank you, Miss Jenny."

"Call me Aunt Jenny," the older woman insisted, pressing a stack of paper plates into Elle's arms. "Kitchen is that way, living room is behind you, and the porch is out back if the heat isn't too much. Or if you and that detective of ours want some quiet time." She winked, then turned to boss another nephew into stirring the pot on the stove. "And watch that jambalaya, Marlon. I see you holding back on the seasoning."

Elle's gaze followed Aunt Jenny for a moment, charmed by her no-nonsense approach. She was also keenly aware of a tingle against her collarbone. The fili-gree necklace lay beneath her top, occasionally tingling as if responding to the hustle of so many people in one place. She swallowed and tried to keep her breathing even. Although magic had taken over so much of her life these past weeks, she didn't want it overshadowing a simple family meal. This evening felt like a capsule of normal life that she had been afraid she would never have again.

She set the plates on a central table as a pair of teenagers raced by, each attempting to wrestle the remote from the other. "That is not how you show guests around," teased Mateo, stepping in to referee. The teens stuck out their tongues, but they settled after a few words from him, letting the older aunt watch the game again in peace.

Slowly, Elle moved around the living room and kitchen, handing out plates and napkins, occasionally pouring someone a drink, and discovering that each new relative had a story about Mateo. A cousin recounted how he once tried to do a BMX stunt to impress a group of friends and ended up with scraped elbows for weeks. Another aunt recalled his quiet ambition even as a child, bringing home stray cats and trying to find them new owners. The stories evoked an image of him as a nurturing boy who had grown into the steady, empathetic man at her side.

Each tale ended with a variation of "We love him," or "We knew he was meant to do good in this city." She recognized how deeply his family valued loyalty and compassion. Despite the volume and the occasional chaos —someone knocked a plastic cup off the table, and children shrieked over bits of spilled juice—the house radiated acceptance.

"Thank you for helping," Mateo said, stepping close to her by the kitchen doorway once the plates were distributed. "I know they can be overwhelming."

She handed him a glass of sweet tea. "It's wonderful, actually. A little wild, but there's so much love." She felt that slight tingle of power again, humming in her chest. She inhaled the heady fragrance of bell peppers and sausage, stirring up a pang of genuine hunger.

Just then, Aunt Jenny plodded back into the main room carrying a hefty pot of jambalaya. "Clear a space on the table," she called, hustling side dishes around. Bowls of potato salad, baskets of bread, and pitchers of iced tea followed. The moment the pot landed, the family closed in like they were starved, grabbing spoons and ladles. Elle found herself chuckling as she dodged an elbow from one of the older uncles.

Mateo guided her in, making sure she tasted a spoonful first. The burst of flavor, spiced rice, tender chunks of chicken, and bits of smoked sausage, made her eyes water in delight. Around them, the clamor reached a new pitch. Chairs scraped, jokes flew across the table, and someone turned the TV's volume down so people would focus on eating.

They ended up sharing a seat on the edge of a small sofa because the dining chairs had all been claimed. Mateo balanced a bowl in his lap while Elle carefully held her plate. Cries of "Pass the bread" or "We need more forks" kept ringing out. She realized her anxiety had eased. A sense of belonging blossomed with each passing minute.

At one point, a baby cousin crawled up to Elle. She set her plate aside and scooped the child into her arms. She gave a soft coo of greeting. The baby babbled, tiny hands clutching at Elle's top. She was aware of how natural it felt to hold him despite the swirling chaos in the house. She looked at Mateo, who watched her with something close to awe.

"You handle babies well," he said quietly, leaning toward her so only she could hear.

She blushed and pressed a kiss to the baby's forehead before handing him back to a relative. "I used to babysit back in high school, but it's been a while." She paused, eyes swept by a wave of longing she couldn't quite name. "Sometimes I forget how sweet it is, being with family."

Mateo nodded, eyes thoughtful. He squeezed her hand. "You're welcome with mine anytime you want," he said, voice low and sincere. The words made her throat tighten with emotion.

Eventually, people began clearing plates to make room for dessert, an enormous bread pudding that Aunt Jenny had planned. Elle helped gather forks and bowls from the kitchen, her steps lighter now. Periodically, she touched the tiny chain at her neckline, noting that the magic had stayed mild. She sensed no looming danger in this house, no illusions whispering at the corners of her mind. If there were small sparks of power dancing under her skin, she let them be, confident they would remain harmless tonight.

After enjoying a bowl of sweet, cinnamon-laced pudding, she walked alongside Mateo toward the back door. Others were busy taking the baby to a changing table or refreshing their drinks, so they slipped outside unnoticed. The porch light cast a warm glow across chipped paint and an older porch swing. Distant street-lamps illuminated the yard where lightning bugs flitted across a patch of tall grass.

Elle inhaled the heavy night air, which draped around them like a damp blanket. Even at this hour, the humidity refused to ease. Mateo stepped behind her and rested a hand at the small of her back. "You holding up okay?" he asked.

She turned, letting herself admire the way the porch light highlighted his angular features. He seemed so steady, anchoring her in a storm that had little to do with actual weather. "I'm good," she breathed. "Better than good."

He nodded, leaning against the porch railing. For a moment, neither of them spoke. The muted drone of conversation from inside formed a gentle backdrop. Elle found herself focusing on the faint chirp of crickets in the yard and the quiet hum of a window air conditioner some-where up the block. She lifted a hand to her necklace again, checking that it was well hidden beneath her top.

She wanted this moment to remain undisturbed by outside fears.

Mateo let out a slow breath. "I'm glad you're here tonight. I've been worried you might change your mind, pack up, and fly back to Chicago."

Her heart squeezed. They had skirted that topic a few times, their fragile new closeness tested by the question of whether she would stay or go. She unfolded her arms and moved nearer to him. "I won't pretend it isn't tempting sometimes," she admitted softly. "I get scared of everything going on. But then I think about how I'd feel if I left. And I realize this city and you, I can't give it up."

He lowered his gaze for a split second, as though letting those words settle in. Then he reached out and brushed a thumb across her cheek, a gesture that sent a pleasant shiver through her. "That means more than you know," he said in a voice that almost quivered.

Sometimes the magnitude of what lay between them made her breath catch. They had faced enough turmoil to forge a bond that felt deeper than she had ever expected, yet so much remained uncertain. Her fears receded. The old wooden boards beneath them creaked as he tugged her a little closer.

Her heart pounded in anticipation. Without overthinking, she leaned forward and pressed her lips to his. The kiss was gentle and warm, woven with a million unsaid promises. She felt her defenses slip away, replaced by the glowing certainty that in this moment, here with him, she was safe.

She drew back slightly, eyes half-lidded, and saw the

faint smile curving his mouth. She ran her fingers along his jaw. "Thank you," she whispered.

"For what?"

"For letting me forget, if only for a little while." She touched the front of his shirt, resting a hand where she felt the beat of his heart through the thin cotton. "All the magic, all the darkness, out here, it's just us."

TWENTY-EIGHT

Morning light seeped through the lace curtains in Ruby's living room, draping the worn furniture in a soft, golden haze. Elle lay stretched across the old sofa, half-buried under a crocheted throw blanket. Her phone rested on the cushion beside her, open to a list of job postings she had bookmarked the night before. She skimmed the titles, marketing manager, social media strategist, project coordinator, yet none of them stirred the old excitement she used to feel. Her thumb hovered over the screen as she scrolled, but her heart offered no spark of interest.

She set the phone on her stomach and exhaled slowly. The air smelled of faint lavender, a lingering trace of one of Ruby's many herb pouches stuffed around the house. It reminded Elle of simpler days when she had visited her grandmother every summer. Back then, she had thought New Orleans was just a quirky place brimming with music and sugary beignets, nothing more. She never imagined the undercurrent of magic that pulsed beneath the sidewalks, or that she herself might be part of it. She certainly had not predicted how much that transformative realization would overshadow her career ambitions.

Another job title slid past her eyes: Associate Director of Brand Innovation. She scoffed quietly. She had once adored brand strategies, pitch decks, and networking events. Now the notion of returning to corporate life felt hollow. Her grandmother's funeral still hung in the back of her mind. The memory of illusions and dimly lit rituals followed her from the moment she had touched that heirloom necklace and discovered the simmering power in her veins. Balancing such magic with spreadsheets and board meetings seemed impossible.

With a weary sigh, Elle clicked off her phone and let the screen fade to black. She pulled the crocheted blanket closer and breathed the lavender scent more deeply until her head felt a little clearer. She was halfway to dozing off again when a gentle knock at the front door startled her upright. Heart pounding, she swung her feet to the floor and rubbed her bleary eyes.

"Hey, it's me," a familiar voice called through the wooden door.

Elle's pulse hitched. She slid off the sofa and padded across the living room. The wide pine boards creaked in soft protest under her weight. When she opened the door, she found Mateo on the small porch, arms juggling a paper bag from an old bakery near the Quarter and a takeout cupholder balanced precariously in his other hand. The aroma of sugar and yeast instantly kicked her appetite awake.

"Morning," he said with a shy grin while adjusting his grip on the pastries. His dark eyes carried warmth that chased away the last remnants of her drowsiness. Sweat clung to his forehead, hinting he had probably walked here in the humid summer air.

Elle held open the door. "Come in before those cups topple."

He stepped inside and carefully lowered the bag and the cupholder onto the round coffee table. The lingering sound of the house made his arrival feel extra intimate. He glanced at the scattered job listings on the sofa and raised an eyebrow. "You have been busy, I see."

She shrugged and gave a non-committal nod. "Trying to figure out what's next. Or at least, I was pretending to try." Her voice held a trace of embarrassment.

Mateo straightened, meeting her gaze. "New Orleans is next, right?" He spoke softly, but the question swirled in the air. For a moment, she could not find the right words.

"Not sure," she finally replied. "I have a flexible leave arrangement with my old job in Chicago, but everything over there feels so far removed from what is happening here." She gestured vaguely at the house, at the faint scent of lavender, at the intangible presence of her grandmother that lingered in every nook. "And I cannot really parse how to live two lives anymore."

When she stopped talking, an uneasy silence settled. She realized her heart was thumping louder than any words she had managed to speak. She wished Tansy were around to interrupt or to lighten the mood, but her cousin was off meeting a friend across town. That left the living room quiet and exposed, just her and the detective who had become more central to her life than she had ever anticipated.

Mateo quietly took a seat on the sofa, beckoning her to join him. She sat, noticing how close his thigh was to hers once she settled beside him. For weeks, she had tiptoed around the deep pull she felt, rationalizing it as some combination of gratitude and fear. But that had changed. The shift had started when they confronted life-threatening illusions together, and it had solidified when she realized he was the one person who never made her feel like her magic was a burden.

He cleared his throat, breaking her train of thought. "I did not mean to barge in so early," he said, offering a small white pastry bag. "But I picked up some fresh beignets. They are still hot."

Elle's face relaxed into a genuine smile. She opened the bag, releasing a flurry of powdered sugar that cascaded onto her lap. "Ah," she muttered, half-laughing, "some things never change in this city." She handed him one of the sugar-dusted pastries, then set the rest aside. The first bite brought on a comforting sweetness, the kind that made her want to believe in simpler joys.

They ate in companionable silence for a few minutes, each lost in private thoughts. Eventually, Mateo leaned forward, resting his elbows on his knees. The soft lines around his eyes revealed concern. "What is making you hesitate?" he asked gently. "I see the way you look at job listings, and I know you are still worried about what might happen if you stay here. Is it the danger you have faced, or is it something else?"

She finished chewing, then wiped her fingers on a napkin. Her throat felt tight. "It is both," she admitted. "Danger, yes. Hints of illusions at every corner. A sense that I will never have normal again. But it is the fear, too. Fear that if I commit to living here, it is not just me picking a city, it is me acknowledging that everything that has been happening is permanent. I am not sure I am ready for that."

Mateo nodded, absorbing her words. He set his half-eaten beignet down and reached for her hand. The warmth of his touch radiated up her arm. "You do not have to decide the rest of your life," he said. "But you also do not have to run, especially if you really do not want to."

She swallowed hard. Her entire body trembled with quiet tension she had been holding for days. "The truth? I'm not sure I want to leave New Orleans," she said, voice dropping to a near whisper. "Even with all the craziness and risk, it feels like home. And you, there's something about this that makes running back to Chicago seem meaningless."

His eyes softened as he moved closer. "Then stay."

That simple statement landed with more force than any complicated argument could have. Elle felt her pulse quicken. Stay. The fear inside her coiled and retreated, leaving a single, clear sense of certainty. She wanted to be with him, wanted to explore the magic that had awakened in her grandmother's house, wanted to transform that intangible promise of safety into something lasting.

She carefully set her napkin aside and inhaled a slow breath, bracing for the admission that hovered on her lips. "I will," she said, her voice thick but steady. "I'm going to stay in this house. I'll make it my home."

Somewhere in the back of her mind, a small doubt asked if she was being reckless, if anchoring herself to a city she had long ago left behind was wise. But she only had to look at Mateo to feel that it was less about wisdom and more about belonging. He was a quiet pillar in a world that had tilted sideways. Being near him felt right in ways she still struggled to articulate.

A faint smile curved his mouth. He reached up and brushed a speck of powdered sugar off her chin. His fingertips lingered, leaving a soft trail of warmth along her skin. "I'm glad," he said softly. "You have people who care about you here. Tansy will be thrilled, and..." He let the sentence fade, but the subtext was clear. He wanted her here too.

She leaned in and pressed her lips to his cheek, hesitant at first. The contact sent a pulse of electricity through her, a subtle reminder that their bond ran deeper than any casual fling. She felt him move, turning so that his mouth captured hers. The kiss was tender and patient, yet underscored by unspoken need. She tasted sugar and coffee on his lips and felt the thudding of her heart roar in her ears.

Awareness of the house, her grandmother's home, did not scare her this time. Instead, it felt like a silent blessing. Ruby had always believed in the power of love and magic.

The walls seemed to hold that promise, urging Elle to let go of fear and embrace the life forming right in front of her.

When the kiss ended, she cupped his face, thumb grazing his jawline. The morning air was warm, and each breath they shared felt almost sacred in the living room. Their eyes met, and it was as if they both realized that all illusions of this being casual had vanished. They were well past that point.

Mateo's voice was husky. "I should let you settle in. Find your footing. I don't want to push."

Her lips curved in a slow smile. "You're not pushing, you're the reason I want to stay," she replied. All the quiet yearnings inside her were throbbing against her ribs, an echo of trust, desire, and relief. She glanced at the hallway leading to the bedroom, aware that Tansy wouldn't be back for hours. The notion sparked a swirl of timid boldness in her chest.

He must have sensed her hesitation. Gently, he placed his hand over hers. "Elle," he murmured, warmth flooding his tone, "I'm here for whatever you need." Yet the raw emotion in his eyes confessed that he wanted her too, perhaps more than words could say.

She didn't answer right away. Instead, she rose from the sofa, her pulse skittering with nervous excitement. He stood with her, never letting go of her hand. She led him quietly through the narrow hallway, past the slightly creaking floorboards that had become a familiar lullaby to her. The house seemed to hum a recognition that this was where she wanted to set down roots.

In the bedroom, sunlight spilled through sheer curtains, illuminating the mismatched furniture and half-open boxes of her grandmother's keepsakes. A hodgepodge of old lace doilies and modern storage bins lined the walls. It was far from pristine, but it felt real, the perfect symbol of what her life in New Orleans might be: messy, complicated, and brimming with authenticity.

She turned to face Mateo, heart pounding. His gaze drifted over her face, searching for any sign of doubt. None surfaced. He kissed her again, more fervently this time, and she responded by lacing her arms around his neck. The world outside dissolved. Her mind swam in the warmth of his closeness, the safety she found in his steady heartbeat.

Closing the door behind them, she inhaled deeply, letting every flicker of tension slip off her shoulders. The bedroom wrapped around them, quiet and comforting. Their kiss deepened. Little by little, the swirl of clothes and the press of hands against soft skin blurred into a tender, urgent exploration. She felt gratitude surge through her, gratitude for this man who saw her, both fragile and strong, and never demanded she hide either side.

The shutters cast shifting patterns of light on the floor as a mild breeze swept through the house. With each soft sound they made, she became more certain that this was where she belonged. Any fear of illusions or looming threats drifted to the periphery, overshadowed by the reality of his hands, his words, and the powerful statement in his every touch.

Moments stretched and blurred, a mixture of gentle laughter and whispered affirmations. She found herself melting into him, body and soul. Outside, the day wore on, but in that bedroom, time became almost irrelevant. What lingered was a deep awareness of trust, a vow they silently forged.

They took their time, rediscovering calm in each other's presence. The tension she had carried about Chicago, corporate life, and unsettled magic seemed to fall away as he held her. Eventually, they lay entwined beneath the rumpled sheets, her head resting against his shoulder, the faint scent of his cologne mixing with the lavender that once belonged to Ruby. A memory of the pastries on the coffee table, left half-eaten, drifted through Elle's mind, and she blinked drowsily.

Mateo's voice was low and gentle. "You okay," he asked, pressing a soft kiss to the top of her head.

She nodded against him, a slow, content motion. "Better than okay. I feel settled," she said. "Like deciding to stay was what I needed."

He murmured an affirmation and gathered her closer. In that comfortable silence, she pondered the future. She would text Tansy later and tell her she was officially moving in. She would start sorting through boxes, making the house hers. Maybe she would convert the spare room into an office nook for the part-time remote work she might try. The intricacies did not scare her as much as they had an hour before. The weight of choosing no longer felt suffocating. She had chosen, and that alone brought a heady sense of freedom.

Eventually, Elle propped herself up on one elbow to look into his eyes. The intensity she saw there mirrored her own feelings, equal parts relief, love, and the still-simmering excitement of all that had passed between them. She stroked a hand across his cheek, letting the silence speak where words felt inadequate.

She pressed her lips to his again, a featherlight promise. And in that moment, the morning's doubts gave way to the rhythmic certainty of their breaths. They might still face dangers outside, illusions lurking in quiet corners, but this bond was unshakable. It was no longer a fleeting flirtation, no chance fling. What lived between them was something deeper, and she could almost feel Ruby's silent blessing hovering in the walls.

Gently, she laid her head back down against his chest and let the sound of his heartbeat lull her toward a delicate, satisfied calm. They had come to an unspoken agreement in that bedroom, a vow to stand together even when the next wave of trouble arrived. They were beyond simple romance. And as her eyelids fluttered, the knowledge settled in her bones, unmistakably real.

She was staying. And in that shared stillness, with the shadows of the late morning drifting across the bed, every illusion that they were a casual fling vanished. Here in Ruby's creaking, lavender-scented home, they built something no threat could break. And for the first time in a long while, Elle felt undeniably certain she was exactly where she belonged.

TWENTY-NINE

Late afternoon sunlight trickled through the aging stained glass window above Madame Laveau's shop door as Elle arrived, her steps jittery with anticipation. The narrow store on Royal Street felt even more claustrophobic than usual, its cramped setting magnified by rows of crystals, bundles of dried herbs strung from the ceiling, and the ever present swirl of incense drifting through the shelves. The moment she stepped inside, the heavy spicy scent prickled her eyes, making her blink as she surveyed the familiar clutter. She spotted Madame Laveau waiting near the back curtain, face half concealed in shadow.

"Come quickly," Madame Laveau urged, lifting one tasseled edge of a tapestry to reveal a narrower, hidden room. The older woman's voice sounded unusually tight, her usual theatrical poise replaced by real urgency. Elle swallowed and adjusted the necklace beneath her shirt as she passed behind the draped fabric.

The back room stretched longer than Elle had

expected, lit by only a few candles spaced on tall wooden stands. Immediately, she felt a shift in the air pressure, a subtle buzzing in her ears that hinted powerful magic swirled here. Rows of intricate charms dangled from the ceiling, each click of ceramic or seashell echoing like small wind chimes. Tapestries draped the walls, dyed in deep purples and reds, while a circle of smoky haze clung to the center of the floor, thick enough to obscure the worn rug beneath.

Elle's pulse fluttered. The swirl of magic in the air left her both uneasy and oddly comforted. She had seen Madame Laveau's front shop plenty of times, but never had she been granted entry to this private space. Madame Laveau gestured for Elle to approach a low wooden table. On it sat a mirror that looked like it had been dredged from an ancient shipwreck. Its edges were encrusted with an odd, coral-like texture, ridges rising around tarnished silver filigree. Faint candlelight made the surface appear slick, as though water still clung to it.

Madame Laveau exhaled a slow breath. "I had my suspicions about your grandmother's lineage, but I needed confirmation." Her fingers flexed around a frayed scarf resting beside the mirror. "You see, my own grandmother kept a ledger recording old families tied to this city's deeper currents. When you mentioned the events surrounding your heirloom necklace, I decided to consult those records."

Uncertainty gurgled in Elle's stomach. She glanced at the scarf, a worn piece of cloth with faded floral patterns, and recognized beneath the discoloration a style similar to what Ruby might have worn in her younger years. She remembered rummaging through old suitcases as a child, noticing scarves and dresses that smelled of lavender and bay leaves. Seeing a similar garment now in Madame Laveau's possession made her chest tighten with longing for the woman she missed every day.

She cleared her throat, trying to remain steady. "You said you conjured Ruby's essence?"

Madame Laveau inclined her head. "Through tokens like this scarf, I can attempt to call upon the threads of your grandmother's spirit, no necromancy, mind you, only a subtle contact that clarifies certain truths. But even that contact can be dangerous if the spirit in question is tied to old secrets." She lifted her gaze, warmth flickering there. "Don't be afraid. I only want to show you what emerged in this mirror when I invoked Ruby's name."

Elle's instinct was to recoil from the mirror's dark surface. She had encountered illusions before, and each time, a part of her dreaded seeing something that would confirm the city's darkest rumors. Yet she forced her feet forward. She told herself that she owed it to Ruby's memory, to her own unraveling sense of identity, to look. Slowly, she lowered herself so she faced the table and gazed into the mirror's reflection.

At first, she only saw herself by candle glow, disheveled hair, dark eyes rimmed with the day's tension, her lips parted with the slightest tremor. Wisps of incense smoke drifted across the glass. Then, the surface began to ripple. It reminded her of how heat waves shimmer on summer pavement. The reflection blurred until she no longer recognized her own features.

Something else emerged. Another face, overlapping her reflection like a faint superimposition. High cheekbones, a sharper chin, and the eyes, they glared with a piercing, almost predatory light. Elle's breath caught in her throat. Her own brown eyes still hovered behind the reflection, but this other visage possessed an uncanny, regal quality. The woman's gaze flickered with cruel ambition, so intense it made Elle's stomach clench.

She tried to tear her eyes away but found she could not. The wavering reflection seemed to stir an echo deep in Elle's bones, as if a distant memory called out. Her pulse thrummed in her ears, and the mirror's frame pulsed with threads of leftover moisture. She could have sworn a faint voice hissed in the back of her mind, though she couldn't parse the words. It felt like a threat and a summons all at once.

Madame Laveau's voice broke through. "The Queen of the Quarter." She set trembling fingers on Elle's shoulder. "A witch from three generations ago whose shadow has never quite left this city. Your grandmother's ledger described her forging dark pacts to expand her dominion. She used illusions and manipulations to entrench her power. She was unstoppable until one day she vanished."

Even the mention of her title made Elle's chest tighten. She had heard rumors whispered among locals about some ancient witch who once ruled entire covens, but no one ever said her name plainly. Now, seeing that face in the mirror made the legends real. The flicker of malice in those eyes spoke volumes.

Elle's heart hammered as she swallowed. "So this is, she's part of my bloodline?" Her own reflection twitched in the shifting surface, as if the other face might merge with it.

Madame Laveau nodded. "According to my grandmother's notes, the Queen was once allied with your ancestor. In fact," she tapped the scarf, "Ruby might have insisted on severing that alliance long ago. But the power left behind, the seeds of that lineage, apparently pass down. You, my dear, stand at the crossroads of it."

The mention of the stolen heirloom made Elle touch her necklace through her shirt. Sweat beaded along her brow. If the Queen's essence ran through her veins, and if her stolen necklace was pivotal to resurrecting that old power, the realization nearly sent her staggering back. She recalled how the filigree sometimes heated whenever strong illusions took shape, how thunderous her magic felt on the nights she tried to contain it. Fear coiled around her thoughts like a serpent.

"How sure are you that this old magic can be reignited by my necklace?" she asked, voice quivering. The mirror still displayed that haunting face, faintly layered over her own.

Madame Laveau's hand slipped from Elle's shoulder to the edge of the table. "I am certain of two things. One, the Queen's line persists through you. Your grandmother tried to contain or break that hold by forging a powerful ward, likely the filigree necklace. Two, the heirloom is more than just a ward. It can be subverted if the Queen or her followers lay claim to it in the right ritual. That stolen purse incident, your sudden illusions, these may be no coincidences."

Elle's knees threatened to buckle. Her mouth went dry, and the copper taste of panic tickled the back of her tongue. She squeezed her eyes shut, inhaling incense-laden air in three shallow breaths. She hadn't wanted to believe that the stolen necklace was anything more than a personal keepsake. The function of it, the bizarre illusions...she realized how naive she had been to assume she could just keep wearing it, keep ignoring the deeper significance. Her grandmother must have known. Ruby had given it to her with that grave expression, cautioning her without fully explaining. Perhaps Ruby had tried to protect her from the truth, that a centuries-old witch's power now lingered in Elle's blood.

The mirror's reflection rippled again, and this time, she felt a distinct push in her mind. It was as if the face in the glass tried to speak, shaping silent words that crackled in the swirling air. She ripped her gaze away, pressing her palm flat against the table for balance.

"Enough," Madame Laveau's voice came in a firm whisper. She tapped the coral-crusted frame with a thin wand of polished wood. The haze in the mirror's surface dissipated, revealing only the risen lumps of coralized metal. "I dared not show you more, for fear that you could be pulled in further." She let the wand rest. "I suspect this is how the Queen ensnares souls, glimpses, illusions, half-born nightmares. Keep your strength, child."

Elle's breath escaped in a quiver. Her shoulders shuddered, and tears burned in her eyes. This city was all she had left of her grandmother, a place she wanted to call home. But learning that her blood carried the imprint of a vile, power-hungry witch threatened every trace of normalcy she had carved out. All the stolen moments of peace she had found with Tansy, with friends, and with Mateo, were they overshadowed by this monstrous inheritance?

She lifted her gaze to Madame Laveau, speaking softly, voice tight. "I need to tell him. Mateo. He's been investigating the bizarre illusions and listening to every half-mad story I've told. He deserves to know that this... it's not just random. It's me."

A sympathetic crease formed on Madame Laveau's brow. "Yes, do what you must. But be cautious. The truth will anchor you, secrets can poison the mind. And right now, you cannot afford confusion. The Queen's reflection is strong in you. You must keep close ties to what you love if you aim to remain yourself."

Still trembling, Elle nodded. She gently touched the worn scarf. For a heartbeat, a faint echo of Ruby's warmth seemed to reach through the fabric. The impression comforted her, reminding her that her grandmother had not stood for cruelty or darkness. Ruby had fought to keep Elle safe, forging that necklace to sever the Queen's hold. Elle closed her eyes, summoning courage to carry the knowledge without collapsing in fear.

"Thank you for telling me," she managed, throat constricting. She felt the older woman's reassuring squeeze of her hand. Then, with as much composure as she could muster, she turned and left the back room. A tangle of emotions whipped through her, terror, sadness, fury, but also a flicker of defiance. She would not let that twisted reflection define her path. She refused to let the Queen leech the life she was building.

Outside, the late afternoon sun nearly blinded her, and she winced at the brightness washing the street. Tourists meandered past, oblivious to the quiet hurricane inside Elle. She inhaled a lungful of fresh air that carried a hint of sweet praline from a nearby confectionery. It brought her a shred of comfort as she started down Royal Street, determined to find Mateo.

Her phone buzzed against her hip, and she took it out. One new message from Tansy, cheerfully reminding her about dinner plans. Elle's fingers shook. She typed a quick reply that she would see Tansy later, but for now, she needed to meet someone. Then she hurried, weaving through small groups of travelers snapping pictures of cast-iron balconies and pastel-colored buildings.

It did not take long to spot Mateo along an intersecting street near the Square. He leaned against a lamppost, phone in hand, probably reading the updates from the precinct that had recently pinged him. Even from a distance, Elle recognized the subtle way tension lined his shoulders. The moment he noticed her approach, a question leapt into his eyes.

"Elle? You look..." He moved away from the lamppost, searching her face for reassurance. "What happened?"

She could not slow down. Anxiety coursed through her, a restless energy that demanded she speak. "We have to talk." Her words came out in a rush. "Madame Laveau called me. She showed me a record, something about my grandmother, my family line." Breaths coming faster, she laid a trembling hand on his arm. The look in his eyes steadied her enough to form the next sentence. "Mateo, the Queen of the Quarter is in my lineage. She's part of my blood."

He blinked. "Wait, that same Queen that's rumored to…"

"Yes," Elle cut him off, near tears. "I saw her, in a mirror. It felt real, like she was there, behind my reflection. Madame Laveau says the stolen heirloom might be the key to reigniting her power. And that means I'm tied to all of it."

Terror laced her voice, and she hated how small it sounded. The confession roiled in her gut. If the Queen lurked in her ancestry, that might explain why random illusions gravitated to her, why her powers sometimes flared beyond control. And if those illusions worsened, if the Queen ever found a way to claim the necklace fully, Elle shuddered at the thought. Everything she cared about could be consumed in the process.

Mateo exhaled sharply, as though the news struck him in the chest. He looked at the street, taking stock of any curious onlookers, then gently guided her toward an iron bench a few steps away. She stumbled after him, tears beginning to slip down her cheeks. The city's normal hustle blurred around them, muted by the roar in her ears.

She half-expected that regal face from the mirror to appear at any moment.

Once they were relatively out of the foot traffic, Mateo turned and pulled her into a fierce embrace. She stifled a sob against his chest, inhaling the faint hint of cologne on his jacket. His heartbeat thudded steady beneath her ear. "Don't panic," he whispered, pressing a hand to the back of her head. "You are not alone in this."

THIRTY

Elle woke the next morning with Madame Laveau's warning still echoing in her mind. She left her bed feeling as if every wall in Ruby's house pressed in on her. The faint hint of incense clung to her skin, a souvenir from the day before when the psychic had shown her that cursed mirror and revealed the long-buried truth of Elle's bloodline. She could not shake the feeling that the city's magic sensed a new crack forming in her defenses.

She found Tansy in the kitchen, rummaging through a creaky cabinet for coffee filters. The cousin's usually cheerful face was drawn into a pinched frown. Tansy produced a bag of coffee grounds and waved it like a peace offering.

"Morning," Tansy said. "You look like you barely slept."

Elle slid onto the worn stool beside the kitchen counter and exhaled. "I got a few hours, but Laveau's words are replaying in my head. It is this sense that the Queen lingers behind every corner."

Tansy nodded. She spooned grounds into the filter and flipped on the machine, movements brisk. "We cannot risk ignoring what that mirror showed you. Plus, there is new graffiti cropping up all over the neighborhood." She gestured at a folded map on the table. "I have been marking spots near boarded-up voodoo shops and vacant storefronts. The same glyph is scrawled on doors and windows. I figured we should check it out."

The coffee machine gurgled. Elle listened to the drip of steady liquid and let the aroma calm her. She forced herself not to dwell on half-remembered nightmares. "I will get dressed. Let us walk the neighborhood and see for ourselves."

Half an hour later, they stepped from the house into a bright morning sun that did nothing to ease the chill in Elle's chest. She carried an old canvas tote filled with a small container of salt and a bottle of homemade cleansing spray Tansy had concocted out of rosemary and lavender. Even though they had tried such remedies before, desperation made them try again.

They wandered past cramped side alleys and old buildings with peeling paint. Every boarded-up doorway or shuttered shop seemed to emit a faint hum. At first, Elle thought she was imagining it. Then Tansy paused in front of a dilapidated voodoo supply store that had closed its doors years ago. The windows were coated in grime. A dark symbol glistened through the film.

"Look." Tansy pointed. Through the haze, Elle spotted

an intricate glyph that looked like twisted vines, or maybe branching lightning. It pulsed in a faint pattern, as if it had its own heartbeat. She could hardly tell if it was painted or burned into the glass.

"Did you mark this yesterday?" Elle asked, pulling out the folded map. Tansy nodded and tapped a small X near the block's corner. A cluster of similar X symbols dotted the page. All of them converged on the neighborhood around Ruby's house.

Elle set her hand on the grimy window and muttered a quick chant from Ruby's old notes. She sprinkled a dusting of salt around the frame. For a moment, the glyph flickered, as if resisting. It dimmed slightly, then flared back, undiminished.

"That is not normal," Tansy said. "Magic wards should at least weaken it. I tried scrubbing the same type of glyph near Frenchmen Street yesterday. It would not budge."

Elle's heartbeat quickened. She dumped more salt, careful not to breathe too deeply of the dust that drifted in the morning air. Nothing changed. The symbol still shone with that eerie inner glow.

A man passed by, arms full of cardboard boxes. He glanced at them with concern when he saw them chanting at the closed shop window. Tansy offered him a friendly wave, which he ignored, stepping around them as if they were only a mild curiosity.

Elle's cheeks burned. She cleared her throat. "We should keep going. There are more. Exactly how many do you think?"

Tansy unfurled the map again. "At least seven or eight symbols are new. A few more might still be undiscovered."

They traversed block after block. The second glyph they found decorated the side of an abandoned laundromat, scrawled in thick red lines. A third waited beneath the boarded windows of a defunct bar. Each mark emitted the same nagging hum in Elle's ears. By the time they circled back toward Ruby's street, her temples throbbed.

An hour after lunch, they took a break on Ruby's porch. The old floorboards creaked as they sat on mismatched chairs. The city's humidity pressed around them, and Elle used the corner of her shirt to dab sweat from her forehead. She felt the necklace under her blouse, resting warm against her skin. It had not flared painfully all day, but the memory of its heat remained close.

"It all lines up right here." Tansy traced her finger over the marks on the map. The lines created a jagged oval, and the center was just one block from Ruby's shotgun house. "It's like the Queen wants everything to point straight at us."

Elle clenched the edges of the map. "Or point straight at me," she murmured. Her voice turned quiet. She couldn't deny the growing link between the city's dark signals and her presence. The stolen heirloom, the illusions, the cryptic warnings. She folded the map and swallowed the tightness in her throat. "We might try advanced wards, but if this is truly the Queen's magic, only something strong will tear them down."

They shared a somber look. Tansy's eyes were full of concern, but Elle recognized a flicker of determination underneath. They would not let a few sinister patterns chase them from the streets Ruby had called home.

Around mid-afternoon, they reached out to Mateo, who had promised to check the precinct archives for any relevant cold-case files. He told them to meet him at his apartment because he had found a match. They arrived at the second-floor walk-up with the sun dipping low behind them, turning the sky a vibrant mix of orange and purple.

Mateo greeted them with that steady look of his. Worry lines creased his brow, but his voice was calm as he invited them inside. Tansy settled on the couch while Elle remained standing by the small table covered in folders.

"I pulled a file from eight years ago," Mateo explained. "There was a series of unexplained vandalism incidents with identical symbols. Back then, nobody recognized it as magical. The official statement called it gang graffiti. But the shape is exactly like the glyph you described." He tapped an old photo in the folder. The image showed a charred wall bearing an elaborate scrawl that curled in loops. "One witness reported hearing chanting echo through the alley. Their testimony was dismissed for lack of evidence."

Elle leaned closer, her pulse jumping at the sight of the symbol. She could swear it was the same design forming beneath the filigree of her necklace. Sometimes, when she lifted the pendant away from her collarbone, she imagined ridges that formed strange lines along the metal's underside.

"It gets weirder," Mateo said. "The case detective

found traces of ash but no accelerant. It was as if the symbol burned itself in place using heat not explained by normal means."

Tansy pressed a palm to her forehead. "So it is definitely more than scribbled paint."

Mateo nodded. "I photocopied everything I could. Officially, the old files were closed. Nobody wants to believe it might be the same phenomenon returning."

Elle's chest tightened. She chewed the inside of her cheek, her mind swirling with images of that same glyph blazing next to shuttered properties. The Queen's illusions. Laveau's dire warning. And now, evidence that the Queen's markings had existed for years.

She noticed Mateo studying her. He reached across the table to cover her hand with his. "Are you all right?"

She managed a shaky smile. "I will be. Let us keep all of this in one place. Tomorrow, we can figure out a stronger way to counteract it. Rubbing salt on the sidewalks is not cutting it."

He squeezed her fingers. "We will get there." His gaze slipped to Tansy. "Do you want me to drop you off at your place?"

Tansy yawned, looking at the clock on her phone. "Thanks, but I can walk. It is just a few blocks. I want to check something in the Quarter before I head home."

Elle gave her cousin a parting hug. She recognized Tansy's typical style, never wanting to be fussed over, determined to handle tasks on her own. For a moment, worry stirred in Elle's chest, but Tansy's confident expression promised she would be cautious.

After Tansy left, the apartment felt quieter, as the tension drew to the surface. Elle used that calm to help organize the new files. Together, she and Mateo arranged the copies and photos into a neat stack. The soft overhead light cast shadows on the pages, making the glyphs appear even more sinister.

By nightfall, exhaustion draped over Elle, thick as a blanket. She let herself lean against Mateo on the couch, her body half-curled into his side. Whenever he moved, she felt that comforting heat that always grounded her. The events of the day weighed on them both, but neither said much. Words would not erase the symbols or quell the faint hum that still lingered in Elle's ears.

Eventually, the lull of crickets and cars outside guided them to bed. Mateo's bedroom was small, dominated by a sturdy bed with navy-blue sheets. A single lamp glowed on the nightstand. Elle changed into an old T-shirt and settled under the covers, the necklace resting against her collarbone. She felt uneasy about removing it, though the memory of previous burns lingered in her mind.

Mateo joined her. He slid beneath the sheets and drew her close. The moment his arms encircled her, she exhaled a tension she had not realized she was carrying. She found solace in the steady drum of his heartbeat, letting it guide her away from the glyphs that had haunted her every thought.

For a while, she drifted in dreamless sleep, pressed against his warmth. She wasn't sure how much time passed when a sharp sting erupted against her collarbone. Her eyes shot open. The room was dark, illuminated only by the lamplight. Panic surged as she realized her necklace glowed with a faint, malevolent radiance. The metal felt hot, almost scalding.

She gasped. The sheet beneath her collarbone began to smolder in a tiny circle the size of the pendant. A hiss of something acrid filled her nose. She jolted upright and clutched the necklace in a desperate attempt to yank it away from her body. The heat was intense enough to make her teeth clench.

"Elle?" Mateo stirred, voice thick with sleep. Then his eyes snapped to the faint wisps of smoke curling off the sheets. He sprang up, hands moving to pat the fire out, though it was no larger than a quarter-sized mark. "Are you hurt?"

Elle tore the chain from her neck, the clasp giving way with a sharp yank. Pain seared across her fingers, and she dropped the necklace onto the floor. She scrambled out of bed, pressing her palm to her stinging collarbone. The bed sheet now bore a small blackened hole, edges burned away in a near-perfect circle.

"God," she gasped, breath ragged. Her heart thundered against her ribs. Shame mingled with fear, twisting her insides. "I almost torched your bedroom. What if I had slept through it?"

Mateo rushed to her and scanned the scorched bedding. He turned on the overhead light. The brightness revealed the tiny ring of wispy smoke. She stared at the necklace on the floor. Its filigree pendant still glowed with a dull red hue, as if refusing to cool. Her fingers trembled, and she swallowed hard.

He slid an arm around her and guided her away from the singed sheet. "You're okay," he said quietly, checking her collarbone with worried eyes. She winced. His fingertips felt cold compared to the heat still tingling on her skin.

Tears pricked the corners of her gaze. "This city's magic won't let me breathe. First the glyphs, now this. I can't control it. What if next time it's bigger and I burn down something important? The house? Or worse?"

Mateo's voice was firm but gentle. "You won't. Fear wants you to believe that you can't stop it, but that isn't true." He steadied her shaking hands against his chest. "You're exhausted, and the Queen's influence is pushing at you when you're vulnerable. We'll get through it."

She looked up at him, tears threatening to spill. "It's just I can't keep walking on eggshells around everything I touch. Ruby's house, your apartment, even the people I care about. The power is too strong, and I don't know how to channel it."

He lowered his forehead to hers and closed his eyes. The warmth of his breath settled across her cheek. "Stop thinking you're alone in this," he said. "I'm here. Tansy is here. We're figuring this out together, no matter how stubborn the city's magic might be."

His words loosened something in her chest. She leaned into that moment, letting the fear slowly recede. The necklace still lay on the floor, its glow fading to a dull shimmer. It seemed to sense her defiance, but she couldn't escape the nagging certainty that the Queen's shadows crept closer by the hour.

THE STORY CONTINUES

The story continues in book two, *Midnight in the Bayou,* coming soon to Amazon

EXCERPT FROM
MIDNIGHT IN THE BAYOU

CHAPTER ONE

Elle stirred before dawn, the faint glow of daylight pressing against her closed eyelids. A quiver of unease fluttered in her chest, as though she had emerged from a half-remembered nightmare. The bedroom was oddly serene, with no signs of the illusions that had troubled her the previous night. Mateo slept beside her, dark lashes resting against his cheeks, one arm draped protectively over her waist. She took small comfort in that warmth, trying to ignore the tremor in her pulse.

She gently shifted his arm aside. He murmured something under his breath but did not wake. Carefully, Elle slipped from the bed, grateful for the quiet that enclosed them like a bubble. Her bare feet met the hardwood floor with a soft groan of the old boards.

The house smelled of the lavender sachets Tansy had stashed in corners to drive away lingering shadows. A single beam of early sun filtered through a gap in the thick curtains. She padded into the hallway, her mind drifting through the tension left by Madame Laveau's warnings and the fresh graffiti Tansy kept spotting around the neighborhood. Her grandmother's house often gave her a sense of security, but she could not deny the weight of the stirring magic inside its walls. At times, she felt as if the entire place listened to her breathing, quietly judging whether she was strong enough to stand against the threat creeping closer. Determined not to wake Mateo, she went to the bathroom. A warm shower might soothe the anxiety gnawing beneath her skin. Every week, more of those symbols appeared, and illusions prowled deeper into the city, leaving residents whispering about sleepless nights and missing pets. Switching on the overhead light, she pulled the door shut behind her.

The bathroom used to be her grandmother's personal hideaway, with pearl-handled brushes and floral bath salts stacked in a wicker basket. Elle's own items mingled there now, evidence of her attempt to make this space hers. She turned the shower handle until hot water cascaded against worn tiles. Steam rose in billowing waves, condensing on the mirror above the sink. She removed her sleep shirt, goose bumps prickling her arms in the sudden chill. With the shower's gentle hiss in the background, she caught sight of motion near the mirror. Thinking it was a stray reflection of her hand, she angled her head. A swirl of steam clung to the slick glass. The shape quivered as though guided by a hidden finger. Spellbound, Elle took one hesitant step forward. Letters, if they were letters, formed in the fog. They curved, jagged lines twisting over themselves like living things. She leaned closer, heart pounding. She did not recognize any language yet dread pooled in her stomach. Her reflection blurred behind the swirling condensation. For a moment, the watery shapes seemed to glow with a malevolent undercurrent.

A faint, almost imperceptible voice rattled at the edges of her hearing, syllables that made her teeth ache. In her peripheral vision, the steam coalesced into something resembling a face, sharp cheekbones, eyes brimming with cunning. Elle's breath caught, and a bolt of terror slammed through her chest. The Queen's face was there, half-formed, inside the twisting patterns of steam. A phantom whisper curled through the steam. "You are mine." The words bled across the glass as the Queen's face surfaced. Elle lurched backward, clutching her towel, and yelled, "Mateo!"

Her legs trembled as she pressed against the wall, the Queen's words echoing in her ears. The steam thinned while she fought for steady breaths.

She slid down the cool tile and stared at the mirror. Mateo burst through the door, half-dressed and wide-eyed.

Samhain was only ten days away, each sunrise a reminder that the Beauregard curse might devour her family if she failed.

She clung to him while he wiped the mirror clean, but the vision had already vanished. "She was in the steam," Elle gasped. Mateo steadied her and guided her toward the bedroom. "These illusions are getting stronger. We can't wait."

Her pulse hammered as she sank onto the bed. "Then what?"

"We hunt down that ritual in the catacombs before she reaches you."

Marielle insisted they had only hours. An old prophecy claimed the Queen's power would surge at sundown, making any attack nearly impossible. They spent the morning poring over Ruby's journals and Marielle's notes, hunting for references to the catacombs where the Queen's coven once gathered. Somewhere in that maze lay the altar meant to anchor her resurrection. If they uncovered it first, they might finally end the nightmare pressing on New Orleans.

OTHER FLORID ROMANCE BOOKS

To be notified of new releases and special promotions from Florid Romance, please join our email list:

https://floridromance.lmbpn.com/about/sign-up-for-our-newsletter/

For a complete list of books published by Florid Romance please visit our website:

https://floridromance.lmbpn.com/

BOOKS BY KELLI ROBYNS

The Enchanted Orchard

The Orchard (Book 1)

Family Curse (Book 2)

Crystal Heart (Book 3)

The Charmed City

Spellbound (Book 1)

Prophecy (Book 2)

Ultimatum (Book 3)

Crescent City Curse

Beignets and Bad Omens (Book 1)

Midnight in the Bayou (Book 2)

BOOKS BY MICHAEL ANDERLE

Sign up for the LMBPN email list to be notified of new releases and special deals!

https://lmbpn.com/email/

For a complete list of books by Michael Anderle, please visit:

www.lmbpn.com/ma-books/

Connect With Michael Anderle

Website: http://lmbpn.com

Email List: https://michael.beehiiv.com/

https://www.facebook.com/LMBPNPublishing

https://twitter.com/MichaelAnderle

https://www.instagram.com/lmbpn_publishing/

https://www.bookbub.com/authors/michael-anderle